Let Me Tell You About a Man I Knew

SUSAN FLETCHER

virago

VIRAGO

First published in Great Britain in 2016 by Virago Press

1 3 5 7 9 10 8 6 4 2

A CIP catalogue record for this book
is available from the British Library.

Hardback ISBN 978-0-349-00760-1
C-format ISBN 978-0-349-00761-8

Typeset in Bembo by M Rules
Printed and bound in Great Britain by
Clays Ltd, St Ives plc

Papers used by Virago are from well-managed forests
and other responsible sources.

MIX
Paper from
responsible sources
FSC® C104740

Virago Press
An imprint of
Little, Brown Book Group
Carmelite House
50 Victoria Embankment
London EC4Y 0DZ

An Hachette UK Company
www.hachette.co.uk

www.virago.co.uk

Let Me
Tell You
About a
Man I Knew

One

All morning she washes their clothes in the yard beneath the lime tree, the metal tub by her side. She hunches on a stool. She unfolds the wet clothes, rubs soap on them and scrubs the cloth against the wooden board. Rinses. Scrubs. Rinses. Wrings the water out.

After this, she takes the clothes and hangs them – on a rope, tied between the lime and the stone wall. She does this with care, a hand's width between each garment. Then with a forked branch Jeanne hoists the clothes so they find the high breeze and they sway above the flattened earth and their own shadows and the stool and the metal tub.

She pauses. Looks across the fields.

The breeze finds the hems of her apron and skirt.

Briefly, Jeanne thinks of closing her eyes – to feel this wind against her, to open her mouth as if drinking it. The mistral, she knows, tastes cool. But this is not the mistral. It's a warm southerly wind – and Jeanne goes back to the tub, grasps its two handles and lifts it until the tub rests against her thigh and like this she hurries unevenly to the west side of their house and the boundary wall where not much will grow except dandelions and moss. She strains, momentarily; then there's a sudden clattering sound and the tub is on its side and the grey water rushes across the ground, runs the length of the wall. Jeanne stands, watches this. When she was young, with every upturned pail she'd imagine it – this water's path, its second life. Where now? What might it do? Jeanne would think of it – the roots, the dark and dark-scented world beneath her feet where worms and busy, velvety moles might feel this surge and pause in their tunnelling, tunnels that took this water to streams or the Rhône itself, or elsewhere. The sea? Could it find distant lands? Princes and kingdoms? Or could it – Jeanne's emptied bucket – make new trees and flowers grow? *Roses because of me.*

She thinks this now, as the water sinks away. Roses that, if pinned to her hair, would leave a rose-scented trail in her wake. They grow against south-facing walls, in June and July. She's cupped them, inhaled.

When the tub is empty Jeanne props it against the wall to drain. Walks back across the yard and goes inside.

They watch for the mistral in these parts. Mostly it's an autumnal wind – yet it came early last year, blew when the chestnuts were still forming. It cracked glass. It threw back every unlocked door so that the town banged on its hinges and livestock kept to south-facing walls. *Mistrau* in the local tongue. Wind of change, of shallow sleep. By November the hills were powdered with snow and, in the fields, there was sleet. Jeanne would see the bluish glow of Mont Gaussier in the afternoons as she walked back through the olive trees, clutching her shawl to her jaw.

'Spring will come,' Charles assured her. In March, green shoots pushed up near the gate; April was the month of dripping lanes and a frailer, younger bleating in the moving herd of goats. It's only now, in May, that there's enough warmth in the sun to dry clothes or walk without her woollen shawl

2

and so Jeanne moves from to room to room, unfastening the windows that have been shut for so long and pushing them wide so this new, warm air can find its way into the corners of their house.

Each window's clasp cracks at her weight, like a seal.

Each view is known to her. From the parlour, Jeanne can see the lane and the olive trees beyond. The kitchen, too, faces the lane – but its second, smaller window looks into the yard with its drying clothes, the lime tree, the wash-house and a hen. She opens this window; the hen looks up.

She climbs the stairs to the bedroom – their shared room with single beds – which sits above the parlour. She's higher now, can see more. More olive trees, in their rows; the eaves of Peyron's house, beside the hospital walls. If Jeanne leans out of this window and looks right she can see Mont Gaussier and Les Deux Trous and the five blowing cypress trees and she used to do this in her early married days – lean out, her hands on the sill and smiling, feeling the sun on her face. Her best view south. Beneath her, the road to Saint-Rémy. Sometimes she sees the tops of heads. The dusty spines of mules.

A second bedroom. It looks into the lime tree – green, dappled walls.

And there's a final room. Was it a cupboard, before they lived here? Or even a room at all? It's the highest part of the house, reached by three more steps, which means it feels safe to her – a little tucked-away land. It used to be the nursery. Here she cradled and fed and sang to each boy – and this made it her best place in the world, for a time. How they'd grasp her finger with all five of their own, how they seemed like fish with their soft, soft sucking sounds and round, reflecting eyes meant they seemed other-worldly to her, made for elsewhere. Jeanne rarely comes here now. But

3

when she comes she feels her heart fill up for them; it fills now as she takes five steps across the floor and pushes back the shutter so that the room fills with light.

Look. Her vegetable plot – where she tries to keep the crows away with spoons tied onto string. The ditch that mules drink from. The same white hen.

And there . . .

Jeanne lowers her hand from her eyes. The hospital. Saint-Paul-de-Mausole. From this room she sees it very clearly: a weathered ship in a sea of olives and grass. Its roof is bleached by sun. The pale-blue shutters on every window are locked, she knows, with rusting hooks that can pinch the skin and they're fastened each night, or in summer for shade – but they're unfastened today. Rows of them, thrown back. Each window, she thinks, is an eye. Or each is like a tiny cave that her boys might have pushed their fingers into, trying to find what hid in its dark. The pale-blue paint is old. It flakes, drifts down into the garden so that some of the patients have thought these flakes are butterflies or butterflies' wings, or snow. Carried them with shaking hands.

This old, known place. A garden of ivy. Its boundary wall and corridors, its cloisters and pines. The fountain that's thick with moss.

And him. A patient is sitting on a bench.

He's far away and partly in shade but Jeanne knows who he is. Hands in his lap.

The mistral can make them worse. All her life she'd heard this – that that wild autumnal wind can awaken grief or rage or bring up the fears which, since infancy, have been locked away. That it can call to the animal nature in a person who's always seemed calm. There are too many stories to count. In the hospital, the breaking of tethers; how a man beat his chest until it bruised. But Jeanne can add stories of her own too – of how Laure would sometimes push herself onto her toes and sniff the air when the mistral was blowing. Or how, once, Jeanne had opened the nursery windows and, at that moment, a bird had flown in. Both black and bright. A hard, clapping sound. The bird struck the wall and her forearms and there was a draught from its panicking wings and the shedding of feathers, and in its wake Jeanne didn't see the blood on her arms. She only thought of Benoît – *my child*. But he was unmarked and unknowing. Sleeping on his side in his cool, black-feathered bed.

Her boys, too. They seemed more quarrelsome in the mistral season, more prone to injuries or strange, vivid dreams. And each of her pregnancies began with that wind – as if it woke a deeper, sleeping, wanting part of Charles.

In the afternoon she lifts the chairs onto the table and sweeps. Makes bread. Scrubs the kitchen floor.

By four, his shoes are polished. His books line up, in wait.

Jeanne is breaking eggs into a bowl when Charles returns. She hears him before she sees him. With half an eggshell in each hand she looks up to see him move through the drying clothes, brush past the hens and she sees, too, that he's frowning, which means his thoughts are elsewhere.

'Are they glad of it?'

'Of?'

'The sunshine, at last. Spring.'

He sits down, exhales. 'Of course.'

'Are they calmer?'

'Most are.'

Charles has coffee at this hour – sweetened, and in the brown cup that seems too small for his strong, veined hands. She offers it to him. 'So it's been a quiet day for you?'

He takes the cup. 'Quieter. But . . . '

She knows. It's too much work for him, even so. All these years at Saint-Paul-de-Mausole and he's growing old. He stoops sometimes. There's looser skin beneath his eyes. 'I saw Rouisson,' she says.

'You did? When?'

'Today. From the nursery window. He was in the garden, sitting on a bench.'

'Alone?'

'Yes.'

'And tranquil?'

'Yes. He seemed so. He was sitting perfectly still.'

A nod. 'He's much better these days. But I fear he'll always be here. Well, you know . . . '

Rouisson. Jeanne doesn't know them all by name – there are more than twenty patients – but she knows Émile Rouisson. He came twelve years ago – a short, strong man from the Languedoc who shook as if cold, spoke of angels. He'd lost his daughter and wife to a sickness – and lost them so suddenly that he came to fear losing more so he'd search for what he thought he'd lost – a pocket watch or coin. On his fifth day at Saint-Paul, Jeanne met him. On her way to chapel, she paused; this new, curious patient kneeling by the boundary wall, searching the undergrowth. He saw her, called out. 'Madame! Will you help?' He'd lost a silver key. Had she seen it? Did she know where it was? Jeanne shook her head but she crouched all the same; she parted the leaves and looked for silver amongst the soil and dark green. Then Rouisson grabbed her. He grasped her wrist and hissed, 'You took it! I know you did! Give it back!'

Jeanne has come to understand that most will never leave. They're like the ivy that finds its way onto the powdering stones, seeks out the cracks and takes hold. Even if they leave physically, something stays – an echo in their wake, their names scratched into the walls. But no, most will stay. Some are so undone that the world won't have them or they won't have the world, so they find their routines in Saint-Paul and live by them – their baths, their food, the doses of bromide, simple food and early nights, the soothing words of nuns. Perhaps they don't mend, but they don't worsen. Nor do they mind that the hospital is far poorer than it was. As for their families, they keep their sick, unfortunate ones at Saint-Paul because it is easiest to – a change might make them ill again, and other asylums would cost far more. And so, with time, the shapes and voices of these patients become as known to Jeanne as the outline of trees. There's Patrice who sings. The woman whose arms are scarred from her youth. Yves whose tongue protrudes as if his mouth is too full to hold it – too full of unsaid words or spit. Michel, like a bear – so strong and tall that they used to fear no straps would hold him if he chose to rage. But he's never shown rage. Jeanne has only heard gentle stories of Michel – how he reads in the library, or takes bread from the dining room to feed the sparrows that bathe in dust by the southern wall. There's Dominique who owns a child's doll. Once, there was a girl who claimed she ate an owl's heart so that she could see in the dark, hear mice – *One day I will fly . . .* – and it was Charles had to tell her no, she couldn't fly, and restrain her. As for Rouisson, he no longer loses things. He's too tired for it. Bromide and age seem to have brought a peace to him, even in autumn weather. Sometimes he sleeps on the floor of the corridors so they wake him like a child, lead him back. *This way . . .*

Rouisson won't go. Nor will Jeanne forget the colours that came to the bruise on her wrist after he'd seized her – ink-blue, apricot, gold. It troubled Charles. He turned her wrist over, studying it, and forbade her from the hospital after that. Ever since, Jeanne may only enter its grounds on Sunday morning, to pray in its chapel that smells of dark.

Charles looks up suddenly. 'The windows. Why are they open?'

'They've been closed all winter. I thought—'

'No, Jeanne.'

One by one, rules came. The hospital grounds are only one restriction from this neat, military man. His old army life has meant structure; his medical ways mean that he fears infections, fevers, broken bones. And so Charles ordered their sons in when it rained, forbade them from walking through the field with Breguet's bull. When there were rumours of the Cavaillon melons causing a sudden loose-ness of bowels he wouldn't let Jeanne walk near the stalls, told her not to touch their sun-bright skin in case she fell ill or brought the illness home. He's wary, she knows, of all things: of prowlers, fires, fast water. Meat must be cooked until dark. And so, for Charles, windows must be closed – all of them, even though it's the first warm day in half a year and the winter's been long, too long.

'Shut them, please.'

'Yes.' After all, he's seen far more of the world. He runs the asylum on his own, or so it feels. He's more tired than any patient, looks older than he is – and for a moment Jeanne thinks of touching the side of his face, of cupping it as she would a rose. Breathing him.

Instead, she closes the windows one by one.

*

8

Their meal is omelette with ham, and bread. His glass of red wine. Their home doesn't yet have gaslight so there's a lantern at either end of the table – his lantern and hers. By his light, he reads. By hers, she watches – how he cuts his food, places it in his mouth and then lays the fork down before turning to *Le Figaro* or *L'homme de bronze*.

She looks down. These plates bear a print of flowers – blooms that have no name, and that Jeanne's never seen in lanes or gardens or any place except on these plates and bowls. They're invented flowers, maybe. Even so, Jeanne feels she could pick them. She's looked at these plates and heard bees, or imagined the sun-warm underside of each bloom, and they seem to glow by candlelight as the paler flowers can. As old as their married life – for these plates had been a wedding gift. A second, undying bouquet.

'Salles,' he says, 'is coming to Saint-Paul. We must set a place for him.'

Jeanne pauses, looks up. 'He is? When?'

'Tomorrow.'

'To eat? Here?'

'Yes. Would that be difficult?'

These are Jeanne's thoughts, on being asked: that they've just eaten the last of the ham, the last eggs. And how much is in their vegetable patch? Not much, or enough. But there's the hen that's too old to lay, and the food in jars, preserved from last year. The market, if she needs it. 'No, not difficult. Why is he coming?'

'He's bringing someone.'

'A patient?'

'Yes.'

'A new one? Really?'

'Yes. Quite new.'

Jeanne turns back to the plate. The truth is that it's been a long time since a new patient came to Saint-Paul – four years, at least – and arrivals are not easy. Patients don't always wish to come. Even if they do, they're often rushed with feelings as they step into the hospital's porch – failure or grief, a disbelief at being there. Some are as tired as children; others have no trust in the world and hunt for the lie, curse the nuns. And while they may have come from anywhere – Marseilles, or Avignon – most come from the same hospital in Arles where they can treat the visible wounds, the childbirths and open sores, but have far less to offer the wounds of the mind. Too few doctors, at Arles. They can't care for the disturbed or the insane. So they talk of the town of Saint-Rémy-de-Provence, fifteen miles to the north – of its asylum that was once a monastery. A place with cloisters. Herbs.

'He's foreign,' Charles says. 'Dutch, I think.'

'Oh?' Jeanne looks up, hearing this.

'A strange man. Wild. And self-wounded, I hear – violently so.'

It will be a wound to the wrists, Jeanne's sure of that. To that smoothness of skin under her thumb, its embroidery of veins. With the women, they might choose the upper arms or thighs; long ago there was a far more secret wounding that took the patient back to Arles with an infection in her blood that killed her, in the end. But mostly it's wrists. 'Will he stay with us?'

'Salles? No need. The spare rooms in the hospital will serve him well enough. The nuns have been told. But we'll feed him.'

'Yes.' She nods. Salles, with his slow way of speaking. His smile.

With that, Charles yawns. He presses the heel of his hand to his brow and closes his eyes momentarily, returns to *Le Figaro*.

*

10

In the kitchen, Jeanne thinks this: *he comes from Holland. Dutch means he comes from there.* Her father had had a faded antique globe, the colour of parchment or yellowed bone. By the fireside he'd turn it and say, What would you like to see, *mon chou*? Anything. All of it. Lands where ebony came from or where volcanoes were or big, white bears or where camels trod through deserts with spices and rolls of silk on their backs. Holland, he assured her, was a flat, flat place – land claimed from the sea, which the sea wanted back. Dykes and walls built against it. A blowing sky.

Papa. Two taps of his fingernail. On finding a country, he'd tap it twice and say to her, See? Just there.

There must be better hospitals than Saint-Paul-de-Mausole. There must be asylums (although Charles is less fond of that word) where the director is well and the paint doesn't peel and the food's more than haricot beans. Where the fountain works, at least. Yet Salles is bringing this new patient here? Jeanne knots her apron, looks out at the fading light and can only suppose that Salles thinks the empty rooms and overgrown garden at Saint-Paul will suit this Dutchman, somehow.

She washes the plates, dries them. She slows in her drying, fingers the stem of a dark-pink bud. In the rue de l'Agneau, there was jasmine; she'd make crowns of it, walk home like a queen. Or she'd press herself into its soft, white curtain with her arms held out, embracing it – and she'd do this still, if there were jasmine here.

Dutch. She washes, dries.

When she glances up, dusk has deepened into night.

TWO

Pastor Salles. Tall, with the broad, strong hands that could have held shears or a plough without difficulty if he'd chosen a field life. But he chose God. He chose a different crop to harvest and chose to preach in the corridors at Arles hospital, whispering his sermons to the fevered and dying. He's done this for too long for Jeanne to count the years. Such a life has given him a doctor's eye, she knows. He can quote from Isaiah or Proverbs, but Pastor Salles can also hear a cough's rattle and name it, staunch a wound. In the weeks after Jean-Charles was born he'd come to Saint-Rémy without warning, knocked on Jeanne's door with a fold of cloth. Inside, greenery. 'For the soreness. Your milk. There's bleeding, I think? Press these leaves against yourself.'

Cabbage leaves, ribbed and dark. At first, Jeanne had felt ashamed. She'd flushed, hurried the leaves into the cool space under the kitchen floor and left them there for a day or two, half-forgotten, and said nothing of them to Charles. But those hard, swollen breasts didn't go. They knocked together like crusted bells and her baby wailed, underfed – so one night she crouched on the kitchen floor, reached down, unfolded each leaf. They were softer by then, less green. Yet she still sighed when she held them against herself, for how

12

cool they felt. Yes, she'd bled. Hers had been a pinkish milk until those fanned, new hands.

How had he known? Pastor Salles, who had no wife?

She stews the hen with onions and the bread waits to be cut.

When he comes to their white house Salles brings more than himself. He brings wine – but also, when he kisses Jeanne's cheek, she smells the musk of churches, pipe smoke and damp wool. Other places. Rooms.

'Jeanne. How long has it been? Thank you for this.'

'*Bonsoir.* Your journey went well?'

'It did. It's been a good while since I left Arles – the winter made it too hard, of course. You managed here? They say the canal froze.'

'Yes, for a while.' She smiles, takes the pastor's coat.

At this meal, there's no quietness and no *Le Figaro.* Nor is there a frown, for Charles has the warm, altered face that comes with good company, with news from the cities he used to know before this warden's life that's worn him down – Nice, Toulouse, the old port of Marseilles. They've known each other since boyhood; they talk of Arles or the Third Republic, of Paris and its World Fair.

Charles says, 'It's an eyesore, Frédéric – from what I hear. The paper says as much. It's made of iron and it's so tall that it can be seen across the city so that the only way to *stop* seeing it is to climb it! Who can want such a thing?'

Salles smiles. 'It might not please every eye, but few things manage that. I hear some are fond of it. Either way, it's a feat.'

'Tactful, Salles. I'd expect nothing less.' Charles raises a glass.

They drink. When Jeanne sips she imagines the vineyards that the wine came from – their months of sun and rain, quiet nights, and the fingers that picked this fruit from the boughs. She holds the wine in her mouth, tasting it. For her, wine is a rarity that she'll only drink with visitors – and she curls her toes at the taste of it. She's still thinking of vineyards when Salles shifts in his chair, leans forwards. 'Tell me, Jeanne. How are your boys?'

She swallows. 'Jean-Charles is twenty-nine now.'

'Twenty-nine?'

'I know.'

'Where does the time go, Madame?'

It feels like a moment ago that their eldest boy was hauling himself onto furniture, trying to stand on dimpled legs, as white and folded as dough.

'He's still in Paris,' Charles says. 'Still a bookbinder. A father too – did I tell you that? He's very well. He writes to us about this tower and how they've watched it grow and grow, how they can see it from their drawing room. He tells me their boy looks like me – the Trabuc nose, he says – but we're yet to see him. Too busy here ... ' Charles pauses. 'Laurent's also in Paris. Still not married, but he seems content enough. When was his last letter, Jeanne?'

'March.'

'March.'

'He's a bookbinder as well?'

'A clerk,' Charles says.

'Ah! *Bien.* You must be proud, both of you. And what of your youngest? I remember his hair ...'

Of course. That hair. A fairish-red, or a reddish shade of fair. As soon as he was born there was sunshine in it. This unexpected colouring from two dark-haired, dark-eyed parents so that Jeanne gasped on seeing her new baby; she'd grasped the bed as if she'd made a child of fire, as if her awe and pain were exactly the same. *Benoît*, for the blessing he was. Brighter than flame. Jeanne smiles, 'Yes, very proud. And he still has that hair.'

'In Paris too?'

'No, no.' Charles feels his teeth with his tongue. 'Benoît's further away than that.'

Oh, he is. On a wholly different part of that old globe. The land and sea between her heart and Benoît's heart is, at this precise moment, beyond measure to Jeanne; too far away to make sense of, in the same way that stars are.

My Benoît. My boys – although they've been their own men for years now. Maybe they were never hers, in fact; maybe they came into this world entirely their own persons, with their own characters set and formed – and Jeanne could believe this. From birth, they cried differently, had their preferences. They slept in their own ways. But she is their mother all the same. She's the one who bore and raised them, fed them and protected them and so she's *in* them, somehow. When Salles asked after them her heart clenched; her heart seemed to rise up, come forwards as if called for or desiring them. *Yes, my boys*. There were hunters here, once. Jeanne knows they used to chant the name of the beast they were hoping for – as if by naming it, it might come. And some-times she does the same: *Jean-Charles, Laurent, Benoît*, she says – as she darns or chops wood or scalds the hair from pork or carries in the washing at the end of the day. It isn't to bring them back home to her. Rather, Jeanne supposes it's done in the hope that they might know she's thinking of them – that should one of her boys need strength or comfort they might hear her, somehow. Wherever they are in the world.

'The Americas,' Jeanne tells Salles. 'Benoît went to the Americas. Caught a boat last summer.'

'The Americas? I didn't know. I knew he was elsewhere but . . . '

Charles nods. 'He loves history. Always has. Even as a boy he was digging and exploring and asking about the Romans, and . . . You remember? Now he believes there's a future in the past – money and purpose in the ruins of things. Lost tribes. Cities. I can't understand it, Salles, and I won't pretend to try. Our last words before his leaving were . . . '

'You were worried,' Jeanne whispers. 'He understood.'

Her husband looks at his glass. He looks without blinking, says, 'Mexico. His last letter came before Christmas and was written in Mexico – but who knows where he is now? Or who with? We've no address for him. He needs to come home.'

'To Saint-Rémy?'

Jeanne looks away. She looks across to the wall where their shadows are and imagines her youngest boy's own shadow – not here but on other walls. Temples or taverns. Holding a lantern up in a cave.

Salles raises his brows. 'And what might Benoît do in Saint-Rémy?'

Charles shrugs. 'I'm an old man, Frédéric. I'll be sixty next year. There is so much to do and I'm getting too slow, too old. We'll need a new warden . . . Poulet is good, but—'

'Ah. A successor.'

'I'm hoping for that.'

Jeanne's voice is quieter. 'Benoît's our explorer. The finder of things. He always was the inquisitive one.'

'You think he wouldn't come back here, Jeanne?'

She smiles, as an answer. But she wants to say no. Or not for long.

There's silence. There's the hiss of a lamp, the movement of Salles's thumb against his glass and Jeanne can sense her husband's stillness at the table's end. He hardens himself, sometimes. He can fix himself, impervious; he can close himself like a door and Charles has never talked of the night before Benoît's departure. How he'd given an order to their youngest boy, said You will not go.

'And how many empty rooms are there, Charles? May I ask this? I've heard . . . '

He stirs. 'Rooms? Ah. There are rumours, I know that. Half. Half are empty now. Thirty, at least, in the men's ward. The east wing is virtually closed. Wasps nested in the library last year and cracks run the height of the wall. You'll have seen how the paths are nearly lost to weeds. As for the winter storms . . . Well, we had buckets in the corridors. And the nuns work tirelessly but there aren't enough, and they're growing old like me. There needs to be something, Frédéric. The patients don't come as they did.'

The pastor nods. Then he tilts his head. 'And how is Peyron?'

A pause. 'Better than he has been. But there are still days when he can't work, or he tries to work but he forgets too much or grows distressed and I have to send him home for the patients' sake. His sake, too. It's grief, of course. But perhaps it's also more than that. I don't know.' He shakes his head. 'He never speaks of her.'

'At all?'

'At all.'

'*Mon Dieu*. Charles, can you find more staff? More help?'

'We can't afford more staff. So what can I do, but work harder? Work on my own and on Peyron's behalf?'

Salles smiles sadly. 'So Benoît . . . '

'Yes. Young. Bright. He knows this place. I could teach him everything. The patients would come, and money, and . . . '

It's impossible for Jeanne to imagine it: Benoît in the striped uniform. Benoît restraining the violent ones, pressing pills onto the tongue.

The pastor places his knife and fork side by side. 'I tell you this: we are all in God's sight. His plan must be trusted for He knows what lies ahead. And we shall be taken care of – Peyron, your boys and ourselves.'

More wine. Jeanne fills their glasses.

Charles shifts in his chair. 'So. This arrival. He's Dutch?'

It's as if they've been waiting for this – as if this matter could not be mentioned until they'd eaten, sat back. 'He is.'

'Does he only speak Dutch?'

'No, no. He speaks French very well. The accent is mild. Would you mind if I lit my pipe?'

'Not at all.'

'Jeanne?'

'Please.'

'You're asking Jeanne? She likes it. Smells of her child-hood, she tells me.'

'Is that true?' Salles smiles.

Jeanne blushes. 'Perhaps.' She knows this smell of old – from doorways, from the men that played boules or cards in the shade. From Claudette, from time to time. 'I don't mind.'

Salles reaches inside his pocket. He fits the end of curved wood between his teeth and strikes the match. Salles half-closes his eyes, sucks twice, three times, shakes the match out and says, 'He's been in France for three years. Paris, first. Came to Arles last year. Lived on Place Lamartine.'

'Place Lamartine?'

'The square to the north of the town, near the river. He

lived in the yellow house there. Perhaps you've heard the stories. Some things will always find their way through the passes, even in snow . . . '

Charles looks at the ceiling. 'Have I? Place . . . ?'

'Lamartine.'

'Lamartine. I think I did hear of a foreigner, yes. An artist.'

'That's him. We've had him since Christmas – in and out.'

Jeanne looks at the table before her. The candle wax, the crumbs that she will sweep with the side of her hand when Salles has left and Charles is upstairs. Once she didn't want talk of madness in the house, but her boys learned the word all the same. She couldn't stop it. They saw it, in the cloisters. Heard it across the fields at night. In the village school it was thrown around like stones so they'd come back and ask her about it. *What's mad? Are we mad, Maman?*

No, we aren't mad.

'What's been diagnosed?'

'Dr Rey didn't know. Mania, anxiety. Epilepsy of some kind. But these attacks are more physical than mental in their nature and there can be many months in between where his mind is perfectly clear. He's educated, this man. He works very hard when he's able to.'

'Your journey here?'

'Without incident. Talked of books, and his dislike of God.' A shrug from Salles. 'I've not met one like this. Unique, I'd call him.'

'And why here?' Jeanne asks this. She looks up, not understanding. 'Why bring him to Saint-Paul? When it's not . . . ' Clean. Full.

'The landscape, Jeanne. With him being a painter, you see. He said he wanted landscape. All these fields and the fresh air.'

She considers this. The days and nights here are all the same. Last night's dusk was like the dusk before. And yet Jeanne remembers coming here, seeing it all for the first time. She'd called it beautiful. She'd known no better word for the land and greenery – and despite the years, there have been moments since when she's stopped in her work and looked at a view as if it's new again. She's seen every olive tree lit, on one side, with sun. Night skies of blue and gold. So yes, perhaps it is a good painting place. And has she herself heard of him? This artist? There have always been tales of patients; the wives of Saint-Rémy have tongues like the drumming of fingers and always did. But Jeanne stopped listening to them. She couldn't heed every patient's story, just as a fisherman's wife couldn't listen to the sound of each wave coming in, over and over – and she's never wished to start tales of her own.

'He harmed himself,' says Salles. 'Did you hear that?'

'I heard. But five months in the hospital? His wound was so great?'

'No, the wound healed as much as it could. But he had to stay with us.' Salles pauses. 'The townsfolk. They felt ... Well, he drank too much. Fiery. Knew the rue du Bout d'Arles ...'

'A petition? I see.'

'Indecency, too. He walked into Place Lamartine one night, entirely unclothed. It was raining and—'

'Think of Jeanne.'

'Of course.' Salles blushes. 'Forgive me, Jeanne.'

She smiles. She tells him she has been a warden's wife for nearly thirty years and can't be shocked, that she's heard far worse. There is nothing to forgive.

Later, in the kitchen, she thinks of Place Lamartine. She used to know it well. Knew the flowerbeds and the dry, flattened path beneath the trees in whose shade the men played their games. That thud, the clack of boule against boule which were comforting sounds to her in her childhood in the way that *Amen* has been in her later life, or the smell of pipe smoke or a candle, blown out. She'd been born not far from that square. A true Arlésienne – who arrived as the bells of Saint Trophime tolled for midday, so her father claimed they sang *Jeanne! Jeanne!* Twelve seconds of joy.

Sometimes she used the square's flat earth for handstands when no one was looking, or no one that she knew. Wrote her name in the dust with her fingertip.

Stray dogs gather there. The Rhône runs by it.

Place Lamartine in rain. The fountains spill, she remembers this. To step over a puddle was to see oneself, looking down. Bowls of reflected sky.

Pastor Salles holds her upper arms when he makes his farewell. His touch is light and brief. 'Thank you. A fine meal in fine company.' He takes Charles's right hand with both of his own. 'I hope it won't be long before we meet again.'

'Will you be back to see him? This patient?'

'He hopes he'll mend here. Maybe.'

The Trabucs stand side by side, watching the light of Salles's lantern as he carries it ahead of him, between the pines and olive trees. It lights his feet, the grass on either side. Explorers must look like this, Jeanne thinks – swinging a light through the uncharted dark as if looking for wild animals, the edge of the earth.

'Our house will smell of pipe smoke for days,' says Charles. 'Ah well.'

He goes back inside. Briefly, Jeanne holds the doorframe and breathes the night air – the pine trees, the earth, the last traces of smoke – before hearing what she knows will come, which is, 'Jeanne, will you close . . . ?'

She turns out all the lanterns except one and makes her way upstairs to where Charles is already sleeping. She thinks of other sleepers. Rouisson. The bear-like Michel. Her boys. The nuns, one by one.

Peyron – his spectacles next to his bed.

Salles with his prayers.

And this foreigner. The Dutchman. Tonight he sleeps in a new bed, far away from Place Lamartine. Bars on the windows. Cypress trees.

Now Jeanne allows herself to think of him – of this patient from Arles and the two words she heard that made her breathe in very sharply, as if touched by an unseen hand. *Entirely unclothed.* Two words. Just two. Salles had brought them to her and, just as she'd taken the gift of cabbage leaves from him years ago and hidden them, she'd tucked those two words away. She'd smiled, as if they meant nothing.

She unfolds these words now.

Entirely unclothed.

Jeanne stares. Here among the views and trees and sounds of her life, the brown cups and flowered plates, his uniform and her pinned hair, Jeanne never sees anything that's new any more. Or if she does, if there *is* newness in her world, it's only old things shifting themselves to a slightly newer state so that she might call them *new*, but they're not: a wearing-down of a shoe she's worn for years, or a new splinter in the same, splintery door. She may see the wheat change – new stalks of it, a new crop, but this crop is the same shade as the crop the year before. A night sky may give her pause, but they're still the same stars. Fruit comes from the same trees. It's taken to the same market square. Laid on the same pale cloth.

I can't be shocked any more. She'd said this to Salles, smiled. Had that been true? As a young mother and a younger wife Jeanne could, sometimes, be shocked at what she saw. But she has aged and grown used to all of it – to the stories of patients who daub their grief on the walls or cry for their mothers or carve their own maps into their arms with stones from the garden or their fingernails. Biting or hating. Soiling themselves. None of that is new.

But this. Entirely unclothed.

Jeanne puts her hand out, finds the bedroom wall. The tale of a man's nakedness in a public square on a rainy night has brought, to Jeanne, a memory from forty years before.

She sits down on the bed and she sees herself again. A young, unmarried Jeanne in the yard at Arles. It had been early morning. She'd been bathing at the metal tub, washing her waist-length hair – and hadn't she dared to undo everything? To unbutton herself to the waist? No matter that other houses looked down into their yard. No matter that she'd been fifteen or sixteen, and knew far better. She'd been bold, reckless. Not caring for rules.

She'd thrown back her wet hair, like a wing. Stood there.

Jeanne turns out the light. And slowly she starts to undress. She undresses as she has undressed every night, for so long – finding each hook and button by touch alone, feeling the cloth, fingering seams. She loosens her ties, unpins her hair in the bedroom's dark.

Three

She's only ever known two homes. The first was in Arles – a tall, thin house at the end of rue de l'Agneau. Shafts of light on the polished floor. A hushed house too; the sounds Jeanne remembers are the scuff of Claudette's broom and how the stray cats padded along windowsills, dropped down. Cats of fleas and bone. She'd talk to them. She'd trawl a bootlace on the ground, reach for their warm, gritty fur and haul them closer to her. *Hello, you.* The sound of the bullfighters – and bulls, from time to time.

Her second home is here. Her married life has been lived entirely in the warden's cottage of a hospital on the southern edges of town called Saint-Rémy. *La ville verte,* too. The green town – because Les Alpilles shelter it. These fields have always been thick with grass or olive trees or cypresses, where vegetables rise up and fruit hang down as if they're trying to touch each other. An artichoke wanting a plum. There are goats and cows for milking. The hospital has its own mules – five of them, which scratch their rumps on the powdery walls or are tethered under the pines, where they swing their tails at flies.

Herbs in the lanes.

She left Arles for this place.

'I think you'll like it,' Charles told her as they boarded the

24

train. They were newly wedded, flushed and both still aware of the ring on Jeanne's finger that wasn't yet warmed by her body's heat. 'Saint-Rémy-de-Provence.'

It was to be a quieter life, Jeanne knew that. Arles had had huge markets and festivals and theatres and dancers and cafés and Les Arènes – but how often had she been in them? Or among them? Her chances to know these places had been rare. A day of truancy, perhaps; peeping into taverns, or the secret following of the dancing girls with bells stitched to their hems so their movements had their own music. As for the Pegoulado, the young Jeanne could never go: her father was too saddened by it and Claudette had no wish to walk through the cobbled streets with candles and tambourines – 'I've better things to do' – so Jeanne would climb up to the attic, throw open its windows and look out. A thousand lights beneath her. She'd cup her chin in her hands and gaze. *Look at those dresses* . . . Boats like dreams on the Rhône.

Jeanne went to school, then worked, then nursed: these were the three stages of her youth. With each she grew used to half-dark rooms. But with each, too, she kept hold of her private curiosity – so that she'd hum Christmas carols in June, name each spider that she swept outside with a broom, crush mint before lessons so that, all day, her palms smelt of gardens and elsewhere, not school. Like this, Jeanne survived. Like this, she reminded herself that there was far more to this world than a schoolroom, or riches, and that her father loved her and she loved him – and so wasn't she fortunate? Small pleasures, then. How he kissed the top of her head, moving past her. Apricot season. Swifts, dipping low.

So when Jeanne, newly married, looked at this white-washed house with its lime trees and yard and nearby olive groves, she supposed that yes, it might suit her. It wasn't as the house in her daydreams had been. But surely there would be new, small pleasures in these four walls. In these fields surrounding them. She'd find them.

'Do you like it?' he'd asked.

'It's beautiful.' Charles by her side.

Years have passed since then. Yet the cottage itself has hardly changed. Its whitewash is greyer, the lime tree is far taller and the ivy has crept up towards the nursery window, spreading itself like a dark-leafed fan. In the wardrobes she hangs lavender – a talisman against moths. There is milk and butter kept in the hole beneath the kitchen's flagstone floor – one of her early, secret finds. But there are no real differences from how it was before.

She stands in the vegetable patch.

Jeanne hardly slept last night. Half an hour, perhaps, before dawn – but no more. She watched the bedroom grow less dark, saw the wardrobe take its shape and the wallpaper move forwards with its simple striped pattern, so she knew the sun was rising.

Such a night has left her with the need for air. So Jeanne stands, digs in the earth. It's too early in the year to find much. Their vegetable garden is less than it was, now that the boys have gone. Part is overgrown and she lets it stay that way, for the sake of the butterflies. The rest is earth that she gathered years ago from the edges of fields, the quarry or from Gilles's wheelbarrow. She formed a rectangle of soil, bordered it with stones. In this she has grown onions, beans, lettuces. She has radishes that fall into her metal pail like rain. Soft fruits, sometimes. There is no skill to it. Charles used to admire it: her neatness, the turned earth and how, in the beginning, she'd try to write the name of each crop on splintered wood so that she might mark out each row, each growing place – as a general might name his infantry or a schoolmistress name her class. Fennel. Radish. Marrow.

26

Chard. Charles approved of this – 'So neat, Jeanne!' – before leaning in and saying, 'But radish has one *d*. See?'

No skill, even so. She'd liked to claim there is, but all it takes to grow a thing is a seed and a finger to push the seed down. Sun and rain. The passing of time.

There are some early radishes now. Onions. And here, in one corner, sorrel: fistfuls of it. Sprawling and bright.

Jeanne's knees click as she bends down. She cuts with a knife, nicking away at the stalks and leaves.

Laure loved sorrel. She used to talk of broths and baking fish; she'd chew it as she gathered it. *Used to* – as if she's dead. Perhaps Laure is dead. How might they know if she was? But it's hard to imagine she could ever die.

'You don't look Provençal,' Jeanne had said to her. Long ago. 'Not even very French.'

'Not French? The freckles? I know. There's strange blood in me, Jeanne . . . '

There was. *Is*.

Jeanne feels the sorrel. It's feathery, with a little dew upon it. And she thinks of all that's still to come – the berries and the stoned fruit – and Jean-Charles, too, comes to mind. His dark, berried hands. For he'd gorged on blackcurrants once. In the summer of Jeanne's fourth pregnancy, he'd come indoors with a stained shirt, stained mouth, stained palms. And Jeanne had tended to him all night. She'd carried purplish, sour-smelling bowls away from his bedside and emptied them into the privy outside, murmuring her reprimands. She'd felt both cross and tender towards him – for having been impatient. For having wanted more.

The sorrel. If she'd discovered this crop two days ago she might have made a soup for Salles. A little cream, if she'd found it. But Salles, she knows, has gone. He'll have signed the papers this morning, left Peyron's room and, placing

27

his hat on his head, he'll have walked through the olive trees and down to Saint-Rémy. He'll be on the train at this moment. Passing through Les Alpilles. Heading back to Arles.

So much sorrel, though. Too much – too much for her and Charles alone.

She looks down at her hands, examines them.

A good life is an ordered, disciplined one. That's what she's come to know. It's what she was taught by her father and has, mostly, obeyed – to wake at the same hour, sew neatly, fold a garment perfectly in half. Jeanne kept this in mind with her marriage to Charles – that here was a man who favoured a crisp, clean shirt and a swept floor. Coffee in the same brown cup.

Jeanne shifts from side to side, eyeing these fistfuls of green. *Look at it all.* And who could resent a kind act? A gesture of goodwill? Aren't there thirty empty rooms or more, a leaking roof and cracks in the walls? Saint-Paul is in need.

Besides, Charles won't even know. At this hour he'll be with the arrival – showing the Dutchman the courtyards and baths and library. Explaining the hospital's rules to him. *We eat at midday. We keep on our clothes.* He won't see his wife in the corridors, discarding – for the first time in years – a rule of his own.

She walks towards the hospital. Beneath the pines trees, the ground is softened by needles that have fallen in the months before and stayed. But the pines are not the only trees. Beyond them, on both sides, are olive groves. A desert of olives. An expanse of them – parched and grey, twisted with age. They stand in pale grass that will be paler by the summer's end, and if Jeanne were to walk in those orchards in August or September the grass would crackle beneath her feet like fire, scratch her shins.

Provence. It's olives, she's always known that. Cicadas and heat and lavender, garlic and asparagus, lemons in the south – but it's these trees that have shaped and coloured this part of France. Their salty crop. Their rough bark. Their lifetimes which are far longer than most human lives.

Let me tell you, her father told her, about *les oliviers* . . . So the infant Jeanne learned of the dove and the great flood, the last shady garden that Jesus knew and prayed in, the place of his betrayal. A kiss like a lie. Her father told her, too, of the city that was made when a goddess threw her spear into the ground and it turned into an olive tree – greenish-grey and bearing fruit.

'Which city?'

'Athens.'

'Is it near, Papa?'

He took the globe, tapped it. 'Look. Just there.'

The path leaves the pines. Jeanne steps into the sunshine, narrows her eyes.

A thousand years ago or more, a monk had come to this quiet farming land in the south of France, between the mountains called Les Alpilles and the town of Avignon. A tired monk, so he rested. He planted his staff into the soil. And at that moment his staff turned into flowers. It blossomed as suddenly as birds take flight: coloured, unidentified flowers tumbling down, shedding their petals and sugary scent. A sign, of course. The monk thought so. To him, the flowers said *stay* . . . So he stayed, built a monastery. Cloisters and cells.

Saint-Paul-de-Mausole. Its proper name. Charles had told

her on their first evening here. Jeanne had replied, '*De mau-sole?* Why that?' She saw no mausoleum there.

'The Romans built one near here, that's why.' She nodded, understanding that her husband knew better and more.

Monks became nuns, in time. Cells became bedrooms. And one by one the patients came – people whose minds had broken or weakened or poured out of them like dark water. Windows were shuttered and barred.

All things weather over time, of course – but four years ago it seemed to weather more quickly. Weathered, perhaps, overnight. For Laure Peyron went, and that one act came down like thunder. It seemed as if the building mourned her loss as much as her husband did, and both are still mourning: in places, it crumbles to the touch. The paths have narrowed and the benches are stained by bird droppings and lichen, and as Jeanne walks towards the building itself she can feel her skirt brushing against thistles and irises and a fallen branch, and she thinks of the bars on the windows, the flaking paint and the leather straps and she feels the ring on her finger, turns it with the pad of her thumb.

'*Bonjour.*' Smiles.

'*Bonjour à vous*, Madame Trabuc.' Sœur Madeleine stands, lifts the key that hangs on a string around her neck and unlocks the hospital's door.

'The nuns are like ghosts,' Jeanne told him once. 'That's what I thought when I saw them.' For they seemed so expressionless. Without sound or colour. They never hurried or slowed.

'Oh, they're strong. You'll see.'

They are. Even the youngest ones – Clemence, Yvette, Marie-Thérèse – can brace or fix themselves like stone against what thrashes beneath them and not wince at the fists or language or teeth: such stories have found their way to Jeanne. How they can push doors against a grown man's weight. Haul a patient from the ground and carry him into the shade, whispering, *There now. Hush.*

Strong in their minds too. Never afraid. Dabbing at wounds with eyes like pools. More than once Jeanne has wondered who they were before they took their vows – but with many it's hard to believe there was ever a time when they weren't as they've been to her. Dressed in grey, guiding the ill.

She shifts her basket as she goes.

Past the library. Past the broom store. Peyron's office with its mahogany walls. The room where arrivals are brought and assessed. The door that leads to the second courtyard, where the worst of them are taken. It's ajar, and a small breeze finds her as she passes. She sees a lone metal chair.

Jeanne pauses on a corner. Holds her breath, listens. A far-off cry, then silence – and she carries on.

The kitchen is easy to find from its heat and smell. She knocks.

'*Entrez!*'

The nun is Jeanne's age or older. She smiles and yet the lines on her forehead are permanent and deep, so that it seems that the nun is always surprised, or in thought. Marie-Josephine. She says, 'Madame Trabuc? *Bonjour.* It's been a long time.'

'*Bonjour.* Yes, it has.'

The nun accepts the basket. 'What's this?'

'Sorrel. Ours. It has grown so well and I have too much of it. I thought—'

'Ah! What a crop! Spring will always come, however hard the winter. You're sure you have no need yourself?'

'I've taken enough. Please.'

'My word.'

'I hope it will help a little.' Smiles.

'I'm sure it will. Everything does. *Merci*, Madame.'

Jeanne nods, looks away. All those mouths are fed by a room not much larger than Jeanne's own – a stove, a table and a sink. A copper kettle and saucepans. Cups and ladles and bowls and a knife with rust on its blade.

'You're keeping well, Madame?'

'Yes. Thank you. And you?'

'I am. Busy, but it's preferred to being idle . . . '

It hadn't always been just Marie-Josephine in here. In the beginning, there'd been a cook. When the hospital had still been full, still known as the best, progressive hospital in France – when Peyron had still been healthy – a man had come. What was his name? Jeanne's lost it. But he had family near Orgon and sometimes he brought in fish from the Durance, borne in his arms as a child might be. As heavy as silver.

'There's a rabbit,' the nun says.

'A rabbit?'

'I know. Monsieur Peyron and his rules on meat . . . But I came into the kitchen to find it on the table, just lying there. Gilles must have caught it or found it. Used the back door. How can meat hurt them, once in a while? I don't think it can. Nor has it cost us anything. It was His gift, after all.'

Jeanne understands: God's gift, not the gardener's. Not Gilles's, whose mouth is lost inside his beard, and when he chooses to speak it's in Provençal. Jeanne can speak it too. It was her only tongue for the first few years of her life – a river of sound, finding its way between stones so that her words could not be navigated by anyone who wasn't from Arles or wasn't the housemaid Claudette. Her father changed that, soon enough. He could speak both Provençal and true, strong, proper French – but believed only the latter would help Jeanne in later life. *Tell me again, but in French this time.* Charles can't speak Provençal. A word or two, perhaps, but no more. So it's French that she has always spoken with him and it's French with her boys, and with the nuns, and with Peyron and Poulet and Pastor Salles. Only in the market does Jeanne sometimes reach back inside herself, use her first language. *Bona matin.*

'The sorrel will work with it. Wouldn't you say? Madame?'

The rabbit. It lies on its side by the basin. It could be sleeping, except for its lifted paw.

'One rabbit will hardly go far, of course ... Even less so now that a new one has come. Arrived yesterday. You heard?' With that, the nun sets to the work. There's the tough, quick sound of her knife against the fur, the unpicking of stitches. The fur is grasped, tugged: four, five, six tugs before it is clear of that body's flesh and the rabbit is shining, a purplish-red.

Jeanne watches. 'Yes, I heard.'

'Foreign. He's having two rooms – two. Needs a second room to work in because he's a painter.' She says the word with emphasis. 'He's painting already, or so Sœur Agnes said.'

'Two rooms?'

'Well. If it helps them. Some write poems, some sing ... He's rather solemn too. Doesn't say much. Yet Agnes says he thanked her for assisting him – thanked! We don't work for thanks, of course, but it's pleasant when it comes.'

That feels unexpected, somehow. Quietness and gratitude from a man who can take off his clothes and walk into rain. Cut himself, and violently.

'He's very striking, I'll say. In a rather strange sort of ... Anyway, look at the time.'

Jeanne knows she must go: she isn't meant to be here and the kitchen is hot and Marie-Josephine has work to do. But as Jeanne turns she hears her own voice. She hears herself say, 'His rooms – do you know where they are?'

'The east wing, I believe. It's almost empty and he says he needs peace to work. The bedroom's on the first floor and his other's underneath. A view of the wheat and Gilles's hut.' The nun stops cutting, looks up. 'Do you know him, Madame?'

Marie-Josephine. She is the only one who found her faith late in life, who didn't take her vow before God until her mid-thirties or later – and so she, of all the nuns in Saint-Paul, had a life before here. An adult life. And what life had it been? Had she travelled? Danced with the dancing girls in Arles? Had she kissed a boy, or far more than kissed? 'No, I don't know him. It's just been a while. Since . . .'

'A new patient came? I know. A long time. We must be glad of his arrival – and hope that he might thrive amongst us. Find the rest he needs.' She smiles. 'Thank you for the sorrel, Madame Trabuc.' Which feels like a dismissal, the closing of a door.

Back into the sunlight. The overgrown paths.

She thinks of the rabbit as she goes. That glossed, purplish-red. The rabbit's hue had been the same as the mucus they'd peeled off each newborn child as she'd heaved herself onto her elbows, tried to see through her matted hair. *Is she alive? Let me see. I can't see.*

She carries her empty basket.

Under the pines. Through the olive trees.

*

34

Charles may have heard. Or he may have seen her there, with his own eyes. The Major, they call him. It's been years since he left his military life but he was a major in it and the name stayed, which he's never minded. How Charles walks is like marching. How he dresses is with military care. When he disciplined their boys Charles would stand before them, his hands behind his back, and click his heels together. Short, hard words. *Enough! Both of you!*

The Major's own wife in the corridors.

Jeanne's heart takes its time to slow. In her youth she used to press her thumb to her wrist after running, feel her pulse move back into its own rhythm, and it never seemed to take long. But she's so much older. And Jeanne remains restless: in the hours afterwards she doesn't allow her pulse to slow down for she sweeps, kneads dough, cleans the windows with a rag and vinegar. Her heart is a bird in a cage of bone.

Jeanne feels light-headed, places both hands on the parlour wall.

This newness that's come. If this were late autumn or early spring Jeanne might think that dark, northern wind was blowing – moving under aqueducts, spinning through town squares. But there is no such wind now. What there is, she knows, is a patient – perhaps violent – in the abandoned east wing of the hospital who, at this moment, is painting. Who is finding something of worth amongst the cobwebs and corridors.

Unique, Salles called him.

Laure used to say that nothing comes alone. That new, strange moments are as raindrops, or swifts, in that they're never on their own. One comes, and then another does. She'd smiled at Jeanne. 'You'll see.'

Charles finds her in the parlour. She's holding the back of a chair.

'Jeanne?'

'I didn't sleep well last night.'

'No? Why not?'

'I don't know.'

'Are you ill?'

'Not ill.'

'You're sure?'

'Tired. I'm tired, that's all.'

'You should rest. I'll feed myself.'

'But—'

'I can. What is there, Jeanne?'

'There's broth. Bread – over there.'

'Good. Any cheese?'

'A little. The hole in the floor.'

'Now, go upstairs. Rest.'

'Are you sure?'

'Yes.'

In the bedroom she lies on her side. Looks at the window. The shutters stripe her face with evening light.

There was no reprimand from Charles. So he knows nothing. He's in the room beneath her, eating cheese and bread and reading *Le Figaro* and sipping his wine with no knowledge of sorrel – fistfuls of it – or a dead rabbit or how Jeanne broke a rule. How she paused in the corridors. Heard a distant crying, the sound of closing doors.

Perhaps this is a fever coming. Perhaps all this strangeness inside her is a fever's beginning, and that's the explanation. *Yes. Perhaps.*

Jeanne turns onto her front. She stares at the wall for a while. She is aware of her body – its temperature, her breath.

Then she shuts her eyes, finds a shallow sleep.

*

36

She dreams. And in her dream she sees the frail, female patient who'd claimed she'd eaten the heart of an owl. Her name? It's gone. But when Jeanne wakes and rubs her eyes she remembers seeing this patient – in the olive groves, once. It had been dusk. Her arms had been held out and her loving, lonely, sunburnt face had been looking up, wide-eyed as a saint, and she'd called out, *Watch this! I can fly!* She'd flapped her arms five times, or six. She'd breathed in and pushed up onto her toes and Jeanne, standing under the lime, had seen every part of this – how the patient beat her arms, how the patient closed her eyes and wrinkled her nose in the effort and wishing for this taking off. And in the last, brief moment before she was found – before Charles and Peyron took the girl's wrists and hips and pushed her onto the ground – Jeanne had believed her. She'd thought, Yes. You can do it. There'd been no doubting it. For a second or two Jeanne had believed entirely – and had loved doing so – that this girl had magic in her, and that birds could lend their flight. That any human – any – could fly away from Saint-Rémy.

As Laure had done. Not a feathered flight, and not seen. But she had left here all the same. Four years ago, exactly. In her dark-red travelling coat. She'd been gone by first light.

Four

Plain people are the better ones.

Never trust a man who wears a hat indoors.

Be afraid of both fevers and hard frosts, Mademoiselle . . .

Those were the words of Claudette. Claudette of the baked-fig complexion who came to the house on the rue de l'Agneau within days of Jeanne's birth. No milk of her own, and no husband, but Claudette knew how to bathe and soothe and raise a child whose mother had died in the hours after birthing it. Claudette hardly needed sleep. She hissed her own strange lullabies. A newborn Jeanne and a hunched maid: both folded, strong-smelling and small.

No hard frosts in Jeanne's lifetime. She's known some cold winters, as the last one had been – when a grainy whiteness found the tips and sides of things – but no frosts. The lone tale she's heard is of a frost so sudden and late that it froze the rising sap in the trees, killed them. But this was before her birth, or Charles's birth.

Yet fevers have been in Jeanne's life since its start. She's always known to fear them; she didn't need Claudette's sharp warning to tell her how fevers can boil or kill or soften the brain. She'd hear the word fever and think stay back. Had no choice but to endure Claudette's strange beliefs in how to keep the fevers out: drinking the broth of boiled artichokes or rubbing garlic on her feet or being bathed in vinegar until her skin turned brown. Later, as a mother herself, Jeanne rubbed ointments on chests. Looked up at each sneeze as if it were a late-night knock on their door.

'A fever can creep up on you . . .'

Jeanne wakes, sits up.

She's damp beneath the arms. Am I hot? But she isn't hot and her skin isn't sore. No fever has come.

Sunday. They dress in their Sunday clothes, which are their cleanest. He wears his spare uniform; she has a dress with buttons that lead up to her jawbone and keep her chin high. The cloth creaks when she looks down.

The tunnel of branches parts to show the chapel in front of her. The carved saints in greyish stone.

'No fever. You're quite sure?'

'Quite sure.'

'You're rested?'

'Yes.'

Charles seems content with this. Even so, he glances across at her. When they reach the door he places his hand on the hollow of her back to usher her inside.

Dust, beeswax, wood. In Arles every place of worship had unnerved her. The statues. The cracked, holy faces that Jeanne stayed away from. They were large too – with naves so high and corners so dark that she felt childish, but not in that she wished to play or explore Saint Trophime. She felt a need to hide. To crouch, hold her breath.

Not here. The chapel at Saint-Paul has no high ceiling, no agonised Christ to make her think of loss. Instead there are unmarked columns she can run her finger up and down. A porcelain Virgin on the left side of the aisle, with her kind, mothering face. Where there are engravings they tend to be of lambs or rising suns – and today there's a glass jar by the altar, filled with flowers – lily of the valley, a poppy or two. A nun's private gesture.

They sit in their pew. Always this pew.

Charles prays.

Jeanne turns around, looks behind.

The chapel is starting to fill. There's a momentary change in the light as a person enters, coming through the doorway and taking off their hat. Peyron glances from side to side as he walks up the aisle, pushes his glasses back up his nose. Poulet too – the second, younger warden; he tries to hide his yawn.

And then Jeanne twists further in her pew and sees the nuns. Most are here, but not all. Some must stay with the patients who've no wish to worship God or aren't yet trusted to, and those nuns will pray this evening when the shutters of each bedroom have been closed. But many are here now. Jeanne names them as she sees them: Celeste, Bernadette, Maude, Clemence, Suzanne, Marie-Josephine, Mère Épiphanie and the nun who is so elderly she's bent over and can do very little but pray and sew. They move like water, parting around each pew before meeting again.

And also there is them. The ones who leave their mark on walls, ivy-like. They, too, pad through the doorway, altering the light. Emmanuelle with her shuffled gait; Yves with the too-full mouth. Some seem to be ghosts of themselves. One – she thinks he's called Maurice, thinks he is from Corsica – whispers to himself from dawn till dusk; reassurances, or quiet reprimands. She sees his lips moving, hears him.

The men sit on the left, the women on the right.

Jeanne searches each pew. She looks at the doorway with

each movement of light, and asks herself how a Dutch face might look, how it might be different from a French or Provençal one. Its shape, its colouring.

His face will be the face I don't know.

But she knows them all. No new face comes through the door – and as the congregation stands she tells herself she was wrong to expect that he might have come. Why might he have done? On their journey here the patient talked to Salles of his dislike of God and surely no dutiful, God-fearing man could know the girls on the rue du Bout d'Arles, or cut his own wrists as if trying to die, or take off his clothes in the rain.

Keep my boys safe. Wrap them in your protection. This is always her prayer.

Also, Jeanne prays for the nuns. For the damaged brains and hearts of each person in Saint-Paul. For him who sits beside her with his neatly parted hair and polished shoes. *Look after Charles in his work.*

As for Laure ... Laure, who must have seen the sun rising as the train passed through Avignon. Who must, just once, have glanced back. So Jeanne prays for Laure, wherever she is. For her husband Peyron who is, she sees, praying too.

Later Théophile Peyron walks back with them. Short and plump, with blemished skin. The last two buttons of his waistcoat aren't fastened. He walks with a limp, though he always has. Spectacles like moons.

The two men walk together, and Jeanne follows them.

He'd been such a gift. Charles and Jeanne had lived in Saint-Rémy for six months before Peyron came. Until then, the hospital's director had been an elderly priest who forgot people's names, talked of the Devil being inside them and starving the badness out. 'This won't last,' Charles told her. 'It can't.' Then he arrived: Théophile Peyron, limping and short-sighted but a talkative, kind, purposeful man who had a history in optometry, more qualifications than Jeanne had plucked hens, and he steered the old priest – with tact and reassurances – to a new life near a seminary in Digne. For Peyron, the patients were worth nothing less than himself. To make them well again. That was what he wanted – to care for the patients, heal them. His way of doing this was gardens, books, regular baths, gentle walking and simple meals with little meat. Sleep. Peace. Nightly prayer. A little bromide. Restraints were to be used sparingly, only when they had no choice. And when Peyron met Charles for the first time he shook his hand and said, 'The military? My word. And I hear you're quite an asset to Saint-Paul-de-Mausole.'

Peyron charmed the nuns. He commended the cook. Listened to the patients' requests and tried his best to meet them. 'I'll see what I can do ... ' Opened up a west-facing room so that families could wait for their loved ones there – on upholstered chairs, with books and dried lavender and a view of the courtyard. 'So it won't feel like a hospital to them, you see? More like ... a hotel!' He admired Gilles's flowerbeds. Asked him to keep the fountain clean. And like this, Saint-Paul unfurled.

A bachelor, at first. Then he married. Had said to Jeanne, Isn't she wonderful?

The former Peyron – before Laure left. The Peyron that everybody knew. Everyone knows him still – but not for his care in the hospital's rooms. One Christmas he fell in the marketplace. Punched the ground until his knuckles bled.

Jeanne watches them. Her husband is a foot taller than Peyron and stoops to hear him as they walk.

'Dominique? I hear she is having a bad spell.'

'Yes,' says Charles. 'She grows distraught at mealtimes so she will eat before the others now – at a quarter to midday, with Mère Épiphanie.'

'Good. Yes.'

'With Yves, I've decided ...'

The tunnel of branches and shade. Jeanne wants them to say Dutch. Say Dutch, she thinks, and looks away to the vines that cover the boundary wall. She hears the stones as she treads on them, twists her heel to make the sound a little louder, which she knows is a childish act but she's done it all her life – in Place Lamartine, or the marketplace – and so Jeanne's thoughts are elsewhere as they come to it: a wooden door in the wall. A rusted, weathered, splintering door that creaks on its hinges when caught by the wind, or opened or closed. Mostly, it's closed. It tends to be shut and locked because of where this door leads, which is into the hospital garden – where the patients are often walking or resting or playing cards. Or they're scratching at the wall as if seeking escape. It keeps them in – this wall and this door.

Sealed, and half-hidden by ivy.

But it's open today.

A patch of light across the path ahead. A space in the wall, that's all. But as she draws closer she glances into it – an instinct, perhaps, or simple curiosity or the mother's reaction, which is to check, make sure, find out. But in those six slow steps that it takes for her to pass this open door with its garden view she sees what she has wanted to.

A straw hat. Blue overalls.

He stands. He has his back to her so Jeanne can't see his face, but she can see his artist's easel and a metal box on the ground. He's holding a paintbrush, high up. Held in his fist, almost proudly – as a lantern might be, casting light.

Then he's gone.

The door and the ivy are behind her. The men talk but she cannot hear them. Jeanne follows them, thinks only of the wild, unkempt irises – as purple as dusk or as old, hidden bruises – and how they were splayed, covering his feet.

She used to spy.

Number 4, rue de l'Agneau. Theirs was a heavy front door. A knocker shaped like a rising bear and a keyhole so large that Jeanne could fit her eye to it and peep into the street or, from the street itself, peep into their house. *This is what others might see of our lives*: the curved end of the banisters, the tapestry. Claudette's shadow on the polished floor.

Or she'd peep through other keyholes. Into other empty hallways, or rooms lined with books. Gardens. Through cracks in a stable door she's seen a horse sleeping. Once she found a space between the wooden boards of a stall and saw two black bulls beyond them, waiting for their deaths in the heat of Les Arènes. Stamping their feet. Working their mouths.

These moments, as brief as a bird flying over.

Jeanne finds Charles a little later. He's sitting in the parlour with *Le Figaro*, doesn't look up but he knows she is there. 'Is there coffee?'

'I dropped my handkerchief.'

'At the chapel?'

'Perhaps. The lace-edged one. I'll go back—'

Now he looks up. 'Jeanne.'

'I know. But it's only to the chapel and there'll still be others there.' Smiles. 'I won't be long. And I'll bring your coffee afterwards.'

We do not tell lies. A rule she herself has encouraged and passed on to her boys – that a lie is a bad seed sown, and it will only grow into a troublesome plant. But aren't there worse crimes? And there can be no injury with this. Just as there was no chance of injury by taking the sorrel to them. Jeanne has no intention except to see – to peek through the doorway, to look a little more at this patient who's come. That's all.

Ma petite espionne. Claudette called her this, having seen Jeanne's dark-brown eye through a keyhole so that she'd crouched and peeped right back. 'I see you, child ... *Ma espionne.*'

Jeanne goes through the yard, under the pines.

Perhaps the door is closed now. Or perhaps the Dutchman has left, gone away. But no, the door is still open and the man is still there.

Jeanne presses herself against the wall, leans in.

The easel hasn't moved. Nor, perhaps, has he – for he stands in the same pose exactly, holding the paintbrush above his head as if he's candle-holding, trying to see in fog or at night. The colour she sees is purple. It's everywhere – on his brush and fist and overalls and on the canvas itself which is so thick with paint it shines.

Irises, on the canvas. The ivied wall.

Turn, she thinks – wishing it. Turn – to the man who stepped out of his clothes as if clothes never mattered, as if decency and order mean nothing to him. Who comes from a far-away, Dutch-speaking place.

Turn. She wants this.

As if he does hear, he turns. It's one movement: a quarter-turn of the head and no more but it's enough for Jeanne to see very clearly – the long straight nose and the heavy brow. And she gasps, then. She gasps because this man is not like other men: this man is on fire or he seems to be burning for his beard is a flame of bright-orange and red. It's copper and autumn and rust. It is fox, perhaps, or the pelt of a deer. The shade of fevered skin.

The patient stands still, sensing her.

Jeanne steps back.

A twig breaks underfoot. At this, the Dutchman turns entirely. His heads snaps round and he sees Jeanne standing there. Then he drops the brush into the grass and he takes four strong, sudden steps towards her, wading through the irises. He doesn't take his eyes off Jeanne.

She stumbles.

He stops.

He pulls off his hat. From this, she sees that his hair is the same bright fire-red as his beard. It's thick, unbrushed, darkened by sweat where the hat has been and he bears a dent from the hat's brim – a crown of some kind – and he stares directly at Jeanne, who is standing in her buttoned dress, her Sunday best, with her hair pinned back.

Blue eyes. Blue as sky.

It wasn't his wrist. It was not his wrist that he sliced at in Arles.

One ear is nearly gone. His left. His left ear. There is no lobe to it. The lower half is missing so what's left is only the upper, hard shell and the hole itself – purpled, obscene.

She clasps her mouth with both hands.

'Is this,' he calls, 'what you came for? To see this?' He points at the wound. 'See? Look at it! See *le fou roux*! Are you contented now?' And he takes one more step to her, flicks the straw hat twice, three times, four, as if to say *Get away! Leave me! Go! Go! Go!*

Jeanne doesn't stop until she's back in the kitchen.

Water. Drinks from cupped hands.

His mutilated ear lies before her. The hole in the side of his head is still in her sight – waxy, scarred. And she can hear his outrage, his accent, how he spat out the words *le fou roux*. The mad redhead. Is this what you came for?

'Find it?' Charles, calling through.

Find what? Her handkerchief. 'It was on the pew.'

'And the coffee? Could you . . . ?'

'Yes.' She boils the water with shaking hands, fills his cup.

Claudette was more than hunched. More than baked by years of sun. An unmarried, sour-tongued creature who spoke her own strange Provençal – shaded and textured, a slurring of words. A maid, a housekeeper and a carer for this child.

'Not like that. Like this . . . ' How to clean a fish of scales.

'Yes. Sorry.'

'You will be. Try again.'

More than a mouth that knew curses, spat out cherry stones. More than a woman who applauded the use of the guillotine – 'Why shouldn't I? It gets rid of the bad ones' – so that Jeanne wondered who these bad ones were if Claudette, with her hairy lip and withered hand, thought herself good and worth saving.

For Claudette had a deformed left hand that she tucked under her apron. Claw-like, a twisting of tissue and bone. For years Jeanne had thought about it. She'd wanted to see it: this fleshy hook that couldn't carry a saucepan's weight or thread a needle or braid Jeanne's hair. She longed to see it properly. Spied through keyholes. Peeped round doors.

'Enough,' Claudette said, one day. 'Do you think I'm a fool? Do you want to see my hand? Come here and see it

47

and let's get this done with.' Laid it down on the tablecloth. 'Take your time because I won't do this twice ... Look,' she said, 'at the thing.'

It looked broken. Bones where they shouldn't be, pushing up under her skin.

Later, tucking the hand away, she asked, 'Are you contented now?'

And had Jeanne been? Perhaps a little. Perhaps the inquisitive part of her had been calmed by what she'd been shown in that room – that mangled hand laid out on the tablecloth. A dried fish. A withered land.

But she still tried to glimpse it sometimes. Seeing it once didn't mean she didn't wish to see it twice or three times. And mostly Jeanne felt that way whenever she spied: that to simply see a thing wasn't quite enough. She'd wanted to touch those bulls – to reach through the boards and pat their sweating sides. To walk through all the rooms that were locked to her. To enter those shady, private gardens whose gates she'd stare through, holding their bars, and do handstands there.

Five

La ville verte. Saint-Rémy. 'It's not too far from Arles. A train ride, that's all. I think you'd like it, Jeanne.'

Charles, on their fifth meeting. Treading around *marriage* as if the word was sleeping. 'I've been offered work in the asylum there. So if . . . '

Verte. Yes, known for its baskets at market that are too heavy to lift. The waist-high grass. Honey that tastes of lavender, or thyme. But Saint-Rémy is known for other things too – for the Roman ruins called Les Antiques, a mile to the south of the narrow streets. They aren't as famed as the aqueduct near Nîmes or Les Arènes, where the bullfighters are – but these two stone structures are Roman nonetheless. An archway and a tower. They stand in a pine-shady place. The tower is the mausoleum for which the monastery was named, carved with gods and warriors. Charles liked it best, perhaps for its solemnity. But it's the archway that Jeanne has always liked more, and feels with the palms of her hands when walking round it – a shelter of sorts, carved with women whose faces have been worn away by the years and years and yet still seem to be looking downwards, onto passers-by. Queens or slaves? Both, maybe. This arch used to span the ancient Roman road between Rome and Spain. *Via Domitia*, Charles told her. A name like a wind.

No road there now. Only pine cones and the droppings of goats. The boys used to play here – *Maman! Look!* – jumping down from plinths so that Jeanne's heart was in their own little hearts in that briefest of moments, as they fell.

Did you see, Maman?

I did. Very good.

Saint-Rémy is known, too, for the quarry from which Les Antiques were hewn. The olive groves. The road to Les Baux – a fortified town in the highest parts of Les Alpilles, a castle built into the rock. It's known for the canal. For the old, dusty monastery which is a mental hospital now. *You must have heard of it. Saint-Paul? It's where the lunatics go . . .*

But these things are the town's landscape. They are the places around it, from which she can see the church tower and the trees in the square: they aren't the town itself.

In need of food, Jeanne goes. It is Tuesday. She walks down towards Saint-Rémy as she always does – hair pinned, basket on one arm. She tries to keep to the shade.

Charles told Jeanne very little of the town before she came here as his wife. What she knows, she discovered herself: the tall, Provençal houses, their backs to the north, with their blue-painted shutters. The chalk-white wall near Place Favier that clothes are sometimes dried against, and can be too hot to touch. Courtyards of vines. Alleyways. Fountains against the sides of churches which spill and attract the sparrows and cats. It is near such a fountain that a man called Nostradamus made his strange predictions about the future, and stars. Plane trees make each road an avenue.

Her boys discovered even more. In the village school Jean-Charles, Laurent and Benoît learned what she had done – the alphabet, how to count, to add and subtract – but they also learned discipline. Charles instilled it: the need to learn, to listen, to do as they were told by Madame Meunier and be polite at all times. No being late. No chattering or daydreaming in school hours. So they came back with a knowledge of gravity and politics, poetry and human bones. As for other children in the Meunier school, they took no notice of the name Trabuc. They didn't mind that the boys' father was the warden at the place where the insane rocked in their chairs, didn't mind that the boys' mother was the strange, quieter kind: Jeanne's sons had friends enough. Not many, but some. They'd play in the cemetery. Jump off the bridge on the road to Maillane, into its stream, on the hot August days.

Those friends have also gone now. Such is the way, perhaps, with young men. *Go.* See those countries whose names they learned when they were small. *India. Mexico.*

Of all things, what Jeanne has come to know in Saint-Rémy is the market and how it can spill into streets and squares but mostly it finds its home in the Place de la République, where mules are tethered under the trees, with the *pat-pat* of their dung. Here, the women bring out what they have to sell; they'll sew or talk or breastfeed, call out to children or husbands or dogs. Cockerels fight in corners. Housewives sweep. There's the smell of mule and sweat and tobacco and the church of Saint Martin stands in the far corner, watching it all – the bartering, the daytime sleep, the fanning to keep the flies from the meat.

One summer, eagles roosted in the crevices of the church. Her boys had been amazed at this. *Real eagles, Maman? Real? With wings?* They played marbles in the warm dust of this square.

Jeanne comes to Madame Arnoux, speaks her Provençal. 'One bunch, please.'

'I don't have many.'

51

Asparagus. Soft, white stems. 'Then just a small bunch, Madame. *Merci.*'

Jeanne takes the vegetables. In return, Madame Arnoux takes the coin warily, examines it as if it might not be a coin at all. 'There's a new patient.'

'Yes.'

'The first in how long?'

'A while. Years.'

'Three years? Four?'

'Four.'

This is Gilles's doing. He rarely works any more, for he's old and can't be paid as much as he was, but when he does work he is watchful. He notes what he sees. If a patient falls down or cries out, if a nun calls for help or if Gilles hears any whispers of blood, he carries the news to his wife – a doll-sized woman who, in turn, passes this news on. She slips up to ears, says, *Have you heard . . . ?* So it's always been. The marketplace lays out rumours, alongside the peaches and dung.

'Foreign,' the woman says. 'That's what I was told.'

'I don't know about that.'

'You must know.'

'I don't work there, Madame.'

'But your husband does. The Major does. Doesn't he run the whole place these days? Since Peyron . . . He must tell you things. And you live where you live, which is near enough to see yourself, surely?' Madame Arnoux narrows her eyes, tilts her head. 'I've heard he paints. That he's painting in the garden – not flowers but ugly, rotting things. Moss and dead wood. Odd-looking too . . . ' With that, the woman leans forwards. 'Madame Trabuc . . . What's the harm in sharing what you see and hear?'

Jeanne smiles, steps back. 'I keep to my house, that's all.'

'Sounds lonely to me. No sons any more. No Madame Peyron.'

'I still have my boys. They're just not at home.'

'Even so.'

'There is Monsieur Trabuc.'

'Of course.' She says those words as if she doesn't like their taste. And with that, Madame Arnoux leans back and folds her arms.

'Thank you for the asparagus. *Au revoir*, Madame.'

Jeanne has never been to Cavaillon or Fontvieille or to any of the other towns, and so she can't know if all towns-women talk so freely – but she could easily believe that Saint-Rémy's women talk far more than most. Nostradamus spoke of what was yet to come; they speak of what has been, or is – as busy as needles at work. That happened from the start. In Jeanne came, her stubborn hair tied in a poor, unpractised version of the Arlésienne way, with her military husband and her plain face. They raised their brows at this arrival of two. Came closer to her, sniffing her. And perhaps they might have warmed to Jeanne if she hadn't been so quietly spoken, with so little to speak of or to bring to their lives, or if they hadn't learned that her husband worked amongst the invalids who bite themselves or others, howl on full-moon nights. With this, they mistrusted her. Mistrusted Charles too – for his job, but also for seeming so distant and hard which Jeanne knows he can be, without meaning it. As if he sometimes forgets he's no longer the leader of men.

They say this of Charles Trabuc: that he killed many men in the army. Shot them. Stabbed. *Throttled too . . . He has the right hands. Look at them.*

Jeanne walks away.

In the early days of her wedded life she wondered if she might tell the women of Saint-Rémy-de-Provence this: that she wasn't simply a warden's wife. She'd been a daughter too. A haberdasher's baby. A shopkeeper's girl. A woman who knew the texture of lace, how to cut it properly. Who knew shells from white coastlines, cloth that had been dyed with indigo. *Lafuye's – Haberdashery –* written above the shop in gold.

Perhaps such tales would soften the wives of Saint-Rémy, if they knew? Make them more accepting? But Jeanne chose against it, in the end. It felt like a disloyalty to Charles. And what good could it do? What change might it make? They'd made up their minds about Jeanne. And their minds have stayed made. Jeanne is from Arles, not here. Jeanne was friends with the wanton Laure. Jeanne has married a hard, pompous man who murdered men in a distant war. And Jeanne lives too close to lunacy for any of these wives to feel safe.

Mostly, Jeanne feels like a shadow in this market, passing through. But they are all glancing up at her today.

'Ah, Madame Trabuc! We hear there's a new patient who . . .'

'Would you like any cherries, Madame? Come here, and . . .'

She gives her tight smile. She says nothing of what she knows of the Dutchman – how his fists were iris-coloured or how he held the brush up high.

Nor will she. *He is mine, all mine –* with his eyes, his sunset hair. She walks past the stalls feeling this hardness, this new certainty: *the Dutchman is mine.*

She buys other things. A tufted ball of early beetroot. Two goose eggs from Madame Lenoir. And as she is leaving the Place de la République, Jeanne sees honey. May feels too soon for it. But what matters is that it's here – from the bee-keepers whose forearms are always bee-stung and who cut

54

out the comb and wrap it in paper, twist it as if it's a gift. A routine as old as the Trabuc marriage: Jeanne buys honey when she can. She buys it instinctively, with the half-gone memory of being young, of how they'd eaten some together in their first married summer, sucked it from their fingers as they'd lain in the grass and thanked the passing bees for it. 'This honey ... Delicious.' And in that moment Jeanne saw the boy that Charles had been. She'd paused in her own eating, looked across at this man – he is my husband now – and smiled at how he sucked his fingertip. How he flexed his toes at this honey's taste, and hummed.

Five births and thirty years later and still she buys honey for him. It is Charpentier. His hives are to the south-east, near miles of lavender. He nods. 'One?'

'Please.'

'Like this?'

'Yes.'

He cuts into the comb. 'My regards to your husband' – as if afraid.

Jeanne nods. 'Thank you.' He has bee stings on his forearms, neck and jaw but his ear lobes are untouched by them – pale, a little downy. Later, walking home, Jeanne reaches for her own and feels them. Delicate, as soft as fur.

'Honey?' Charles cracks his knuckles. 'And is there bread?'

There's bread. 'How was your day?'

He takes his time with his mouthful. He takes one thumb, sucks it clean. 'Charpentier's?'

'Yes. He asked after you.'

'Kind.' A pause. 'Not a good day. We had a problem. With Rouisson. He's been calm for ... well, years now, as you know. But last night his terrors came back – as strongly as they had been when he first arrived, so that he asked where we'd hidden his daughter, thought we had caged her, struck out . . . ' Shakes his head. 'It was wretched, Jeanne. Poulet restrained him. Rouisson's sedated now, but . . . Well, he's not well. Bit his tongue very badly. The blood was . . . ' Charles looks at the honey.

'I'm sorry.'

'He's still restrained. Must be. For his own sake.'

'Yes. Here.' She offers him more.

Charles holds his bread up. He watches as she pulls the knife along the side of it, leaving the honeycomb on it, and thanks her. Takes a bite. 'I can't understand it. Why now? No change in his dose or routine. I looked at Rouisson's old papers – no anniversary of any kind that might have awakened these troubles and no visit from a friend that might have undone him like this. He was kicking the door. He's broken a chair and damaged the wall. I'm surprised we didn't hear it.'

'From here?'

'From here. Benoît did once, didn't he?'

Jeanne remembers that. It hadn't been Rouisson, for Rouisson hadn't yet come to Saint-Paul. But their third son had woken in his nursery one night to hear a distant wail making its way over the fields, and he'd padded down to her. *Maman . . . ?* Not afraid. Benoît was never scared by the world. Jean-Charles could be, at first – wary of dogs, a little anxious of tasks he felt that he might fail in and, sometimes, the mistral was too loud for their eldest son, so he whimpered. But that was only Jean-Charles. Neither Laurent nor Benoît ever seemed afraid. Laurent was too wilful for it. As a schoolboy, it was Laurent who'd come home with a torn pocket or a missing shoe and give no proper answer as to how, or where; in his teens, he'd flout his father's rules. He'd swear, sulk. They could pace this house like wild cats, Charles and a growing Laurent. But Benoît? He was unafraid in a far softer, slower way. Benoît the watcher. Benoît the opener of boxes, the taster of fruit. Of all three, it was Benoît who'd watch the patients in their pews on Sunday mornings and whisper his thoughts and questions to Jeanne during a hymn: who is that one talking to? Or, why does that lady cry? Never fearful of them. He just wanted to know as much as he could about his life and others' lives. And that night he'd tugged at Jeanne's nightgown to tell her about this strange, ghostly wail from the hospital that he didn't know or understand. *Don't worry, mon chou,* Jeanne told him. *Someone can't sleep. But we can, can't we?* Fetched blankets. Led him back to bed.

'He did. Yes.'

A week before he left for the Americas, Benoît had come to her. He'd found Jeanne in the vegetable patch, dark-handed, and asked if she minded his leaving. His going away. 'Because I can stay. If you want me to.'

Stay. She could have said it. For a moment, Jeanne had wanted to grasp Benoît and absorb him back into herself, keep him safe and with her. She could have said, Don't go. But she felt something else far more, and far stronger – which was that she wanted Benoît to walk down the lane and board a train and walk out across the globe that she'd spun with her finger on winter nights. To see oceans. Run. She'd smiled. 'Don't stay.'

'Rouisson.' Jeanne looks up. 'Which wing is he in?'

'East,' Charles says, swallowing. 'He always has been. For years it was just him in there.'

*

The days pass. They take away the milder heat of May and asparagus; they bring in June and nectarines, a slight scent to her body when she rises at dawn. This is a landscape in need of water now. Slowly, the canal reduces itself. The goats stay in the shade.

With each Sunday that follows Jeanne looks to the door in the wall. Closed. Even so, when Charles remains in the chapel to pray a little deeper, Jeanne walks home and feels the ivied door – testing it with her fingernails. Is it locked? Could she force it, as she once forced a door in Arles because a dog had slunk under it? She'd wanted to follow that dog. But she can't force this door.

In the evenings she asks the same thing: 'How is Rouisson today?'

He doesn't mend quickly and doesn't sleep through the nights. When Jeanne lies awake and looks into their own bedroom's dark she imagines Rouisson, and how it must be for him. But she also imagines the others – how his voice must echo, how they hear his crying out. The sound of their dry heels being drawn across sheets as they sigh and turn onto their sides, wanting to find even the shallowest of sleep. As for the Dutchman, she wonders if he can lie on his left-hand side, or if it hurts him to – and if a severed ear could still hear the crying out.

'The sorrel. It's growing better this year than it's ever done. We've too much for us. Shall I take some?'

'Where to?'

'To the kitchen. To Marie-Josephine.'

'No,' says Charles.

'Or just to the entrance, then? Charles, there's so much.'

'Not with Rouisson as he is.'

'Restrained, you said.'

58

'Jeanne.'

She shifts her jaw, turns away. With her father she had two choices: to obey a rule, or pretend she had. Mostly she obeyed. But other times she'd walk down the Chemin de Brissy at dusk, despite the tales of beggars and gamblers meeting there; she'd stand at the end of the rue du Bout d'Arles and look down. Would sit down by the men playing cards in the shade, ask them to explain their game. Nor did she ever stop trying to entice those cats inside with slivers of fish, or chicken skin.

'Have those cats been in here?'

'No, Papa' – wide-eyed. And after he'd closed the door again she'd peep under the bed and tell the cat – licking its lips, with its fleas and sores – that it could stop hiding now. 'Don't tell anyone . . .'

With Charles, she's been different. Her vows in church did that, perhaps. Or being the warden's wife. A sense of duty came with it.

But look, she thinks breathlessly. She is like the cats in Arles that slunk into shadows, kept to the sides of things. Gave no sign of their daytime wanderings when they sat by the hearth at night.

He paints in the garden, Madame Arnoux said. But if the door in the boundary wall is locked, and if Jeanne has been forbidden from taking the sorrel past Sœur Madeleine with the key round her neck, then how can Jeanne enter the hospital grounds? And without being seen?

She kneads dough. She hangs out the clothes on the line, and it's as she hoists her aprons and his uniform into the air that it comes to her. *There is a back door.* For hadn't Sœur Marie-Josephine said so? That Gilles had used the kitchen's back door to leave the rabbit, still warm?

*

Jeanne chooses the height of the day – when lunch has been eaten, the tables cleared and the saucepans washed and laid out to dry. Some of the patients will be sleeping, their shutters closed for a temporary night. He might be too, of course. But reddish hair belongs in heat and light. Benoît could never sleep during the day.

She pads down the lane. Peels away from it, through the olive trees. She touches the northern end of the boundary wall, uses it to guide herself round the side of the hospital. Past a mule's dung heap. A splintering cart.

There. The kitchen door.

Through the kitchen and the corridors. She pauses in archways, peeps round corners. She ducks beneath ivy, steps outside.

In the early days of Peyron's directorship this garden – a courtyard, bordered by a brick wall and three walkways – had been beautiful. Now the pathways have greened. The fountain – a twisted fish of stone on a plinth in a circular pool – merely leaks into the bowl beneath it, where water spiders live.

Her heart grows faster.

Hush ... hush ... Like a broom. Or a bird's wing on a nursery floor. Or it's a painter's brush.

There's no difference in the Dutchman when she finds him. He wears the same blue overalls, the same straw hat. He holds the brush high, lantern-like, but then he brings it down with force, pressing the brush against the canvas so that it spreads out like a fan; sometimes he hauls the brush up and down through this thickness of paint and this is the sound she hears – the *hush* ... He holds a palette. Beside him, a folding stool. By his feet and half-hidden by grass is the metal box; tubes spill from it.

Around him, moss. The trees meet overhead so the light

is strange, half-green. This is the corner where Gilles will bring his grass and branches and unwanted earth and his dead, softened wood.

'*Excusez-moi.*'

His turn is instant – as if a stone's been thrown and struck him and he's turned to see if more are to come.

'We've met. *Excusez-moi.*'

A pause. 'By the irises. You came to see my ear.'

'Not your ear. No, that isn't why.'

'Of course it was.'

'No.'

'Then why?'

She stares. Why? She doesn't know. She stands, finds she has no answer for him – only that she wants to be here in this garden, this place of undergrowth, looking at him. Yet she doesn't say that. 'We don't have many new ones.'

'New ones?'

'Patients. Coming here. It's been four years since any came.'

His face remains fixed. Shadows pass across it when the branches move overhead but his face itself doesn't change. 'Your name.'

'Jeanne.' Her voice halves itself so she says it again: 'Jeanne. Trabuc. The warden's my husband. We live in the white house—' and she gestures to it, even though it can't be seen.

'The Major?'

'Yes. The military. Used to be.'

'He's your husband?'

'Yes.'

'Ah.' He glances away. He tilts back the brim of his hat with the back of his hand. 'Not all people are kind, but they seem kind enough here. Your husband and Peyron – is his name Peyron? They gave me two rooms when I asked, and that's kind.'

There isn't a colour on his palette that's brighter than his own. Even in this half-light his hair's like rust to her. His beard is metal left in the rain, an unused bolt that won't open or shut. 'In the east wing. I heard.'

'Yes. The morning sun moves across my wall. A warm room too.'

Salles said the accent was mild. And it is: Jeanne might not have known he was foreign from these words so far. There's only the slightest edge to his French, as cloth might fray when cut with old shears. She hears it with *kind*, and *morning*.

'There's wheat. Through the bars of my bedroom I see wheat fields, and a hut, and the hills. What are these hills?'

'Les Alpilles.'

He turns away. He talks to himself – a whispering that Jeanne doesn't catch. His own language, perhaps. She keeps her eyes on him: she sees how he works at his lower lip with his teeth and tongue, how his hands are gloved in paint of green and dark blue and black-green. He tilts back his hat a little more and by doing this she sees his ear – the right, untouched and perfect one. An ear like all ears. Pink and ridged, with the paler skin where it's stretched over its frame.

'Do you like it here?' Quietly said. There is such a long pause that she thinks he hasn't heard her, and she nearly says it twice.

'Like it? I seem the least ill. I've never been in a place where I seem the least ill. Others are far worse than me. There's a woman with a doll. And some poor wretched soul who—' He glances back. He narrows his eyes. 'What do you want, Madame?'

'Want?'

'You say that not many patients come. So are you here to stare? Do you want something from me? A story to tell? What?'

Briefly, Laure comes to mind. Laure wouldn't be afraid if she were here now; she wouldn't tremble or lack the right words or feel her heart beating. Then Jeanne looks down. From her apron she retrieves a single bunch of lavender, a dozen stalks, dried and tied with straw. 'Here.' Offers it.

The patient doesn't move.

'It's lavender. We keep it because moths don't like it and it saves our clothes. It grows round here. But they also say it helps you sleep.'

'I painted one. Yesterday.'

'A moth?'

'Yes. A death's head moth. In this garden – just there. You think I can't sleep?'

'His name is Rouisson. The man who's been calling out in the night? I know his room is near your room.'

'Rouisson?'

'Yes. Émile Rouisson. From the Languedoc.'

'Rouisson . . . ' The Dutchman shifts his jaw, looks down. 'That's an ill man. The nuns have patience. Your husband too – I've heard the Major's voice in the corridors, trying to calm him down. Your husband seems to be the zookeeper in this crumbling zoo, doing his best with his orders and chains. Whips, maybe.'

'No chains. No whips.'

'No. But perhaps he should have them. There are lions and lionesses.'

'No whips. He's kind. You said so.'

'Yes.'

'You painted a moth?'

He glances back at her. 'It surprises you?'

'When I heard a patient was coming here, I wasn't sure why. Saint-Paul isn't as it used to be, and Salles knows that. But he said he was bringing you for the fields, not the building itself, that you would paint the landscape – and I understand that, because there are so many flowers in spring and the light can be like gold. But you've chosen a moth? It seems ...' Tiny, perhaps. Even for Jeanne, who has had her small joys.

'Dull? Do you mean dull?' A sudden anger in his voice. 'You think it's all seascapes and festivals? Picnics in parks? Portraits of queens? Of course you do ... Theo would like me to paint such things because such things sell in the galleries, but I'd rather have weeds. The stone benches. There's a dead tree in these grounds that they say was struck by lightning, and I'll paint that tomorrow, or the next day. The moth matched the bark I found it on – so plain and brown that no one else saw it, but I saw it.'

Theo? She isn't sure who he is. 'You painted the iris bed.'

'Yes, that too. No neatness to it. There was a lone white flower amongst the rest that needed to be painted and I wish I could paint it again, paint more irises. But the irises are gone now. Their season's passed.' He looks up into the branches. 'I'd paint far more, if they'd let me. Outside the grounds, I mean. Those hills. What are they called again? You told me.'

'Les Alpilles.' Jeanne tilts her head. 'You can't go outside the hospital grounds?'

An animal sound from him. He spits – a thick ball of saliva – into the grass, wipes his beard. 'Me? Too soon. *Le fou roux*, remember ... I'm the newest beast in the zoo and they aren't ready to untie me. I may yet kick or snarl.'

She looks at the place where he spat. 'Shall I ask?'

'Ask?'

It surprises her too – this question. Her voice comes again. Or, at least, it sounds like her voice; it's coming from her mouth and yet it sounds different, as if this dank corner and the half-light has altered it. 'The Major. I could suggest it. That it would good for you to go outside. Into the fields. Paint.'

A birdish stare from him. He neither blinks nor flinches, and when he speaks it's slowly, as if in warning. 'And why would you do that, Madame Trabuc?'

Jeanne looks away. Because he's new, yes. But it's more than that, far more. What would her truthful answer be? That she has been here for thirty years. That every day and night feel the same. That she used to think of other countries, force doors, wear yellow silk – but those days feel like a dream she had, and she hasn't really thought of them but she's thinking of them now. Dreaming of women who thought they were owls. *You make me think of Benoît. You make me think of Laure.* And how the words *entirely unclothed* had made her sit on the edge of her bed that night, aware of her body underneath her dress. She's aware of her body now. How she sweats. How she's breathing in and out.

But Jeanne says none of these things. 'Charles might not listen to me. But I'll try.'

For a moment the Dutchman stands like a painting himself. No movement. A single drip from his brush. Then he turns back to his work abruptly, decisively, as if he's done with Jeanne now. But Jeanne calls out, 'One more thing, Monsieur? My husband can't know that I've been here. I'm not meant to come here.'

'To the hospital?'

'The hospital or the hospital grounds. It's forbidden.'

The Dutchman glances back. His lips are parted – not in a

smile, as such, but she sees his reddened gums and brownish teeth. 'And I'm not meant to leave them. So what does that make us, you and I?'

He wipes his mouth on his sleeve. Turns back to his painting of the ivied wall.

Her father's illness had come in the last days of autumn. The mistral had rattled the locked shop door. He was well, and then he was not well – and he'd never be well again. Jeanne became the talker between them, making up for his new, slack silence by reading parts of books to him or telling him what she'd seen in the sky as she'd risen at dawn. How Arles smelt. Who she'd seen in the rue de l'Agneau. Jeanne made things up, sometimes. She imagined a flock of birds, moving like a shoal of fish, for she'd heard that birds could do this – so told him she'd seen some, lied.

The cup to his lips. *Drink, Papa.*

In time, he could hold her hand. His muscles remembered how to loosely take a spoon. But he was never able to turn the globe again. So this, too, became his daughter's role – to hold it and spin it, to find countries and say their names as he used to. Her own tap-tap. And just as this illness changed his life, and hers, and Claudette's and their house on rue de l'Agneau, so it changed that old, cracked globe. It felt different in her hands – smaller. She'd hold it like an egg that could break under her touch. Because now Jeanne's mind could not be on a future of foreign countries; it had to be on the cutting-up of food, the emptying of chamber pots. Her life moved around her father, and loving him more closely – and how could she resent this? He was her father. The man who'd tucked her into bed, who'd carried a butterfly to her on the back of his hand to show her its vibrancy. Who'd talked of the Camargue. Who had explained the gargoyles on the sides of Saint Trophime and shown her lavender and the succulence of pears and who'd told her that her mother was safely with God, but that she still loved Jeanne, even so. As he, too, loved her. Jeanne knew he did. She knew, too, that she loved him. She was *Jeanne-Jeanne*, his spirited girl – and as he slept by the hearth she vowed she would be good, dutiful. *I will take care of you.*

So Jeanne stayed with him. Reduced her world down to this house with its yard and cats and thick blankets, its kettle that puttered as it boiled. Its dust in corners. Its small view of the rue de l'Agneau.

Six

Her father had been Camarguais. He – Didier Lafuye – had been born in the southern marshy land where the cattle are black and the horses are white and there are, he said, flamingos. 'That sky. There isn't there a better sky in all the world . . . ' As if he knew this for sure.

If his own father – Jeanne's grandfather – hadn't died in that watery world, Didier might have stayed there. Never left. Looped ropes around bulls, turned as dark as their own dark hide. But his father did die, without warning. And so Didier, his mother and a hard-eyed sister came inland, away from the land of far horizons. Arles. Arles was their choice – where the Romans had fought and drank and cheered, and where the Lafuyes were called *gitans* in the street for their colouring, their own way of speaking and their lack of height. They were mistrusted by some. 'We never begged. They thought we'd beg but we never did.' Instead, despite their strange accents and squatness, the women found work as maids. The house had five storeys, a cellar and a piano. It also had a tiny-waisted mistress who rustled as she walked, fanned herself with feathers made by no bird that Didier ever knew – and many birds had flown through the Camargue in his lifetime. He'd look up, as a boy, to see them. Not just flamingos.

'I've never stopped missing the marsh. But the wind was a cruel thing there. Horses died. And Arles is a good place to be.'

Didier worked in that five-storeyed house too. He polished boots and saddles, swept hearths, cleaned the brass of candle wax and once, on a rare day of rain, Didier had glanced up to see an even rarer thing: his older sister smiling. Her face had been lit up.

'Lit up at what, Papa? Smiling at what?'

'A pair of gloves,' he said. 'Edged with fur, and beaded. Her mistress had many gloves, Jeanne, but this pair was her best. That's when I knew.'

'Knew what?'

'That all women – even those as sharp and sour as your Aunt Marguerite – are drawn to fine things. Silk or ostrich feathers.' He winked, tapped the side of his nose. 'For beauty, there's always a franc or two ... '

So Lafuye's Haberdashery was born. At first, it was tiny – a pocketful of buttons in an alleyway beyond the city walls, near the shady graveyard of Les Alyscamps. But Didier told himself, *work hard* ... For wasn't this Arles? Where a statue of Venus has been dug out of the earth, so all of France believed this was beauty's home? Where beauty lived abundantly? *They're the most beautiful women of all, les Arlésiennes ...* France thought so. As did men who came to Arles with this in mind. And so a year later Didier had a shop on the rue Diderot – so close to Les Arènes and the theatre that it seemed the whole world walked past his door. He lost his dialect. He practised proper French and learned how to bow when his customers came in: *Bonjour, Mademoiselle ...* Revolutions didn't matter. Nor did droughts or foreign wars or sea mists that blew in and settled for days. Ladies still craved what was soft to touch or jewelled or bright; they would still gaze at the tortoiseshell combs or the velvet bows or the stitched handkerchiefs or the linen or the veils and sigh. 'Look . . . ' Gentlemen bought for their wives; fathers bought for their daughters. The bullfighters, still bull-scented, came in to buy gifts for the women who loved them – ivory buttons or a blush-coloured silk.

All this, in a little wood-panelled shop. Run by a man who'd been born in the marshes.

'Beauty, you see . . . '

Jeanne saw. When she was still small, and had to sit cross-legged every morning and late afternoon in a schoolroom near the Place Voltaire, she'd look at the other girls in the room. Were they beautiful? Or might they be? She considered this and a hundred other things in that school: the fate of a fly on the windowsill, what was for lunch, if Madame Desmarais's legs were as hairy all the way up. But such distractions didn't last. Nor did they stop Jeanne from longing to be elsewhere – away from the boredom, away from the children who all seemed to have mothers and distrusted this girl whose own mother was dead. She thought of the Rhône, and gardens. Of the market stalls. But it was her father's shop that Jeanne longed for most of all – to be in his wood-walled cave amongst his pearls and elephant tusks, to be polishing silver or measuring silk of such colour that she hardly dared breathe. Brooches made of amber that looked like caramel. Lace. Lapis lazuli. His glass jars and cabinets that refracted light.

'Let me come to work with you, Papa . . . ' Pleading.

By eight, at last, he agreed. 'Well, *ma petite* – if you aren't happy, and aren't learning . . . '

'*Merci! Merci!*' Jeanne danced, and he laughed. And so those were Jeanne's days from then on. Rolls of velvet, coils of gold thread. She learned her mathematics from measuring lace: Point d'Angleterre, Valenciennes, the black Chantilly, the Mechlin that ladies might tie into their hair in the evenings like a dusting of snow in the dark.

As for her own beauty, Jeanne also thought of this. In their single mirror she turned from side to side. Black eyes and black hair, a dimpled chin. Her forehead, she felt, was too large. And there were moments when she might pin a flower to her hair and pat it and consider herself a little prettier now, and she had a certain dress she liked in her teenage years, when her body had formed itself – of the brightest yellow silk. It was a shade that no one else in Arles had dared buy from her father's shop, so he gave it to her and she fashioned a dress from it – and to wear it felt, to Jeanne, like wearing summer sun. But mostly, Jeanne knew what she was. Claudette called her plain. The boys in the street didn't seem to look twice. And the rumours of her handstands on Place Lamartine didn't help with this; a motherless girl, curious and watchful, and who rarely pinned her hair so that it swung down her back. Jeanne overheard two ladies once: 'That's Aurélie's daughter? *Her?*' As if it wasn't possible. 'You must be mistaken.'

'No, I'm not. That's her.'

Jeanne pauses beneath the lime. She believes she can smell the shop for a moment – leather, polished wood. Sees the sun on that yellow dress. Can hear the bell above the door – *ting!* – and that was a good sound. But Jeanne folds these thoughts away as she'd fold cloth and place it in a drawer, using her hip and body's weight to close the drawer entirely – and returns to sweeping the yard.

*

In the days that follow it's Rouisson's name she hears. 'He gets no better, Jeanne. Less violent, perhaps, which will be the bromide's doing, but he's still unwell. Fretful.'

'Does he still think he's lost things?'

'Lost, yes. Or he thinks we've stolen from him. Last night it was letters. Said we'd taken old letters and burned them, said he could smell the smoke and it was Sœur Yvette's fault – but he's never had any letters in all the time he's been here. No one's written to him. What can be done? We don't want to keep restraining him. It distresses him all the more and restraints don't cure the thing. We need to know the cause of it.' Charles sighs. 'I'm writing to Salles.'

Salles. She nods. The pastor, too, knows Rouisson. Rouisson also came from the hospital in Arles. 'Do you think he can help?'

'Perhaps. We can try.'

So that night, after a meal of liver and haricot beans from their vegetable patch, Charles writes a letter to him. Jeanne dries the floral plates and watches: how he dips his nib into the ink and, by lamplight, writes. Sometimes she thinks she sees her boys in Charles – a gesture that she has seen in Jean-Charles, or how Laurent holds his head. But at other times she sees only Charles. And when she has dried the plates and stacked them she comes into the parlour, sits down beside him. 'After this, shall we write to the boys?' The ink is out. He has his pen.

'Of course. Which?'

Benoît can't be reached. Jeanne considers. 'Laurent?'

'It's his turn?'

'I think so.'

'Very well.'

Laurent writes far less than their eldest boy. But Jeanne accepts this entirely, knowing that he was always the son

72

with the strongest will and least concentration. Hopping from rock to rock, grasshopper-like.

There's the slow scratch of his nib, the rhythmic pause for more ink and, from time to time, he blots the ink with paper as if tending a wound. When he's done he passes the pen to Jeanne – 'There you are.' Rises from his chair.

'Are you going upstairs?'

'I'm tired, Jeanne.'

'I won't be too long.'

He leaves, and Jeanne looks at the letter. She pulls her chair closer, lifts up the pen. He's left her a quarter of the page or less, but so it goes – he writes better, has more to say – and she looks at Charles's words before she writes her own. Several times, he's written *Rouisson*. There are also lines about Peyron, which she follows with her finger-tip. *Peyron is having a good spell. Mère Épiphanie assures me he's eating well.* But Jeanne's eyes carry on, scan down the page – nuns, Paris, Gilles, honeycomb – until she finds, at last, the word *Dutch* – and on seeing it she leans closer. *We have a Dutch patient who cut his own ear, and has seizures. He paints a great deal, and his style is very unusual – uncomfortable, even. Some of the nuns are rather wary of his work but painting keeps him tranquil, which is all we can ask for. His canvases dry quickly here.*

She sits back. What to write to her middle boy? There is what she wishes to write and what she will write – and they won't be the same. Charles will no doubt read her words before sending them, so she can't write of lies or a fox-red beard, or this restlessness in her, or how she hopes Laurent is being bold and unfettered. *Enjoy being young.*

Jeanne writes: *We think of you often. This is a hot July. The canal is only half full. I am well and so is your father. He has written of Rouisson and the new arrival too so I won't write more, only*

*that it's quite strange having a new one here. We saw Salles and he
asked after you.*

Would Laurent wish to know that he was made on mid-
summer's night, when there were fireflies under the pines?
With Charles being a little unshaven so that, later, she found
her chin was pink? Jeanne smiles, thinking of that. She ends
by saying, *Stay safe and well, mon chou.*

Upstairs, she whispers, 'Charles?' He had frowned, on
seeing her sore, pink chin. He'd said, *I did that? Oh Jeanne.*

She wants to tell him of this. To tell him that she hadn't
minded, that she had liked it. It was proof of their love, as
Laurent would be.

But Charles is already sleeping. He lies on his side, faces
the wall.

In the chapel, the glass jar by the altar holds broom and lavender. There is the sense of trapped heat that comes in the
summer months. A trapped bee too.

Amen.

Afterwards, as Charles speaks to Peyron, Jeanne makes her
way back into the light and sees Marie-Josephine with her
furrowed brow. They're too close not to pass an exchange.
'*Bonjour*, Jeanne.'

'And to you. You are well?'

'Very well. And you? Your sorrel?'

'Less well, since it grew warmer. It's wilting somewhat.'

The nun smiles. 'Might that be said of us all? The kitch-
en's a poor place to be in this heat.'

'Can you open the back door? A breeze?'

'I can, but there's no breeze to be had. Very still.'

'Yes, very warm.'

'I told your husband that it might be the heat that's
brought the trouble to poor Rouisson. You've heard about

Rouisson? Never mind the mistral: I've been at Saint-Paul long enough to know the heat can be a real hardship for them all. It makes them eat less and sleep poorly . . . ' She moves her hand as she says this, rolling out her thoughts.

'Poor man, Rouisson.'

'I know. As for the Dutchman, he claims he doesn't sleep or eat in any weather, rain or shine, so this heat means nothing to him.' She smiles. 'Forgive me, Jeanne. I must . . . '

'Of course. *Au revoir.*' Jeanne watches the nun go, through the shade and light.

There's truth in it. In Arles, the bulls were far fiercer in July or August sun. Those baked afternoons were always the strangest too – when the human world was drowsing so the streets were deserted save for a lone trotting dog or a beggar, making his way from church door to church door. Fights, in the Place du Forum. Perhaps the nun is right. Perhaps the heat is the cause of Rouisson's worsening – why he plucks at his own skin, believes that everything is lost. Tries to break his leather straps.

'We heard he's gagged.' Jeanne is asked this in the market.

'No one is ever gagged, Madame. My husband would never do that.'

'What if they bite?'

'Even then.'

But Rouisson has known far hotter summers than this. Jeanne can't shake this off: that in the decade since Rouisson came to Saint-Paul there have been droughts that have dried the canal, a summer of such heat that fires came, crackled through the orchards to the south of Les Baux so they saw the rising smoke, smelt it on their clothes. Kept pails of water near their doors, in case. In those pails, the sparrows came to drink. And there have been thunderstorms. She remembers how Charles dressed at two or three in the morning and ran through the rain to the hospital, fearing the nuns would not cope with the patients' distress at the noise, the flashes of light. And Jeanne went to the nursery to be with her boys, watched the sky with them.

Summers so hot that she'd lick her arms, taste salt. And yet for all of this Rouisson stayed calm. No tales like these tales she's hearing now.

It can't be the weather that's damaged him. Made him afraid, cry out at night.

It's him. Jeanne knows this as well as she knows the view from each room. For how could the Dutchman have come to Saint-Paul without being noticed, or making his mark? Fire-haired and paint-smelling? Rouisson's ill, but no fool. He must know who sleeps in the east wing. That the man they petitioned against in Arles, who walked bare into Place Lamartine, lies in the room next to him. At night, a few inches between their sleepless heads.

A day of cicadas, the washing of clothes.

Charles walks home beneath the pines. He unfastens his cravat as he goes.

'Coffee?'

'Please.'

She brings his brown cup into the yard. A metal bench sits beneath the lime tree. It's rusted in places and rickety – and sometimes the hens will lay here, but there are no eggs today. A cobweb or two.

Charles sets himself down and she sits beside him.

'You look unwell. Tired.'

'I'm always tired, Jeanne. I'm old.' He smiles, takes the cup. '*Merci.*'

'No letter from Salles?'

'Not yet.'

This man used to cradle her. When they still shared a bed and had only been married a couple of years, he'd fit himself around her. He'd felt so much larger than Jeanne – a cave for her to shelter in.

'It will come. Salles is a busy man.'

'You are too.'

He's aged more in these past four years than he did with fatherhood. That day, at Christmastime – the incident where Peyron fell in the square, punched the ground – damaged Charles too. Not physically, but if the wives of Saint-Rémy had always thought Charles to be humourless and strict, he gave them proof of it that day. Jeanne saw all of it: how, for a second, Charles had seemed unsure – was this a joke, an act of some kind? But then he saw Peyron's blood. He saw the fists, the open mouth, and Charles became the Major then – hauling the man to his feet, seizing his fists, giving him such orders as *Get a hold of yourself, man!* He ordered the crowds too – to stop staring, get back to their work. The women sucked their gums at that.

Perhaps they're all mad up there . . . Even the workers.

Jeanne heard this. And she'd wanted to say, You don't know how hard he works. How much he cares. You don't know.

'I've been thinking,' Jeanne says.

'Hm?'

'Rouisson. When did it start? This trouble of his? Before the hot weather came, I think.'

'Mid-May. Yes, before the hot weather.'

'This new arrival came in May, I think?'

'We wondered that. If an arrival after so long may have troubled him, and I know that this Dutchman's the first to come in so long. But there have been others before him. Ten years, Rouisson has been here – think of the comings and goings in that time. Marcel, Thérèse, Yves, the owl girl. They've all arrived or left – and Rouisson never fell so ill with those.' He brings the cup to his lips again. 'Not arrivals. Can't be.'

'But Charles, what if it's . . . him. *Him*, Charles. This one.'

'The actual man?'

'Yes.'

'Why might it be him?'

Jeanne needs to be careful. 'I've heard he's strange-looking.'

'Several here could be called that.'

'Because he paints? The smell of the paint? I don't know. But didn't Salles call him unique?'

Charles sits back on the bench. He closes his eyes; his face is dappled under the leaves and she looks at his features. The jawline, the nose. When he opens his eyes he says, 'He *is* unique, I suppose. How much he paints, and what he paints – the undergrowth and corridors. You know the tree that was struck by lightning years ago? He's done several pieces of that. And his manner of painting, Jeanne: I'm no artist and I don't understand those things but I've got eyes, at least, and I think he paints . . . Well, childishly. It's disordered. Layered. The floor is already ruined in his studio. He's shown me a few pieces. I've seen some too, drying outside, and I told him they were splendid because what else can one do or say? But I find no beauty in them.'

'The nuns are wary of them? You wrote that, to Laurent.'

'One or two. Sœur Maude. But she was afraid of the wasp's nest last year.'

Jeanne smiles. 'What does he do with them? The paintings?'

'Sends them north. He has a brother in Paris who takes

them, tries to sell them. It's this brother who pays for the Dutchman to be here at all, so Theo must be fond of him. Or perhaps there's a sense of obligation, I don't know.' He sips again. 'You think it's the paintings? That the paintings might have upset Rouisson in some way?'

Jeanne looks beyond the yard. The sun has caught Les Alpilles, lightening their western sides. In the groves, too, she sees at that moment that the western side of every tree is golden with sunshine, row upon row, and there's a brightness in the depths of the waist-high grass. Laure would have walked through this. Jeanne, if alone, would want to lie down in it. 'Maybe.'

'We can't stop him painting. Painting keeps him well, he says.'

'Could you move Rouisson?'

'He's always been in the east wing. He's had the same room for years, Jeanne. And to move him might worsen him.'

'Move the Dutchman?'

'He says he needs the morning light.'

'Well ...' Jeanne shrugs. 'Maybe the Dutchman could paint elsewhere, by day. Far away from Rouisson? In the olive trees, perhaps. Look at them now.'

But Charles doesn't look. 'Leave the grounds? No, Jeanne. Patients must stay in the grounds at all times.'

'That's not true. Some have been allowed out, in the past.'

'Ones we know. Can trust to be well.'

'But you say he's calm. You say he's well.'

'Enough. Stop this please, Jeanne. I'm the warden, am I not?'

With that, the conversation ends. Jeanne makes her way into the kitchen, cuts bread and rinses the herbs. Charles stays beneath the lime till it grows dark. When he comes indoors he places the brown cup next to her – gently, and with care – and touches her back as he moves past. It's the first time he has touched her in weeks, she thinks. Months.

They eat by lamplight. *Le Figaro.*

'No reply from Laurent?'

'Not yet.'

Let him be in love, Jeanne thinks. Let his slow reply mean Laurent's in love. Let Jean-Charles be with his infant son. Let Benoît be with kind people in the land called Mexico.

When Laure came to Saint-Rémy for the first time she'd shaken the hand of each Trabuc boy. Never mind that Benoît had only been five, and his brothers not much older; Laure had shaken all their hands in a proper introduction, as if they were all gentlemen. Said *Enchanté, Monsieur.* They'd blushed, twisted their toes into the ground. This fair-haired woman who still seemed girlish, somehow. 'And what are your names?'

Laurent had whispered *Laurent* . . .

'Laurent? Mine is Laure! What a thing! So our names aren't too far away.' And all night the eight-year-old Laurent had peeped through the olives, towards Peyron's home.

Remembering this, Jeanne looks up. 'What's he called?' she asks.

'Who?'

'The patient. The new one.' Jeanne doesn't know.

Without taking his eyes from the newspaper, Charles tells her.

'Van . . . ?' She blinks. 'I didn't—'

Charles says the name again.

'That's it? His name?'

80

The Major looks up now, half-smiles. 'I know. It's Dutch, remember. And we've all struggled with it. But he knows that we do, says the French can pronounce his first name, at least – and so he goes by that. His first name alone. Easier.'

In the kitchen, Jeanne says it: his first, given name. Her bottom lip tucks itself under her top teeth; she hisses its tail.

It's a name that sounds like two words. Two numbers, in French: *vingt* and *cent*. Twenty and one hundred. The first number is not so large as to make a difference to her days and nights: what might twenty seconds be, or twenty olives plucked? But one hundred, she thinks, is far more. Wouldn't one hundred of anything always carry a burden, a weight? One hundred francs. One hundred patients. One hundred days of cracked earth.

Two numbers in one name. Large and small – both.

Her own name has no meaning. She knows no reason as to why it was picked for her, or which parent chose it. But she likes her father's claim – that on her arrival the church bells were so overjoyed that they sang out *Jeanne! Jeanne!*

It is neither one hundred days nor twenty before she sees him again. Three days, that's all.

She's in the old nursery, late in the afternoon. She looks out, and sees him – in the olive groves, walking with his easel under his right arm. His sunhat is pushed back; his gait is easy, slow. And he walks, Jeanne thinks, as reapers walk back from their fields, or as fruit pickers walk back from their trees: a sense of a day's work done. And does he glance at the white-painted cottage as he goes? Jeanne likes to think he does. A glance, as if in gratitude. This newly untethered bird of blue overalls and gold.

*

Vingt and *cent*.

At night she wonders if she might have ever thought of this name for a fourth son, or a fifth. But there couldn't have been more sons. Benoît, they knew, was the last.

Jeanne had named their youngest boy. She'd stated it, not requested – *He is called Benoît* – and Charles had agreed without any word of protest. It went unsaid, but they both knew of the two losses that had preceded him, that there would be no other children now. His birth marked the closing of a door. And after Benoît, they took to separate beds. Charles talked of restraint, the need for rest and Jeanne had agreed to this, at first. Her body was tender, after all. But she'd imagined a time when the beds would be pushed together again, so when they weren't she came to reinterpret their meaning – two beds with an expanse of floor between them: her job was over now. Her purpose as a wife was done. She'd given her husband three healthy heirs; what else might he want from her body? Or perhaps he now valued his sleep far more. Did not wish to share himself. Jeanne also needed sleep.

It's done. She said nothing of it. Rather, she chose to find a frail relief in sleeping alone for the first time in years – in knowing that the bed's warmth or any human smell came from her body alone. It reminded her of childhood. It made her dream more vividly. Also, it was easier for her to rise, in darkness, and make her way to a calling child without waking her husband who mostly slept through the night-mares and storms.

Twenty years have passed. It's felt longer but also, some-times, far less. Jeanne's body, she knows, is so very, very different from the last time Charles saw it – slacker, with parts that she can cup that she'd never even had back then. And him? Has his body altered? Are the dark hairs fewer, or grey? She hasn't forgotten the way that he used to climb on

82

top of her, lower his weight very carefully and say, Is that too much? It was never too much.

Twenty years. But Jeanne hasn't lost how it felt, the different tastes of him.

The cicadas sing out as she approaches him. And how she approaches him is how she'd come to any beast that she isn't yet sure of – mules, or cattle. Like them, the Dutchman has his own odour. A musk.

Jeanne's ten feet from him. He's crouching, setting his easel into the grass, and she thinks he hasn't seen her until he says, 'Les Alpilles? Do I say the name right?'

'Yes.'

'The small Alps?'

'Yes.'

'You've seen the true Alps, of course? Compared them?'

'No. Have you?'

Still crouching, he looks up at the hills. 'I know flatness better. Fields. When I walked in the fields in Nuenen I was the tallest thing. No trees or houses. I'd walk and feel as if a thousand eyes were watching me, or just one pair. God's eyes. I believed in God there. So much sky.'

The easel is done. He straightens up.

Jeanne says, 'That one? It's Mont Gaussier. And to its left there's a rock with two holes in it, so we call it Les Deux Trous. I've heard it sing.'

'Sing?'

'The mistral. When it blows through it, it makes a high sound. There are stories of ghosts in Les Alpilles.'

'There are no ghosts.'

'Some people think there are.'

'No ghosts.' The Dutchman turns his head. 'You spoke to him, didn't you? The Major?'

'Yes.'

He scratches his beard. 'Why? I asked you that but you never answered me.'

'You said you would paint far more if they let you out, into the fields. It seemed the right thing to do.'

'To help me to paint?'

'Yes, simply said.'

'Do you help all the patients like this? You don't know me. I might be a monster. I might be the worst of all of them and you've helped to set me free.' A thought comes to him, and he seems to rise up with it. 'Or you paint, perhaps? Do you paint, Jeanne? Understand the need of it?'

'Me? No.'

'Draw? Write?'

'I don't draw at all. I can write a little, and read.'

He seems disappointed by this. He spits, slowly wipes his mouth with his sleeve. Lowers onto the folding chair. 'A little? Not well?'

'Not well.'

'You were never taught to?'

'Yes. There was a school in Arles for a while but I left when I was eight. I didn't want to stay.' She shrugs. 'It felt a waste.'

'A waste?'

'Of days. Of being young. I wanted to be outside. Or to be with my father in his shop. So when I was eight I left and went to help him. It was a wonderful shop. Lace, and cochineal, and—'

'It's not a waste – to read, or write. You were foolish to leave, to be so impatient. We can't just leave the places we don't like. That's a child's way of thinking. Sometimes we have to stay because it's right that we do.' He points his thumb behind him, at the hospital walls. 'You think that's where I wish to be? Same conversations, same meals ... Beans. Always beans. But it's the right place for me, being as I am, and so, for now, I'll stay.'

Jeanne looks down. She watches as he reaches down to his metal box, lifts out tubes, and she feels like a girl who's been chastised.

'What made the holes in Les Deux Trous? Do you know?'

'Some people say—'

'Walk round.' An order. It is brisk, sudden. He points at the grass by his left side. 'Come here. I can't have you behind me. I've had bad dreams of voices behind me and enough people have done it. Come here.'

Jeanne steps forwards, nearer. His smell grows stronger: it's rodent, sour.

'Let me see you.'

As she draws alongside him he looks up. The Dutchman, seated, is lower than her. She must look down – and like this, Jeanne can truly see his face. It's half-shaded by the hat's brim yet she can see where sweat has dampened it, where age has made its mark. How old is he? She might guess that he's forty, at the very most; thirty-five, perhaps. And yet this face is marked and worn down. It makes her think of Les Antiques, which have altered themselves through the years of neglect and bad weather. There's a darkness under the eyes. The flaking lips are slightly parted and show his brown, uneven teeth; there are fronds in his moustache that are longer than the rest of it so they are damp at their ends – from sweat or spit, or water he has drunk. His eyebrows too. They're thick, almost blond. And his eyes themselves might have matched the sky above the Camargue if she'd ever seen that sky – the bluest blue, with birds and shadows blowing through, and yet she can imagine these eyes growing dark.

'The holes in Les Deux Trous. You were saying.'

She can't take her eyes off his eyes. 'Water. That's what I heard – that ancient rivers ran there and wore the rocks down. It must have taken years to make the holes, if so.'

'Water takes over a place. I knew when the Rhône would flood, in Arles; I could tell. I lived with a man who mocked me. He was a painter too. I said the Rhône would flood and he laughed but it did flood and he lost his work. He should have listened to me.'

'I lived in Arles. Rue de l'Agneau.'

'Rue de l'Agneau? I never went there. What do you want from me, Jeanne?' This isn't rudely said. It isn't said as it might have been in her youth, when she'd peeped through keyholes or followed Claudette like a beady-eyed fly. He says it as if he wishes to know – nothing else. 'People don't come to talk to me, you see. They never have. But you're standing here. Have you brought more lavender, or want to see my ear?'

'I want to say thank you.'

'To thank me?'

'Yes. You didn't tell Charles that you saw me in the grounds.'

'You asked me not to. So I didn't.' He shrugs. 'Shouldn't I be thanking you? I'm in these fields because of you, it seems.'

With that, he turns to paint. Jeanne also turns, but as she starts to leave he calls out her name so she glances back – his hat, his back that's darkening with sweat. 'Jeanne? No more lavender. It was useless. I've never slept well and never will until they bury me so a bunch of dried flowers won't help.'

*

86

In time, she learns this about him: that he paints as if he's late or there's no time left to work. He'll scoop the paint with his hands. Or he'll stand, use the brush like a spoon and throw the paint onto the canvas, not caring if it colours his hands or overalls or the grass about them. Sometimes he paints as if he's at war. Or sometimes it's as if the easel's sleeping, and he has no wish to wake it – the softest *dab . . . dab . . .* And when he paints, he has no awareness. He might have no knowledge of Jeanne standing beside him or sitting in the grass. He won't hear the cicadas or see the day passing, or the mules or the goatherd that leads his goats through the olives at dusk with their curious eyes and chiming bells. All he sees is the paint. And he'll hold his breath or roar at himself; he'll pick up a tube and squeeze the paint onto the brush directly, or onto his palette, or his blackened thumb. He'll throw down a brush. Spit. Curse. Speak Dutch. Walk into the trees as if furious before coming back, sitting down. And when it's all done he lowers brushes and paints, puts his head in his hands.

'Not good enough,' he says. 'Look.'

'I like it.' She does. She longs to touch each painting, to bend closer to these rectangles on which he makes a second olive grove, a second Saint-Rémy. 'It's wonderful.'

'No. Not good enough.'

His strong, unwashed smell. His eyes. And she sees, too, how he licks his lips when deep in thought, how his tongue runs from one corner to the other, which is why those fronds of his red moustache are slightly matted and damp.

Impatient. He'd called her that. She couldn't have disputed it: oh, she had been that. She'd wanted too much too quickly – to have those cats on her lap, to walk on her hands, to grow breasts, to leave that room of alphabets and blackboards and to wear that yellow dress every day or see the bulls in Les Arènes and the aqueduct near Nîmes. To kiss, or be kissed. To smoke a pipe. These things: *now*.

'Papa, will you tell me about ...?' His own parents, or the history of France. Who she might marry, and where she might live. And Didier would try to find answers for her – if he wasn't too tired or it wasn't too late.

But this changed. Her father fell ill, and in the days that followed this Jeanne learned that nothing could happen quickly now. She had been wishing life on. She'd been hurrying it, looking ahead – and the days of looking ahead were gone. *I will stay here with him.* Where her own daily pace could only be as fast as her father's new, slurred speech. And if she'd ever found pleasure in the little parts of life before he fell ill, she came to love them now: the jasmine, the rain or a candle, blown out. Her only sense of hurry came when Didier was sleeping, and Jeanne could slip into the streets at dusk and run so fast that her footsteps echoed off the buildings – *slap-slap-slap!* – and faces would come to windows to see who was running so fast.

She'd had to change. To shape herself to fit this new life. Jeanne put away the dreams she'd had before.

Perhaps Rouisson did this. Perhaps, over the years, with bromide and baths and ivied walls he managed to bury the dreams he'd had, to deaden the sense of waste – and want – for the wife and daughter he'd lost. Perhaps he'd tried, before Saint-Paul. But it was only at this hospital where, at last, he managed it – to take his rage and broken heart and seal them in a box. To eat. To sleep, even in corridors.

Impatient, said the Dutchman. And yet he is too, he must be. He does not paint like a patient man, nor does he speak

88

like one. And where was the patience in his life before Saint-Paul? Which rules has he obeyed? If he curses and spits and smells of his own breath and no longer has faith in God and has hacked at his ear and taken off his clothes in a town square and lived so that others petitioned against him, and goes by his first name? There is no change in him. He throws paint against canvas, gives orders. He has buried nothing, and what Jeanne feels when she's with him is that all her own impatience – her quickened heart and her wanting of things – is waking up after so long asleep. Stretching itself.

What do you want? Jeanne sits on the edge of her bed.

A dark room. A ticking clock.

She thinks, *To be the soil when pails are upturned. To soak it all – this, you – into my parched life.*

Seven

'You'll need to work hard. Say yes, if asked.'

'If asked what?'

'To marry someone.'

'But what if . . . ?'

'Say yes. Trust me – it won't happen twice.'

Claudette. The maid with the pomegranate skin. The splayed, large teeth that meant she whistled slightly when she said *s'il vous plaît*, which she rarely did. She'd never married. Nor did Claudette imply that she'd ever wanted to: how she spoke of marriage was how she spoke of bullfighting – a choice for fools, a danger, a thing she didn't want and had no wish to see. Something she wasn't built for.

'Who'd want this anyway? Love this?' Her withered hand, held up.

One night Jeanne crept to her father, tugging her thumb. 'What did it?'

He took off his spectacles. 'Did what, *ma petite*?'

'Claudette's hand. Was it a curse?'

'No curse. She was born with that hand, that's all. Just as you were born with yours.'

'But why is hers like that? Not like everybody else's?'

'Who knows? It can happen. And it's harder for Claudette here, I think.'

'In Arles, Papa?'

'Yes, in Arles.'

No husband for Claudette, then. Who'd pick her, when there were true beauties? With two working hands and stainless teeth? Women who'd buy lace from Lafuye's shop? The maid had her views on that too. '*How* much? For *lace*? For flimsy cloth with holes in?' As if she knew better than everybody else. No time for beauty, or wish to speak of it. 'It's pointless,' she said. 'And it fades.'

The space where Jeanne's mother should have been, with the handful of truths that Jeanne knew of her – long lashes, wide hips, a girlish singing voice – was filled by Claudette, and Claudette lacked all these things. Instead, she crushed spiders with her heel, dismissed flowers or festivals and scowled at the globe – for what good was dreaming too high or too widely? 'Take what you're given and say yes, if asked.'

'Was my mother beautiful?' Jeanne asked this, just once. But Claudette never answered – or rather she sniffed and turned her back – which was an answer, in its way.

The Dutchman is not the first patient to be allowed out of the grounds and into the fields and lanes. There have been others – ones that have been well enough to walk with the nuns under the pines, sit on the benches. In autumn, when the leaves have gone, there's a view of Avignon to the north and some of them ask to walk out and see it; some have come from that town. There was also the grey-haired Marseillais who wished to see Les Antiques. An educated man. He was a man whose brain had broken in many ways, but not in his wish to learn more, said Charles, so he'd take him to those old stones. They'd walk beneath the archway as the Romans had done.

So no, the Dutchman's not the first. But he's unaccompanied and this is much rarer – so rare that Jeanne can't list any other patients who've been unaccompanied as she moves the undergrowth, looking for eggs. Who have they trusted enough? To walk out on their own? Then a name comes to her: Deschamps. Gone, now. But for a time he was allowed to walk by himself to the five cypress trees that sway to the south and to sleep beneath them. He'd asked for that – said the sound of the wind blowing through them was like a river to him, that a river had been a comfort in his childhood. So he'd curl up at the feet of those wind-filled trees. A form of lullaby.

She moves through the undergrowth, thinking this – of Deschamps. Then, seeing an egg, she crouches – and it is whilst she's crouching that Jeanne hears two voices. She knows both of them. Poulet, the youngest warden. He of the shrug and the downy beard. He and her husband are standing in the lane.

'How does he seem?' Charles.

'I spoke to him. He's well, I think. His hands are covered in paint and there's paint in his beard that might never come out – but yes, he seems well. Monsieur, is this wise?'

'Wise?'

'The episodes in Arles. The madness, and the ear.'

'I know his history. I know. But I talk to him daily; he's shown nothing but lucidity since he came here. He eats enough and he's civil to the nuns. And he assures me that his paintings are part of his cure, that such work is restorative – and what reason do I have to disbelieve him? He wants to paint the olive groves. I'm a warden, not a gaoler. Do you think I'm a gaoler, Poulet?'

'No, Monsieur Trabuc.'

'That I'm too stern?'

'No, Monsieur.'

'Besides, it's only the olives for now. We'll see how it goes. And Poulet? Don't call it madness. I won't have that word. A little respect to them, please.'

'*Oui. Pardon.*'

'The hat, too. I've ordered him to wear a hat in this weather. His colouring is the kind that would burn within minutes and so we must ensure he wears it. Do you hear me, Poulet?'

Jeanne waits to be told these things herself. It takes a while: when Charles comes home he speaks of the nests of mud and clay that are being built under the hospital eaves, and the birds that dart through the corridors. But then he moves behind her as she breaks eggs into a bowl. 'Did I tell you? The Dutchman? He's allowed into the fields now. You'll recognise him if you see him, I'm sure – red hair and a red beard. You know to avoid him, of course. But I rather think you'd choose to anyway; he has baths twice a week as the others do, but even so . . . '

She waits until the sun is at its highest. Then she carries a cup of cold water out into the fields, finds him.

'You're working in the heat of the day. Most people sleep now.'

He turns. 'I don't mind the heat. I like the heat.'

'Water.' She offers it.

'It's the cold that troubles me. The damp English days. I felt them in my bones and couldn't work or sleep, and the cold can lead to far worse.' He takes the cup.

'It will get even hotter.'

'I know.' He drinks.

Jeanne watches him. 'You lived in England?'

'For a time. Didn't care for it. It rained constantly. Never a day without rain and it was so cold that I lost feeling in my feet and hands. Couldn't paint. That country gave me a cough.'

'An island.'

'Part of an island. I wouldn't go back.'

'What are you painting? May I see?'

The Dutchman half-smiles. 'What else could I be painting but the olive trees? Their bark and branches, their shadows on the grass. See the shadows? As the afternoon goes on they lengthen and turn a violet shade. Provence is different from the north.'

'Because of its shadows?'

'Shadows. Cicadas. Many things. You have cypresses.'

'I thought cypresses grew everywhere.'

'Not everywhere. I think they're like churches.'

Jeanne frowns. 'Churches?' This line of five trees near Les Antiques. Charles once called them soldierly for being so straight and lined up. All that height and dignity. 'There was a patient who used to sleep beneath them. He could only find sleep by the cypresses.'

'A church to him too, then. Sanctuary.'

She looks back. 'You don't go to chapel. I've never seen you there.'

'No. If there's a God He's found in other places. I don't have to kneel in a house of stone. I preached for Him once. Lived for Him. Spoke and moved for Him. It was what I wanted to be more than any other thing – to be a preacher. But I was wrong to want that. They laughed and I failed. I don't want that now.'

'What do you want?'

'To paint. To be well and no burden.' He says this as if *burden* is a heavy, hated word.

A small breeze comes. Jeanne feels it on her arms, takes the empty cup from him and decides that she too has found

God in other places – in a sleeping boy, or her friendship with Laure. In Charles. Yes, Charles, who used to breathe on the nape of her neck as they slept. 'You're settled here now?'

'My room's pleasant enough. Flowery patterns on the curtains that I don't care for, and having to wake and retire at the same time every day is . . . Well, I find that tiresome. But my dread of the thing is less at Saint-Paul.'

'The thing?'

He holds out his left hand and flicks it, beckons angrily. 'Stop standing behind me. Don't you remember? What I said? I don't like you standing behind me.'

'Yes.'

'There.' Without warning, he takes hold of her. His right hand seizes her left wrist and Jeanne flinches – but he holds her as gently as he might a child. He coaxes her, halts her. 'There.' Then he takes back his hand. He looks down at this hand, checking it. 'When I can't see who is speaking . . . ' A pause.

'I know. You said. I forgot.'

He nods. 'Your little white house. How long have you lived there?'

'Thirty years. Nearly.' She turns her wrist over too. Looks for a mark or proof of his touch – a little paint or, perhaps, a pinkness to the skin. But there is no mark at all.

'A mere afternoon for an olive tree. You know they can outlive a man? They can last for centuries. And the yew. What do you know of Monsieur Peyron?'

She doesn't expect this. 'What? Peyron?'

The Dutchman scratches his beard with the end of his brush. 'He's an intrigue to me. The director of Saint-Paul and a doctor himself, and yet I barely see him. I see your husband far more. People talk,' he says, 'of the Major far more than they talk of Peyron. Why's that?'

Peyron as an olive tree. It would be easy to believe it,

somehow – aged and withered by a frost that came suddenly, that no one had predicted. 'What rumours have you heard?'

'That he's widowed? Or not widowed? I've heard both.'

'Not widowed.' Although some thought to suggest it, afterwards. Charles himself had offered it – the thought that Laure's death might have, in fact, been easier for Théophile Peyron to bear. The rumours, too, of death – that she'd fallen, or drowned in the canal, or that she'd been hurt in the fields at night by an unseen man and dragged away. That she'd died in childbirth, even though Laure had been past forty when she went. So it goes, in Saint-Rémy. Madame Gilles and her restless tongue. 'His wife went away.'

'Went away?'

'Left a note on the kitchen table for him. Went north.'

'Does she mean to come back?'

'No, I don't think so. I don't think she quite knew herself. She just needed to go.'

The Dutchman pushes back the brim of his hat, squints. 'Do you know why? She was your friend.'

'Yes.' And for a moment Jeanne feels like telling him all about the bright rarity of Laure – how she'd listen to fruit when buying it, as if its ripeness had a sound. How Laurent would blush when she greeted him. There had been such energy in Laure. That's what Jeanne thinks of, when she thinks of her: her physical self, jumping a ditch or urging Jeanne to hurry up. How she'd set to work on the mules, picking burrs from their sides, not thinking the mules might nip or kick out. Her naivety too: an unwavering belief in the world. The romance novels she read. 'I think it felt too small for her. Saint-Rémy.'

'To be left by one's wife . . . I've not heard it before. Men have left their wives, of course. Men venture elsewhere and come back and there's a tolerance of that. But the wife . . . '

'You asked about Peyron. It changed him. Laure went, and he became forgetful, very anxious. Too talkative. He lost weight and prayed for hours on his knees. Then at Christmas he broke down. He fell in the market square so that Charles had to carry him back, or as good as, and everybody saw. You said he's a ghost and I think he is – a ghost of the Peyron he was before.'

'Can he work? Is he able?'

'Sometimes.'

'He can't leave? Find a quieter way of life?'

'But what if she does come back one day? And Peyron has moved so that Laure can't find him? I think he thinks that way.'

They're quiet for a time. On the canvas before her she sees each stem of grass in a copper-gold paint and they're ridged so that she could grasp them.

'Laure? Her name?'

'Laure. Yes. Peyron doesn't talk of her.'

The Dutchman scratches his beard again. 'Half the people in this world have been undone by grief, in one of its forms. Some can endure it, some can't. I've lived in places of such poverty that they must tie their clothes to themselves with string or the clothes fall away and if one harvest fails they're dead. Bury child after child. I worked in mines.'

'A preacher and a miner?'

'I didn't always paint.'

'I lost my mother. When I was born.'

'Then you know.'

'Yes. Do you have a mother still?'

'In Zundert. Does your husband know that you see me?'

'No.'

'He's forbidden it? As he's forbidden the hospital grounds?'

'Yes.'

'Yet you come.'

She looks down. She touches her wrist. 'Do you mind that I do?'

'Mind it? You're a strange thing. But you aren't throwing beans or sobbing in corners or dragging a doll ... Or not so I've seen.'

She looks up from her wrist, smiles. 'No doll. No beans.'

'Not yet, anyway.' He catches her eyes, smiles too. 'No, Jeanne – I don't mind.'

As if the chant of the Provençal hunters were true – as if Peyron were summoned by her talking of him – he comes to the white cottage, in the late afternoon. He walks up from the village, fanning himself. Striped by light as he walks beneath the planes.

'Ah! Madame.' The slight limp.

She straightens from the vegetable patch, brushes the earth from her hands. '*Bonjour.*'

A ghost, yes. But Peyron is real enough now. He carries his jacket over one arm; in places, his shirt has darkened with sweat. He pauses in the lime tree's shade, retrieves a handkerchief and dabs at himself – forehead, upper lip. '*Mon Dieu*. And it's only July.'

'Yes.'

Such polite exchanges with him. In the past four years, if she stitched such greetings together she might make an hour, no more. Jeanne can't recall the last time she really spoke to Peyron. When she knocked on his door after Laure's leaving and offered a pie or a little help to him, his words had been uncertain. But perhaps they've never talked freely, Jeanne and Peyron. Even before his wife walked away they'd only handed pleasantries back and forth. *Your garden is very beautiful.* Or, *How are your boys?*

He seems so far to her. She could reach out and touch him, yet is he far away.

Peyron folds his handkerchief. 'It will be a fierce August. I've heard there are wild fires near Sainte-Croix.'

'Oh?'

'But don't worry. I'm sure they won't reach us for this breeze is small and we're upwind of them. But it's proof that it's hot. Are you keeping well, Madame?'

'I am.' She watches him. 'Would you like a little water, Théophile?'

'No, no. *Merci.* You're busy, and—'

'Not busy. You seem—'

'I have something for you. And for Charles too, of course.' He reaches into his jacket pocket, holds something out. 'I've just come from the village. Here.'

It's a cream envelope with ink on it. For a moment, Jeanne stares. Then she steps forwards, takes it, knows it comes from Paris and knows who's written it.

'One of the boys?'

'That's Jean-Charles. That's his handwriting. See the slant?'

'Good,' says Peyron. 'That's good.'

Jeanne wonders how Peyron might miss Laure. Which moments? Which sounds? Jeanne misses her boys, but boys are meant to go; a husband's love is different from a parent's or a friend's. And she knows that the nuns wash his laundry these days, that every day Sœur Clemence or Sœur Bernadette will come to set his fire and dust and straighten his linen and sweep away the ash, and Peyron eats the hospital food so he has no need to cook in his home. But Laure must have left her scent on things. A hairbrush on her nightstand. An echoed hum. 'How was the village?'

'Quiet. The heat. But I had things to be posted, you see. There were canvases from the Dutchman that I had to carry down. Heavy. It's why...' He opens his arms, presenting himself. It's why he sweats as he does.

'Perhaps you should take a mule next time. Let it bear the weight of them.'

'I shall. I didn't think they'd be so ... The Dutchman paints in the fields, did you hear?'

'Yes, I heard.'

'Charles was quite right. His idea. It suits the patient and Rouisson appears to be calmer too.' He stiffens, gives a small bow. 'Well, I must return to my duties ... *Au revoir*, Jeanne.'

'*Au revoir.*'

Charles unfolds the letter.

Dear Papa and Maman,

   I hope this finds you both well. Mimi and I are finding Paris too warm, too soon, and Petit-Jean is not sleeping – but I imagine Saint-Rémy is far warmer. The cicadas must be singing now and I can't say I miss that! Otherwise, we are in good spirits. The boy is walking, and strong. He has a taste for the Spanish oranges we can buy at Les Halles, so Mimi wonders if he'll turn the same colour as them, or have their scent! He has also grown fond of a caged bird on boulevard de Clichy and insists on seeing it when we walk near there. I'm not sure what kind it is but its song is fast and sweet. As for work, it progresses. The office is not a good working place in the heat, but we have the custom, which we're grateful for.

The wife and son they've never met.

We see Laurent from time to time. His business strengthens, and he seems optimistic for what lies ahead. He asks me to send his assurances to you that he is quite the Parisien these days, and content. He thanks you for the letter too. Being Laurent, who knows when he'll write – but he's safe and well, Maman. We haven't heard from Benoît but he is Benoît. He'll change the world yet! We all send our love to you. Affectionately . . .

Charles smiles. 'A good letter, yes?'

Later, Jeanne reads the note alone. Charles sleeps, but she chooses to stay downstairs and breathe the paper and ink. Holds the letter to her chest. She presses her hand onto each place where Jean-Charles's hand has been. *Maman* – which might be her favourite word. Touches it with a fingertip.

The boy is walking, and strong. Surely it was only an hour ago, or two, that Jean-Charles himself was pulling himself up onto furniture, trying to fit each new thing in his mouth. A quarter of her is always with Jean-Charles or Laurent or Benoît; only the last quarter is here in Saint-Rémy. It's part of motherhood's truth – that to release a little life into the world means that part of you runs with it, totters in its wake. The Dutchman's mother is in Zundert but, perhaps, a part of her is in Saint-Remy too.

In the heat of the summer there is a shuttering of things. Stalls and shops and all the houses in Saint-Rémy fasten the shutters at sunrise; they don't push them back until evening, when it is cool. Underarms and spines and the base of spines stain cloth; dampness on each upper lip. There are fans in the chapel – not feathered, nor with handles of bone or elephant tusk like the ones her father used to sell, but paper ones, simple, used by the nuns.

Dogs pant. Even the hole under the kitchen floor – where Jeanne once kept the cabbage leaves – feels only less hot than the rest of the room. She notes the foam on working mules.

The market is over by twelve. At the height of the day, Provence sleeps. Workers find shade and children are laid down in their cots. In the hospital the patients return to their rooms at this hour, with their soaked skin and tiredness, a need to drowse – and the nuns rest too. Charles himself refuses: he sees rest as a gift for the end of the day, not before it. But even so, he retreats to the cooler parts of Saint-Paul. 'I did my paperwork in the cloisters today. I took a chair, and . . . '

Jeanne lays a damp cloth on the back of his neck when he comes home. 'How's that?'

'Better. Thank you.'

Simple evening meals. The deep longing to throw the windows open at night, all night, for the breezes to find their way into every corner of every room. But he says, 'No, Jeanne. Please.'

Every living thing rests in the shade at noon except one.

'A new painting?'

'Don't you have other things to do? Hearths to sweep or bread to make?'

She smiles. 'Are you mocking me? It's too hot for sweeping. Certainly for baking bread.'

'You won't rest now? Everyone else is resting.'

'You aren't.'

'No. Just us two, then.'

Jeanne smooths the back of her skirts, lowers herself into the grass. 'Will you tell me things, Vincent?'

'I'm painting. What things? About my ear?'

'Not your ear. You always think I want to know about your ear. I was thinking of the cicadas. I've grown accustomed to them, I think. And I've never seen one, even though I'm Provençal – and I thought that if you'd painted a moth you might have painted other unseen things.'

'Cicadas? I've drawn them.'

'What are they like?'

'Like . . . insects. Legs and wings. A head.'

'That doesn't help me. Can I see the drawing?'

'No, it's in Paris now.'

'With Theo, your brother.' She knows. She plucks a stalk of grass. 'We had a letter from our eldest a few days ago. He lives in Paris with his wife and child. Do you know where Les Halles are?'

'Les Halles? Right bank. Market stalls that go on and on. You know that cicadas are Greek, by the way? Socrates thought so. I like to think they sing to us in Greek.'

'I don't know who Socrates is.'

'Because you daydreamed in the classroom and don't read books. He was a philosopher. Dead now.'

She watches him. And to watch him paint is like watching any skill she knows nothing of – the blowing of glass or the taking of honey from bees, both of which she has seen in her life – in that she feels awe. How he mixes the colours. How he selects the brush, for he has many brushes.

'They didn't seem violet to me. The shadows.'

'There's colour in everything. The darker the shade the more hues are in it.'

'Are these your paints? In the tubes?' He doesn't answer – so she moves her weight across the grass to reach for the box and pulls it closer. There are dozens of tubes. Some are dented, half-used. Some had been rolled from their base so that their empty lower halves are curled as a snail's shell might be. Others are still untouched.

'Their names,' she says. 'Ult—'

'Ultramarine.'

'This one?'

The Dutchman looks across. His tone is that of a parent with a child he's enduring. 'That? Vermilion. Lead white. Ochre. That one?'

'I like that one.'

'Prussian blue. They say there's no such colour as that in this world, but I can tell you I've seen it. Night skies and water. I used it in cypress trees. Those irises had it – the ones by the boundary wall that you found me painting. And this. See it?' He lifts up a tube.

'Yellow.'

'More than yellow. Cadmium yellow. It's in grass and dry earth, in mornings. I did sunflowers in Arles. This colour –' he speaks more softly now, as if confiding – 'this is the colour of life to me. This, and the blue; I favour them together because there are some colours that bring out the brightness in another. I've told Theo this. I'll need more Prussian blue soon.'

Colour. In Arles, it was everywhere – the bright, bleached squares, the red and orange flowers that spilled down from window boxes, the flash of bathing birds, the many shades of tablecloths shaken out at the cafés of the Place du Forum and the lanterns placed upon them. The baked white brick. The black gloss of bulls as they were led through Arles.

And the shop. She thinks of the shop – the silks of pale pink or turquoise or apricot; the velvets; the amethysts and jade in brooches. Cochineal, from beetles. Indigo from the far, far east. And that egg-yellow silk that made others gasp at how bright it was, how it glowed by candlelight. And now? Now Jeanne looks into hedgerows as she walks. In the market she lifts a peach to feel its firmness and, as she does so, looks at its flecks and the cleft in its flesh, or how leaves on a stem are never single-coloured. 'Buying? Or are you just bruising my fruit?'

Madame Lenoir's brown eyes.

The figs too.

Later, the sagged, swollen teats of a dog that's borne puppies every year of her life. She looks at these things.

On her way back she sees how the bark of the plane trees is peeling off, discarding itself – and these parched strips of bark are white and grey and brown.

What Jeanne wants is to tell Charles. That's what she finds she wants, in the evenings – to tell Charles of the tubes of paint and their names, to ask him to describe the shade of the peach that he's eating at this precise moment, its flesh, inside and out.

'Good peaches.'

'Madame Lenoir's.'

'Ah.'

What colour would he call Jeanne's own flesh? For her own skin is two colours, she knows this – that which the sun finds and bakes into a hard brown, and her much paler, hidden kind.

It's been a long time since Jeanne's seen it. She might

wash in the wash-house or, in the winter months, bring the metal tub into the kitchen and bathe by the hearth. But even so, she doesn't look at herself any more. A little after Benoît, Jeanne had stood fully bare in the second bedroom; at night, and by lamplight, she'd had her full reflection in the window's glass. And what she'd seen had been a ruination. Her belly and breasts had lost all definition from her pregnancies and births; linking her fingers, she formed a cradle on which her belly could rest and she could rock or lift it, as she'd done with each boy. Her breasts felt both empty and weighed down. Her thighs and buttocks had grown and reduced themselves five times over, were tired, hanging with skin. *This.* A body that was a world away from the hardened, fast, teenage Jeanne. The Jeanne who'd stepped breathlessly out of her wedding dress, let the dress drop down and said, *I want you to touch me.* She'd whispered that to Charles.

Jeanne passes the last days of July and the first days of August by finding the Dutchman and sitting down beside him. She opens the tubes of paint. She looks at their colours, wonders what could be this shade of red or blue. A flower? Or a nameless kind? She smells them, closes them again.

He has his own routines. He won't look at Jeanne when she comes. He'll paint as if she isn't there at all, and when he does speak he does so without looking at her, without any greeting. He'll simply talk of lunch, or ochre. Of the bars he misses in Arles.

'Which bars? I might know of them.'

'Know of them? You won't know of them. You didn't drink in bars.'

'No. But I smoked pipes with the card players sometimes.'

'You did?'

'Under the trees, not in a bar. But when I walked past a bar I always peeped in.'

'Café de la Gare? If you ever walked past that place you'd walked too far.'

So he's slow to talk. But not Jeanne. He pauses in his work and speaks to her, and Jeanne talks freely after that – or as freely as she dares after a mere two months of knowing him. Her vegetable patch, and what's in season. How many eggs she found. Or she talks of the airiness of ostrich feathers or what her dreams have been or how there had been a wasp's nest in the hospital's library last year, and has it returned? How she feared wasps, when the boys were young. 'Jean-Charles did too. He was the most anxious. He feared falling in water and dogs – but he feared wasps most of all. Thought they might seek him out.'

'Was he stung?'

'They all were, in the end. But I'd put sugar on their tongues to stop their wails. Charles never knew that.'

'Wouldn't approve?'

'Not of that. But he's a kind man.'

'I know he's kind. I told you – remember? When we first met.'

'They don't always say so in the market.'

'And what of me? They must talk about me down there. Ask you for tales.'

'A little.'

'Of course they do. Don't pretend. My hair and my ear . . . Your husband should make a circus of us. Think of the money they'd spend to come and see Trabuc's Menagerie, gnawing on our bars.'

'Don't talk like that.'

He looks up. 'You don't like it? Nor do I, and I've had a lifetime of it. *Le fou roux* and stones thrown.' At that moment he stares with such intensity that she can see his pupils grow smaller in the light; the skin by his eyes is creased and grey. A second of this. Then he softens. He looks down, thumbs the end of his paintbrush. 'You know you'll be seen? Coming here?'

'Seen by whom? It's midday. They're all sleeping.'

'Someone will wake, and see.'

Jeanne shrugs. 'What can Charles do? He can't tether me to the bed like he did with Rouisson. I'm not one of his patients. Not a soldier.'

'The disobedient wife.'

'Obedient, until now. Patient. I've done as he asked since our wedding day.'

A shadow passes over the blueness of his eyes. 'Be careful, Jeanne. I'm saying that to you.' He lifts up his paintbrush, returns to his work.

The hot, airless nights. Jeanne sweats in her nightgown, turns onto her side.

Strange dreams. One in which she moves down corridors. There's music, and all the wives of Saint-Rémy are walking with her – Madame Gilles with feathers, Madame Lenoir banging a drum – and the beekeeper with his bee-stung arms. *Show us the patients! Show us the caged animals!*

When Jeanne wakes, she is breathless; she pads downstairs, fills the brown cup. Drinks.

He's right: the Major will know, and soon. What can be hidden for long? In a place where a rumour can grow from a moment as small as a seed, or a crack in a wall? Jeanne knew that the mistral would take the old rumours and blow them under doors and over roofs so that her father would ask her, Is this true? That you've been in Place Lamartine? That his daughter had been climbing trees or had no care for school.

This time Jeanne speaks first.

The Dutchman hasn't heard Jeanne approaching. He's standing, adjusting his hat, and when she speaks he flinches. He turns very suddenly, drops the hat.

'I want you to know I don't think you're ill. I've never thought it. I've lived here for thirty years and I've seen enough and heard enough to know what it means to be unwell, and you don't seem it. You don't seem ill at all. You paint, and you talk, and I like sitting beside you. And this isn't a menagerie of curious beasts. This isn't a circus.'

'I don't seem ill? Look at my ear. Look!'

'Yes. I know.'

'I was ill when I did that. I was raging, Jeanne.'

'I know.'

'They petitioned against me. What does that say?'

'But you don't seem ill now.'

'How can you say that? What do you know of illness? Of' – he taps his skull with his forefinger – 'diseases in here? You with your safe, calm, comfortable life? You with your days of washing clothes? You don't even read books! How can you sit beside me five or six or seven times and, from that, think that you know me? Or what my illness is like?'

'I've seen—'

'Many others. Thirty years. I know.'

He moves his hand as if dismissing her, turns away – and for a moment she looks at his hunched, damp back. Wants to reach out, touch him. Say sorry. 'I like how you paint, and—'

'Go, Jeanne.'

'But—'

'The chapel bell will chime soon.' Saint-Paul will rouse from its daytime rest, open its shutters. 'Go.'

That night, she lies awake. To her left, her husband sleeps. She hears his steady, sleeping breath.

The Dutchman had smelt, in this heat. Her boys never did. Sometimes she'd press her nose to their shirts on washing day – and like this she could tell they were growing into men, leaving their boyhoods as they'd leave footprints in the dust. But theirs was never as strong as the Dutchman's sour, fox smell.

Charles too. He is a man of ointments and neatness, combing his moustache every dawn and dusk; if there's a scent to Charles, it's of pomade. But in the August nights of their early married life, when their beds were still pushed together to form one large, shared bed, Jeanne would sometimes detect a darker scent to him. Sometimes, she'd seek it out; she'd lift his arm, move herself into the haired, damp cavity of him and breathe in what she found there. A hunger for him. 'Jeanne, what on earth ...? Charles was embarrassed at first. But those were the days when each new thing they did had shyness to it, or did the first few times they tried it. Then the shyness went. They came to part limbs without asking. They'd unfold the places on each other that tended to be folded, day and night. Look at them. Touch them. Inhale.

Sometimes, Charles would pause and say, Am I hurting you? He never hurt her. Or he'd ask, Like that? And each time Jeanne would rise up from the bed, put her mouth by his ear and whisper to him, Yes. Yes, like that.

Eight

There is a light, metallic sound as she steps into the yard, fastening her apron.

Bells, which means the goats are near. The slopes of Les Alpilles are their grazing ground; a herd of three dozen goats or more, of every size and colour, spend most of their year neatly treading through thistle and dust. Some are horned, some are bearded. Some sway with milk or unborn goats. Some have bells tied to their necks so that they make a gentle music as they make their way through the morning fields and olive groves. They pause to grasp at weeds with their teeth and pull.

She watches. They aren't alone. It isn't just the patients and workers of Saint-Paul – and the wives of workers – that people whisper of. The goatherd too. There have been plenty of rumours about him. And she's moved through those tales as she'd move through flies, using her hand to be rid of them. Nobody knows his name. He is only *the goatherd* – in his sixties or older, leathered by years of wind and sun. They say he has no home and this is the only part that Jeanne might believe in – that he sleeps with his herd on the hillside, rests his head on their dusty sides and warms himself against them in wintertime. She's heard he drinks their milk. Perhaps he does.

Jeanne can't ask. No one can, for the goatherd's mute. He has no tongue at all, or he's known such sadness that his tongue has lost its purpose – and here's where the deepest rumours are. That he's seen a foul murder, or committed one. That he saw a ghost and it silenced him. He's a foreigner who told a lie and had his tongue cut out in punishment. Or he does in fact have a working tongue but no voice to use it.

He comes into view. He walks with a stick, knocks the goats along with it. She's seen him as rarely as she's seen falling stars but here he is, keeping his eyes on the ground, with trousers worn bare at the knees. A beard that reaches his chest. And he makes his way to the east, along the side of the boundary wall, so she watches three dozen rumps heading away from her.

The Dutchman nods. 'That explains it. Thought I heard bells – and look.' A peppering of dung near his easel. 'I've heard the bells before.'

'They keep to the lower slopes, mostly. They only pass through when he's leading them between grazing land or when the harvest's been and gone. He's mute, you know. In the town they say he lives amongst his goats, no matter the weather. That he has no home so he sleeps and eats with them and takes milk from their teats.'

'You listen to them? Their prattle? Do you prattle yourself?'

She shakes her head. 'No. I'm saying it's not just you they whisper of.'

She was wary of seeing him again. How he'd been, when she spoke of illness – sharp, dismissive, hissing *You with your safe, comfortable life* – has stayed with her, like weather. Perhaps it has stayed with him too, for there's a greyness under his eyes. He frowns so deeply that the groove between his eyebrows looks like it's carved into him. She thinks of the carved things she knows: churches and ruins, gravestones, words etched into a plinth.

'Olives again?'

'Yes, olives.'

'Why olives? There are other things.'

'I know,' he snaps, 'that there are. You think I don't know that there are?'

Jeanne shifts. 'What about Les Antiques? They're not far. I could show them to you. They're Roman remains – a tower that was a mausoleum, and an archway too. Weathered, of course, and they used to be whiter than they are now but they're still very beautiful. You could paint them.'

'I don't want to paint them.'

'Why not?'

'I told you: I don't paint dukes or duchesses. I've no interest in painting what others have already seen and admired. I'll paint what they don't look at. A street. The backs of things.'

'Like the moth.' She tries to smile at him.

'You know Les Alyscamps? I painted them. And when I painted them, I painted what I saw, which was the graves and the trees, and the railway works beside them. Gauguin didn't paint the railway works. He painted a fiction, a falseness.' Spits.

'Who?'

'Why paint at all, if you paint falsely? If you don't paint what is true? So yes, I'm painting olives and yes, I've painted them before but in my studio are a hundred thousand paintings and drawings of things that are not olive trees and I don't need advice, and not from you.' He pushes his brush into the paint on his palette – a dark orange hue. 'Go. Do you hear me? I'm telling you.'

*

His own private weather hasn't gone. When she'd said what she did – that he did not seem ill to her – she'd meant well by it. Hadn't meant harm. This man who she likes speaking to.

I offended you, I think. Upset you.

She says this in the mirror. Practising.

When he doesn't return to the olive trees the next day, or the days after that, Jeanne looks for him. She goes to the cypresses, begins to walk up and down the olive groves in case he might be hiding in the brittle grass. She goes to Les Antiques all the same. Feels her way round the boundary wall. On a day of such heat that the lane seems to shimmer, Jeanne straightens and shields her eyes. Is that him? Straw-hatted? Wearing brown, not blue? But she sees it's Monsieur Charpentier, with his bee-stung arms.

'*Bonjour.*'

'*Bonjour à vous.*'

That night, she looks at Charles. She eyes him as she might eye a stream for a hidden way across. 'How are they all? The patients? Does Patrice still sing?'

'Still sing?' He reads *Le Figaro*. 'Yes, he does.'

'Evelyn?'

'The same.'

She pauses. 'And you? Charles, how are you?' A sudden wish to know.

He looks up. 'Me? I'm the same, too. Tired.' Shrugs. 'And Rouisson's bad again. These past three nights, he's been fretful. Calling out for whatever he's missing . . . It doesn't end, Jeanne. It goes on and on. All of this.'

'I thought he was calmer. What can have changed, in four days?'

'Jeanne, I think you were right. I think it's the painter that troubles him. He began sleeping and eating again when

114

we let the Dutchman into the fields, and he has stayed well since. But now the Dutchman's indoors. I don't know why, but he no longer seems to want the olive trees and he's working in his studio from sunrise till dusk, and has been for the past four days. For four days, Rouisson's been worse. So yes, I think you were right.'

Jeanne would see him if she could. She wants to. She wants to take his wrist as he had taken hers and say, *Is it me? Are you hiding from me?* But with Rouisson's distress, the east wing will be echoing with footsteps and whisperings, with the buckling of straps and locking doors. Nuns with reassurances. Slopping bowls.

She waits.

She stands in the nursery, with the high view. Looks at each movement – the goatherd, a nun, Peyron – in the hope it is him. So when she sees, at last, blue overalls and a wide-brimmed hat near the boundary wall, Jeanne gathers her skirt in her right hand and carries a cup in her left, and hurries; the water spills. 'Why have you been inside for so long?'

'Sometimes I paint inside.'

'I worried.'

'Why? Why worry for me, when I'm in an asylum?' He drinks, wipes his chin. 'Isn't that the safest place?'

She searches his face. She isn't sure if his sharpness is still there, waiting to strike, or if it has gone now. 'What I said, Vincent. About you being well ...'

He looks at her. There are pink veins to the whites of his eyes, and a thicker smell to him than he's had before – and Jeanne thinks he will ask her to leave him, to let him paint on his own. But he smiles. He gestures to the grass beside him, as if saying *Sit*. As if his weather has passed through.

*

115

'I've been painting well,' he says. 'A single canvas. I've been working on one painting and I thought you'd be pleased because it isn't of olive trees.'

Smiles. 'What have you painted? Tell me.'

'Stars. I didn't take kindly to your talk of Les Antiques – telling me what you think I should paint. But I thought of it in my room that night and looked out, through the bars. I've painted night skies before. One of the Rhône from the Place Lamartine, with the street lamps. You'd have recognised it. But this one ... I thought, at first, to paint the view I had – of Les Alpilles and the wheat, under the stars. But there were such skies in Holland – those wide skies above the flat land – that as a boy I'd look out of my attic window and stare and stare ... So I thought of my childhood skies, Jeanne, and I painted a Dutch town. It's very Dutch, with its church steeple, although there's a cypress tree which wouldn't have ever grown there. And so I've been sketching at night, in my room, and by day I've been in the studio turning those sketches into a single canvas of a huge, starry sky with movement and light, and so why would I have come outside? To the olive trees? I haven't wanted olive trees, for once. I might have come out at night to paint the stars themselves, if they'd let me, but I must be caged after dark – and there's no manner of talking to your husband that might change his rule on that.'

'Movement?'

'Yes. Stars move. They live and die. Pass me the blue.'

She passes it. 'You weren't keeping from me?'

'Keeping from you? Those are mad words.'

She exhales, closes her eyes. A longing, now, to see his bright stars. A longing to see his studio and everything in it.

'Why would I keep from you? I told you. You don't cling to a doll. You're company. The only other face I spend any

116

time with is my own, when I'm painting it, and I grew tired of my face long ago.'

'You paint yourself?'

'I'd sooner paint others. I'd paint the other patients if I could, or if they'd sit for me – and I tried. But the Major has forbidden it. Said it might excite them too much or cause distress, and how can I argue? I know he's right. There's life in painting, I know there is. It fills my veins. It opens my eyes so that I can see most clearly with a brush in my hand. But there's life in being painted too. When I painted the postman's wife in Arles she wept afterwards and thanked me, and what if a patient felt the same way? So I paint myself, sometimes. The white, now.' He points. 'It's there. Near your left foot.'

She leans forwards, passes it.

This was always Laure's language – to speak of life, of living. Of doing what made her feel alive. Like swimming in the canal or tucking her skirts into her waistband to climb trees, picking fruit. When she'd heard that Jeanne could do handstands she'd said, Show me! But Jeanne had refused. Too stiff, too old.

'Laure would have liked you, I think.'

'Nobody likes me. Look at Arles.'

Laure, who wore a single pearl. It rested by her throat on a silver chain. A gift from her husband because he called her that. *Ma perle* – believing his wife to be pearl-like in how bright and unexpected she'd been. How she came into Peyron's life after years of still water, years in which he'd come to think there'd be nothing in his future except Saint-Paul and prayer.

That's a good story, Jeanne told her.

It's a short life, Laure replied. We should be happy, shouldn't we? Said a little forlornly, fingering the pearl.

*

Handstands had been Jeanne's joy. When young, it was through that brief, upturned moment that she felt freedom, a quickened heart. Never mind that they said it was indecent. Or maybe it was because of its indecency that she'd loved it – practising in the yard when Claudette was sweeping indoors, pushing her weight down onto her splayed hands and seeing the world upside-down. She'd count the seconds. *Four, five . . .* Later, the soft earth beneath the trees on the Place Lamartine was perfect for it and she found she could hold a handstand for ten seconds or more. Later still, she'd walk on her hands. Past the men, playing – the clack of boule on boule.

If asked, when young, what she'd want in a husband Jeanne might have said she wanted that: a recklessness, as she'd had. A joy that rose up without warning; a daring glint in the eye. *Quick, no one will see . . .* But then everything changed, and she married Charles. And how could Jeanne walk on her hands for him? Underclothes showing, hair brushing the dust? Charles was never that kind of man. He folded everything perfectly. The Crimea seemed to follow him – a shadow on his walls.

Nor had it only been handstands.

She'd felt a quickened heartbeat in the rue du Bout d'Arles too. Of all the streets in the town, this was the one she was meant to keep away from, the street that both Claudette and her father forbade. *Why, Papa?* He talked of immorality. Of selling what should not be sold, and how his only daughter was to keep far away from the women who lived down there. *Do you hear?* She heard – but ignored it. The men who'd travelled the globe had disobeyed rules, after all – and for a time Jeanne didn't really see what was different in that street. She wondered what they might sell, that meant its name was only ever said through gritted teeth. Then, in her teens, she came to know exactly what they sold. That young, dark understanding of her own body stepped forwards – and on a hot day, as Jeanne stood at the end of the street and peered down it, she saw one of its girls. A woman, in fact, larger than most, with combs in her hair. She came out, sat down on a doorstep; she dabbed the sweat from her chest, hoisted her skirts to cool her legs. Lay back against the baked wall.

This was what Jeanne knew, as she stared: that this was a world of light and shade, of a hundred thousand choices, of good fortune and bad fortune and chances to turn left or right. The *tap-tap* on the globe was not enough. Cupping her own small, new breasts and considering them was also not enough. The haberdasher's shop was scented and strange and secretive but that, too, would not be enough for the rest of her life. There was far more to know.

The next time she sees him she wants to tell him – that she, too, knew the rue du Bout d'Arles. That she hadn't been afraid of it.

But the Dutchman stops her. 'Jeanne. It's happened.'

'What has?'

'You've been seen. Didn't I say you would be? Sœur Yvette. She came to me this morning, asked if you didn't find the midday heat too strong, even in the shade of the trees. So the nuns know. And if they know, the villagers will know – tattling over their stalls in the square.'

'Charles?'

'Yes. Charles will know.'

The man they call the Major sits before her, looks down at the floral plate. Lentils and beetroot, a little salted ham. He is perfectly still.

119

'How has today been?'

He takes up his fork. 'They rest, in this heat. It's quiet. We're giving them cool baths.' He pushes the fork into the ham.

She waits.

'Not all of them rest. But you know that.'

'The Dutchman? Yes. He paints sometimes. In the olive trees.'

'How do you know this?'

'I've seen him. Spoken to him.'

Charles looks up. 'So I've heard.'

'I've taken water.'

'Water?'

'It's hot, Charles. So very hot, and he works in the hottest part of the day which seems—'

'Water. And then you leave him, of course.'

She knows this tone. It has been a long time since she heard it, but he'd use it with Laurent when Laurent was at his most wilful. Also, with Benoît. When Benoît had talked about going to other countries, of crossing seas. On his last night before leaving Benoît had pleaded – and Charles had spoken exactly like this in return. *You won't go, of course.* 'I've stayed. Talked with him a little.'

'Jeanne.'

'He isn't in the hospital grounds. You told me to stay away from the grounds.'

'I did. Because of the patients inside them, not because of the grounds themselves. Why might I worry about the foun-tain or a tree? It is the patients that I ask you to keep from!'

'Why? He won't hurt me.'

'No?' He pushes the plate away. 'Are you sure of that? Him, of all people. You heard Salles, when he came. You know that they petitioned him? That he lived in squalor?

120

Drank absinthe and smoked and lived quite indecently? And this man's come from Arles with a list of ailments and troubles that have lasted all his life, most of which we cannot give a name to or understand. He has committed an act of violence against himself that none of us have seen before – not Peyron, nor the nuns. And you've seen his art! Do you think that's the work of a settled mind?' He pauses, breathes. 'I'm the warden. I'm the director of this place as well, or as good as. And I must think of his health too. The patients need a routine. I thought you understood that.'

'I speak to him! Speak – that's all. And he likes that I do. Who else can he speak to, in there? Yves, or Rouisson? A nun?'

'Yes, the nuns! Me. Peyron.'

'Peyron?'

'Jeanne.' He closes his eyes. He breathes in and out, calming himself. 'Perhaps you misunderstood. Fine. But let me be clear now: you're to stay away from him. Do you hear?'

In the haberdasher's shop they used to keep a single, large jar of buttons. It was so heavy that Jeanne could hardly lift it; it flashed with colour when carried into the light. And sometimes, just sometimes, Jeanne would imagine taking that jar and emptying it – not just picking one button out but pouring the jar onto the polished floor so the buttons would clatter and run to every shadow and corner, skittering like rainbow-coloured rain. A way of saying *there. See?*

'Charles, what of me? Who can I talk to? There's no one here.'

'Talk to?'

'Since Laure went away.'

'Then . . . ' – he looks around the room, as if an answer might be there – 'the market. Can't you go there? Talk to the other wives?'

'They don't like me. This idea that I'm tainted with lunacy for living up here, being married to you ...'

Charles lays down his napkin. 'Don't speak like this, Jeanne.'

For a time, there's silence. She hears the tick of the clock behind her. She thinks she can hear her own heart, which knocks against her bones.

Slowly, he retrieves the plate. Lifts up his fork. 'He's asked to go back to Arles.'

'Arles?'

'A day trip, that's all. He still has some paintings there, and wishes to retrieve them.'

'He'll go on his own?'

'Of course not. Poulet will take him, or myself. He needs to be accompanied because he's unwell, remember? Everyone at Saint-Paul is unwell. You need to keep that in mind. And Jeanne, please don't speak to him again.'

The final knot in their words.

They eat in silence. When he's finished, he rises and goes.

Sometimes Jeanne can't imagine Charles Trabuc at war. How he cradled his sons, or used to kiss her with a wet, wanting, open mouth: these were not warlike things. They were the things that war was not. But there are times when she sees the major that he must have been. Thinks of the rumour that he'd strangled men.

Perhaps. Perhaps he did those things. And as she carries the plates to the kitchen Jeanne feels a hardness forming inside her, an anger. She thinks, *the Dutchman is mine.* She thinks of stars through the window bars, of the body under her dress which gets older with each passing hour. She thinks of his studio, how it must be filled with light. And Jeanne wonders, too, if there are other wars – wars that take place in kitchens or bedrooms and that aren't, in fact, for God or money or emperors or land.

On a Wednesday, Charles goes to Arles with him. He rises, takes his coffee from Jeanne and tells her that he and the patient will catch the train to Arles that morning. From Saint-Rémy, through the passes, down onto the plains where Arles sits beside the Rhône.

'Today?'

'Today. Peyron is having a good spell, and Rouisson has settled into a new room in the north wing. So . . . '

She nods. 'How many paintings?'

'A few. He stored them in a café. Wants to see Salles, if he can.' Charles drains the coffee, hands her the cup. 'We'll catch the last train. I'll be home by nightfall.' A pause, and he looks at her. She looks back. There are words, she knows, in his mouth – words he feels he cannot say, and nor will she.

'I'll leave a little food for you. Cheese and fruit.'

'*Merci.*' Places his hat on his head and walks out.

Jeanne watches them go. These two men, walking under the plane trees with their hats on and their coats folded over their arms – coats in case the summer's heat breaks into thunder, as it can. The Dutchman is not in his overalls. He wears a grey shirt. Frayed trousers, a little too long.

They grow smaller, out of sight.

Jeanne waits a while, in case they should return – a broken train, or a change of mind. But they don't return.

Jeanne goes – through the grass, past the tethered mules and the boundary wall towards the kitchen's back door. No

Marie-Josephine. There are signs that she'd been there – an onion's papery skin on a plate, the knife by its side. But the kitchen is empty.

Jeanne goes to the east wing.

She knows it when she finds it because she can smell paint. She can smell him too – the musk, the stale breath of him. On the floor above, where his bedroom is, and all the other unused bedrooms, she knows that doors will be open, that there'll be a sense of light. But she doesn't seek his bedroom. And this corridor is dark.

She stands, breathes.

All these doors are shut. She tries them, leans against them. She puts her eye to the keyhole but only sees more darkness. Feels their sides.

All locked.

Then a door gives way to her.

It opens, and she stumbles in.

A sudden gift of light. It overwhelms her. It rushes in; a huge, bright whiteness comes at Jeanne like water so that she winces, raises one hand and keeps her other hand on the door. The light pours past her.

There'd been a bell, in the shop. It hung by the door and chimed every time a customer came in – a soft, hopeful *ting* so that she'd look up or step out from the corners. That was the sound, to Jeanne, of entering; that *ting* heralded, in others, an intake of breath at the sight of such things of which they had no understanding, and yet knew had worth and rarity – lace, or cream-coloured hair pins made of elephant tusk. That sense of being small, as in a cathedral. The urge to speak under one's breath.

There is no *ting*. And this is no haberdashery. But to see what Jeanne sees makes her gasp as she did in Saint Trophime; it makes her reach for a sturdier thing than the

124

door – a chair, or a wall. But there are, she sees, no walls. Where there were walls there are canvases. Where there had been any square of wooden floor there is also a canvas, for this is a world of them – propped or hung or lying down, back to back or on their own. Wet or dry. Vast or so tiny that Jeanne can't see what they show.

She stands, stares.

Many olive trees. On every wall she can see them; some she knows as she might know a face, having seen them being made. But most are new to her. A bridge. A street. An avenue. A marsh. A single branch. A tunnel of trees she thinks she knows from her youth, so she takes a single step to it, bends. Les Alyscamps: the graveyard of heroes, where they said that Jesus had knelt and left a print but she herself had gone there to climb over the gravestones or sleep on their flattened tops. She ate almonds there, one day.

And just as that childish, almond-eating Jeanne would tread between each type of lace and whisper their names – Chantilly, Pag – as if their names were precious things, so she moves now. A universe is here. A whole, extraordinary world is in this room, or perhaps a hundred worlds. Perhaps every place he's ever seen, he has painted – and those paintings are here: a lane beneath a moon, a café with a billiard table, the cypresses, a single pine. The courtyard of the hospital in Arles, with its trees and yellow paintwork. A factory. When Jeanne kneels down it's to look more closely at a painting of a night-time square that she thinks she recognises. Place du Forum? In Arles? It looks like it – with a café, lantern-lit, and an awning and some stars.

Beside this, wheat. A pencil sketch of the bell tower at Saint-Paul-de-Mausole that she's seen every day for thirty years, and has seen in every season. A river like the Rhône. Rooftops. Undergrowth. A wicker chair.

A room with a single bed in it. At this, she pauses.

All this ... All this is part of his life. And Jeanne might take a year to look at each canvas, touch their ridged surfaces and breathe their oily dust – but she doesn't have a year. She doesn't have much time at all. A nun might hear, or come. By the day's end the Dutchman will return and may find her here – and would either not mind, or mind very much and rage or feel betrayed by her. He of the moods that blow in like wind. She can't stay here long. So Jeanne moves as swiftly as she can. She steps over the empty tubes of paint and discarded cloth; she takes the sides of canvases and, very gently, tilts them towards her so she can see behind them, where other paintings are. In doing this she finds his face. His fox's hue and hard, cold stare. In one, a bandaged ear.

Other faces too. A bearded man in a postman's hat. A distant man in a field of wheat. Sleepers in grass, in the midday heat.

A nude: a woman, hunched forwards. She rests her head on her forearms so Jeanne can't see her face, but she can see her belly and breasts. They sag, as her own breasts do.

She turns. And as Jeanne turns she sees it: how has she failed to see it till now? It's the largest canvas in the room. It rests against the southerly wall – dark blue and dark green and orange and grey. Stars. Yellow, swirled stars; they are stars with tails – like comets, or stars falling to earth as she knows they can – that seem to move across the little sleeping town with its cypress and church spire. As Jeanne looks, she smiles. She smiles because if other painters said there was a way of painting stars, Vincent has ignored them and lifted up his brush. He has done what he wanted to, no matter that they might call him mad. A cypress tree. Balls of moving light.

*

126

At home, she goes up to the nursery. Lowers herself onto the floor.

Jeanne stares at the wall.

Do not forget what you saw. As she ordered herself to remember her father's face in his last days, or as she ordered herself to remember the first night of her mothering life – a sleeping Jean-Charles and a sleeping Charles, too, and her sore, bleeding body, and beyond the window a crescent moon.

The nude. The stars. His blue stare.

With that, Jeanne twists. She lies on her front, peers beneath the single bed and reaches into the dark. Her hand feels the shape of each thing that's hiding there. The bottle of iodine and the bandages. A blanket. And when she feels a leathery hardness she grasps it, hauls it out and sits up so that she's facing it.

A trunk. Jeanne's – which she has neither seen nor opened for years. A trunk far older than her lifetime. A trunk that's veiled with dust so that she blows, smooths the dust away with both her palms. Two buckles. But also four letters – two pairs of them – pressed into the leather so that they can't be undone. *JL* is clearest. Her unmarried initials; Jeanne Lafuye, as she had been for her first twenty-five years of life, and she traces these with her thumb as she might feel for a pulse. *JL*. On their wedding night Charles had said, But that's not your name now.

And there's a fainter pair of letters. *AP*. Older, worn away so that others might not notice them, but Jeanne notices.

In 1859, newly married, Jeanne had brought this trunk to Saint-Rémy. And in it she'd carried all that mattered most to a wife, or a good wife at least – a needle and thread, a corset, an apron, a mirror, a cookbook that Claudette had left. Her wedding veil, folded. A little talcum for its scent. Rouge she

127

never used. A single ostrich feather from her father's shop that she used to brush her cheek with when she missed him or missed Arles.

All these things are long gone. The mirror broke; the cookbook served no purpose. The boys found the feather and it became a sword for them; they fought with it, it snapped and was lost to the breezes, found its final flight. The wedding veil greyed, fell apart when touched.

It is an empty case now – except for two things.

The first is a letter. She's had it for four years. It sits, looking back at her.

The second is a dress. A dress of the brightest, warmest gold. A yellow dress that is, surely, too small for her now – after so long, and pregnancies. And yet how could Jeanne have discarded it?

Waist-length hair, in that gold-fiery dress. She had been movement. She'd danced, at night.

Yes, I had been beautiful. And, perhaps, Laure was right. Perhaps she was right in saying life is short, too short – and shouldn't there be happiness? In filling life with life, and taking opportunities? Perhaps Laure had been right in deciding to rise up and go.

Nine

It was the glass that she heard first. The jar found the floor before his body did – the huge, hard handclap of glass. It smashed, and then she heard the buttons racing free across the wooden floor – spinning on their sides and rushing to every part of the room so that they knocked against walls and the counter, the feet of the ladder that Jeanne was standing on. These sounds, first. She flinched. Then Jeanne turned – and as she did she heard the heavy echoless thud of her father's body falling down, felt the floor shake with it. From her height, she looked down. Cloth in hand. *Papa*.

She knows that she jumped down. She dropped to his side and said his name over and over, placed her hand between his head and the wooden floor and Jeanne knows that she only left his side to run into rue Diderot and call for help – a doctor, a carriage that might take him to the hospital, or anyone who might know how to save him, make him well – before running back to him again. She is sure of that part. And yet sometimes she thinks she paused before she jumped. That on her perch, momentarily, she stood and stared. For she can see it so clearly despite the passing years: her father's body, splayed like a star; the buttons made from the homes of distant sea creatures spinning over the floor like fragmented light; and that, very briefly, those buttons had looked beautiful. Bluish, pink and bright.

The intrusion of illness. By his hospital bed, Jeanne felt they'd been intruded on – a senseless, sudden, cruel interruption. No reason to it. Unfair.

Everything's changed.

In the hospital, she saw it all. She stared through the window at the blowing sky and saw the dismissal of Claudette, his bed coming downstairs to the fireside, the need for easy, softened food. The gentle lifting of his limbs to clean under them, or between them, and how much that would hurt them both – not physically, but with a deep, inner pain. Jeanne saw the selling of things – the shop, but also the candlesticks and the spare lambswool rug, the globe, his pocket watch.

More than illness too. Illness wasn't the only visitor that came and stayed. In his dreams, Didier tried to speak, and mostly Jeanne couldn't decode this new, damp, damaged speech of his. But sometimes there were words she knew.

Aurélie.

Her wounded, dying parent made her think of the other, long-dead one. A ghost came into the house after that: a mother-heavy creak of the floorboards overhead or a mother-shaped patch of sunlight in the hall. These new tasks – the slow, cautious shaving of him, the bathing, the holding of his hand when it seemed to shake for no reason – felt like they weren't Jeanne's to perform. That her mother was watching, beside her.

'I'm turning you, Papa. Ready?'

She missed her mother. *Maman* . . . Thought of her as she kneaded her father's cold, sore feet and rubbed his heels with salve.

*

Jeanne leans against the wall. A late-afternoon light. Aurélie's trunk remains beside her. The nursery's air is still, as if
it's holding its breath.

She has felt her mother's ghost in this room too. As she
crouched by a sleeping son, or tried to feed a disconsolate
one, Jeanne would feel her mother flit through her head like
a bird in the trees – and sometimes she wanted to halt her
and bring her into focus. *Show me how* . . . To feed a child,
starch shirts, cook. How to finish a stitch, or start it. Clean
a wound.

Show me. Help me.

The things a mother shows her daughter. But this daughter had had no mother to follow. No mother to listen to, or
watch. No one to copy as Jeanne whispered, *Like this?*

That's right.

Charles first asked Jeanne about her dead mother on the
boulevard des Lices. It was their third meeting. She understood that this, now, was courtship; she recognised that here
was a man she missed when he wasn't with her, so that she'd
look at the space he'd been standing in and imagine him
there. Charles. A soft, soft, beckoning name.

'She was called Aurélie. She took a fever in the hours after
birthing me, and the fever killed her. It took three days, but
she still died.'

'Ah. I know fevers. I'm sorry to hear that.'

'*Merci.*'

A natural sorrow in him. Some gave condolences with
a flatness or uncertainty, but not Charles; he gave his with
meaning, as if he'd known his own loss and was truly sorry
for hers. With that, Jeanne looked across. He walked with

hands behind his back and, at that moment, she wished he didn't walk in that way because she'd wanted to reach for his hand, or rather, have him reach for hers. She'd never held a hand that had not been her father's.

'You know fevers, Monsieur Trabuc? You've had them?'

'Once, yes. But I've seen fevers in others far more. My army days ... I know medicine, you see. Or a little. In the war there were illnesses of such ...' Charles paused then. A silence in which she supposed he was packing away the memories of dying men and sealing them up. Instead, he talked of Les Arènes, of the Roman craft in its Roman walls and how the stone was hewn by Roman hands – and wasn't it remarkable? That two thousand years later these structures remain? 'What a thing ...' – in amazement. So Jeanne came to sense that he had feelings inside him, but that he wouldn't speak of them – or of his life before her, and its cost.

Jeanne's rarely talked of Aurélie since. Once or twice. On their wedding night, Charles had seen the trunk with her *JL* beside the *AP* and mentioned her. 'That trunk had been your mother's?' When Jean-Charles's hair lightened in the summer months she noted it and compared it to the hair of the woman she'd never known. With her own reflection, she sometimes wondered if the shape of her nose or roundness of her eyes had come from the woman whose surname was Pin. *Do I look like her?* This face, these hands. And with the two daughters who died at birth, it was Aurélie's name that she'd wanted to scream, as if begging or summoning her. But that was long ago.

Her name had been Aurélie Pin. Not from Provence, so she didn't speak Provençal; her language had been the true, strong northern French. Had Didier – the Camarguais, the *gitan*, strong-minded – not chosen to learn this second tongue for the sake of his shop, and selling his lace, might there have even been a Jeanne? Any conversation between him and her?

'Where, in the north?'

'The western side, near the sea. Your mother had come a long way.'

'And why did she come to Arles? To meet you?'

He'd smiled. 'How could she have planned it? She didn't know I even existed when she left the Loire. No, she came with a maiden aunt to spend time with another. In Marseilles.'

'That's near here.'

'Not far.'

Aurélie had taken the train. And perhaps it was the rumours of beauty in Arles, the Venus they found or the lavender fields, or simply that her train needed fuel and water – who can know, now? But Aurélie paused on her way to Marseilles. Left the aunt in a lodging house. Walked down the rue Diderot.

'It was a Tuesday. October.'

Of course. The mistral's early days. 'What else?'

Sometimes, her father wouldn't want to speak of his wife. Jeanne came to know the signs of that – a looking down, or away; a long sigh or a slight shake of the head so that she wouldn't ask about Aurélie Pin for a while. A sorrow he'd succumb to, if tired. But mostly, if Jeanne asked, he'd try to answer her – to offer her something for her own sake. A button, held up to the light.

'She came to the shop, Jeanne. I was measuring velvet . . .'
The end of the day. The sky was beginning to darken, and leaves had been blowing outside – so when Didier felt the

room darken further and heard the slightest tap on the glass, he hadn't looked up. Thought it was simply October, and dusk. But then he heard the tap again. 'And there she was. A young woman I'd not seen before. She was standing in the street with one hand on the window pane, looking in at the tortoiseshell combs.'

'The ones from Asia?'

'Yes, those ones. She was frowning, as if she didn't like them.'

'Didn't like them?'

'A frown! Then she looked up, and saw me.'

She'd been a little taller than the man she would, in time, marry. A girl with a sideways smile, a smile that gathered in one corner of her mouth as if she were teasing. Blackish hair, but not as black as his. Plaited, but only very loosely. And she opened the door so slowly that the bell didn't even say *ting!*

'She came in looking at me. All those things I had – buttons and glass beads and pearls ... But she was looking at me.'

'What then?'

'We talked. She came back the next day. I asked if she cared to see more of Arles ... And so.' He smiled.

Jeanne thought about this. All those streets and terraces. The view of the Rhône from the Place Lamartine. 'How long was her hair? As long as mine?'

'Longer than yours. It grew lighter in the summer months. Curled at its end, if she left it uncut.'

'Mine can curl too.'

'It can, *mon chou*.'

Even as a child, Jeanne knew the potency of *Maman* as a word. A word all of its own. For with *Maman* there were layers of meaning: a sudden fever, an absence, a loss. In that tiny schoolroom of chalk dust and flies the other children would chirp out the word: *Maman said,* or *My maman knows . . .* And Jeanne would watch the shape of their mouths with it.

A new potency, to *Maman,* when Jeanne bore her first child. Suddenly it was her own name. Above all else, the name meant her – and if *Maman* was called out by one of her sons she didn't think of Aurélie: she thought of herself, of her boys, and she'd hurry upstairs saying, Yes, I'm here. The feeder. The dabber of grazed knees. The one who'd fit her arms around each son and tell them how proud she was, how proud. So *Maman* altered itself, in time. It stopped meaning the woman she'd never known, and meant this woman she'd become – Madame Trabuc. With her wide hips and milk-stained dress.

But *Aurélie* never lost its strength. Not for Didier Lafuye. His own private mistral, in that the word blew right through him. Whistled through holes.

'Did you ever meet her, Claudette?'

Claudette sucked at her teeth. 'Me? I didn't know anything about her, or you. I just heard that the short little man who sold buttons near Les Arènes was a widower now. Was looking for help with his house and child. So I came.' She shrugged. She'd needed the work.

'No stories about her?'

A sniff. 'None.'

All Jeanne knew of her mother came from her father, and no one else. How Aurélie could play chess. Had disliked artichokes. Loved Christmas and ducklings, and talked in her sleep. 'And she knew you were a girl, when you were growing inside her. I don't know how she knew but she was sure of it.' And, one day in the haberdashery, Didier paused in his cutting of silk, looked up and said to Jeanne, 'She'd had no care for any of this. Did I tell you that? No interest in Chantilly lace or feathers. I offered her gifts, of course. I'd have given her the whole shop, if she'd wanted it. But she only ever smiled, thanked me, placed the brooch or comb or fan back in my hand ... Said she had no need for such things. And she was right. Your mother needed nothing more than herself. All the diamonds in the African earth would have seemed dull beside her.'

'She was that beautiful?'

He looked back down. 'To me.'

He isn't in the olives. He isn't by the cypress trees.

Jeanne walks along the boundary wall, looking for blue overalls or trying to smell paint in the air. It is only when she's made her way to the far eastern side of Saint-Paul-de-Mausole, where the wheat fields are, and the smooth, curved back of the chapel, that she sees his straw hat, his blue overalls.

She shields her eyes. To reach him she must climb over the boundary wall. There's no other way. She looks about her. At the furthest end of the wall, it has half gone. The wall that had once been twice her height and reinforced yearly by Gilles and other, younger men is crumbling here. Weeds grow through the broken stones. Jeanne used to climb the fruit trees with Laure. She'd jump from grave to grave in Les Alyscamps – and she can see the Dutchman reaching down for his tubes of paints, lifting one up. So she lifts her skirts, steps forwards. Climbs over the wall.

He sees her as she comes towards him. 'The wheat. Look at it. They'll be harvesting this soon and so I must capture it now, while we have it. Did you think I was hiding from you again?'

'How was Arles?'

'We couldn't bring all the paintings. I'd left more than I'd remembered, but we brought back most.'

'Pastor Salles?'

'No. Away for a time. Your husband seemed as regretful about not seeing him as I was. But still.' He spits. 'Wouldn't let me drink.'

'Charles?'

'No. I wanted absinthe. *La fée verte.* I was thirsty and I know a place that sells it, but he refused.'

'Of course. He's the warden. He had to.'

'The Major.'

'That's right. How could he have let you?'

'He could have joined me.'

'Absinthe?' She laughs. 'Charles? Not Charles.'

The painter tilts back his hat. He looks up from his stool at Jeanne and squints. 'What did he say to you? About our meetings? He must have said something, although he said nothing to me. Perhaps he's blessed our acquaintance. Perhaps he's decided that I'm perfectly well and needn't be here at all.'

Jeanne exhales. 'No. He wouldn't listen to me. I told him that I like your company and you might like mine a little, and what harm can it do? But he said no. For your sake as much as mine, I think. I'm still forbidden from talking to you.'

'And from climbing the hospital wall, no doubt.'

She sees a stone, kicks it. 'I have more rules than you.'

The Dutchman eyes her. Then he looks back to the wheat. 'I'm learning a great deal about marriages by spending time in Saint-Paul. All these nuns who are married to God. The absent Madame Peyron. You. And I've had news from my brother. His wife Jo is expecting a child.'

'A child?'

'To be born in the spring.'

'That's good news. Spring is the best time for a child. Blossom and birdsong ...' All her own boys had been spring-born.

'Yes. This news. It's a curious thing – to hear something that gives you such happiness for someone who you love but that also brings a sense of loss to oneself. A sorrow. I can't hide that I feel it.'

She considers him. 'You hoped for that too? For yourself?'

'A wife?'

'Yes. A child.'

He looks away. 'I had one. Or she wasn't my wife for we didn't marry but yes, I've loved a woman and I loved her like a wife. Her children weren't my children but if she'd stayed I'd have made them so. Loved them as if they'd been my own. I treasured Sien, while I had her.'

Jeanne can only stare.

'Now, I wouldn't try. I'm too unwell, and too tired. Who might have me? And what might I offer a wife? The paintings don't sell.' He pauses. 'Still. Theo will be a father. I shall be an uncle.'

'That's a blessing in itself.'

'It is. Yes. And it was also a blessing to return to Arles, in fact. I feared it, but when I saw the yellow house and the hospital and the river I was so calm, Jeanne. The last time I'd seen these places I'd been unwell and alone, bleeding. And yet there I was with your husband, walking by his side as if we weren't warden and patient but simply two men, walking in Arles as men do. I wanted Salles to see me like that. I wanted him to see how I am now – with colour and a little meat on my bones. All these paintings that I've done. Still.' He exhales. He closes his eyes, feels the sun. 'Perhaps I'm mended, Jeanne. How long have I been here? Three months or more – and no attacks, no nightmares. All these paintings too. Perhaps this place has cured me entirely – with its weedy garden and diet of beans.' And he turns, looks up at her so that the sunlight falls across his nose and beard but his eyes remain in the hat's shade. Half dark, half bright. 'You look sad. Why are you sad?'

'I'm not sad.' She's simply looking at him.

He shows his teeth when he smiles.

The final days of August. Jeanne has sat silently in the chapel's dark. She's bought the last apricots of summer from Madame Lenoir, eaten them on her walk home with the juice running down her wrists. She's returned to the trunk, touched its *AP*.

To her husband she says, 'Charles? Do you remember how I told you that I was expecting? With Jean-Charles?' It had been late autumn. She'd turned to him in their warm, shared bed and said, I have some news. Are you ready? He must have known to expect it. But perhaps there is no way to prepare for such news, or some things.

Jeanne is under the lime again, when it comes. *It* – as if the word *attack* had heard its name when the Dutchman spoke it.

There's a change.

The cicadas stop. They don't grow quieter: they stop entirely, and so abruptly that it feels someone's commanded them – *stop!* Sometimes the birds are like this when a hawk passes over them. Sometimes the market wives are motionless when she herself walks by.

Jeanne drops her basket of clothes. She walks out of the

yard, then starts to run. Over the lane. Through the tunnel of pines that leads to the hospital and, as she goes, she hears a shout. One shout, that's all: she knows it's him.

He's not sitting, brush in hand. Nor is he standing, wearing his hat. The Dutchman is swimming, or seems to be – lying in the waist-high grass and thrashing, his arms flattening the stems, his legs kicking out, and there's a strange, jerked motion of his head as if he is breathing above the pale waves. For a moment she thinks that he's playing. That this is a game Jeanne doesn't know.

But it isn't a game. She hears him shout again and again and so Jeanne picks up her skirt and runs into the olive groves and catches herself against rocks and branches and she calls his name as she goes and twice she nearly falls, as he has clearly fallen. She runs until she reaches him. Drops down by his side.

'Vincent.' Grasps his arm. He's thrashing on his front, his face half-buried in the parched earth so she turns him onto his back, using both hands. He drops onto his back and like this she sees that his eyes are open – wide, pink-veined – that he has grass in his mouth, which his mouth is working on, and so she reaches for the grass and clears it away, despite the teeth and the noises he's making and that hard, fighting tongue. She clasps both sides of his face. 'Vincent!' But he answers in a language she doesn't know and rolls back into the grass where his easel has splintered and his canvas has been torn.

She stands and runs. 'Charles!'

Down the length of the boundary wall until she reaches Sœur Madeleine with her key around her neck and she cries, 'Let me in!'

When they all return to him – Jeanne, Charles, Poulet, Peyron, three nuns, all out of breath – the grass isn't pale

140

any more. The patient still swims in his high, grassy sea and he's still calling out, but there is more colour now. Blue. And why? What is blue in the olive groves? Or in nature at all, other than the sky? But she reaches him first and kneels down and she sees that he holds a blue tube, or what's left of it, in his left hand. His teeth and lips and tongue are all blue.

'Eating paint. Salles said he did this in Arles. Poulet?'

The two men kneel by his side. They take his wrists and his waist, brace themselves. Secure their feet in the rough ground. Charles counts to three.

'Ready? Up!'

They lift the Dutchman as they might lift a boat, or a splintered wheel that can't be left; he's a heavy, awkward weight and the men stumble, call out to each other – *careful! Watch out!* – as they carry him home. The nuns move round them like fish. The Dutchman himself roars like a god, arching his back as if freshly woken, fighting their hands and speaking his language, drooling his blue-coloured blood. Jeanne thinks of nets, and spears.

She stands alone.

A hush in his wake.

In the grass, the broken canvas and tubes of paint.

She kneels. Ultramarine. Lead white. And there's blue everywhere. The tube itself is empty; the paint it contained is marking everything – blue earth, blue tips to the grass, a blue handprint on an olive's bark, and, looking down, Jeanne sees blue on her hands which must have come from when she held his face and said his name – *vingt* and *cent*, over and over – as he drooled his own blue.

Ten

Charles sits in front of her. Palms on the table.

The ticking clock.

'The attack in the field wasn't his first. His first at Saint-Paul but not the first in his life. It was entirely consistent with the notes that he came with, that the hospital gave us; Salles, too, has talked of these episodes which they couldn't name in Arles and couldn't control in any proper way. No clear diagnosis. Like epilepsy, but if it were pure epilepsy he'd have no consciousness during the attack or recollection of it afterwards – and he remembers. Mania of a sort? It's some acute, overwhelming distress of the mind that we'd hoped a healthy routine would cure – regular food, fresh air, his painting. And it did help him for a while. But now we know he isn't cured and, Jeanne, I rather doubt he ever can be. We can't know the cause of this. And if we can't know its cause ...'

'He ate paint.'

'I know. He's tried to drink turpentine before, in Arles.'

'Why?'

'The doctors there thought it might be to take his own life.'

'He'll be an uncle. He told me.'

'He told me that too. Why were you with him? I forbade

you from being with him and yet you came for help. So you must have been with him.'

'No. I heard him. From the yard.'

'Heard?'

'Sensed it.'

'Sensed it?' An edge to his voice.

Jeanne stiffens, lifts her jaw. 'Yes, sensed. I felt something was wrong.'

Charles shifts in his chair. 'Why do you think I give orders? To you or the patients? Tell me.'

'It's what you know. From the army. It's how you live – coffee at the same hour, *Le Figaro*. You want the windows shut and a wife who stays at home.' Her voice is tired, as if longing for rest. 'For thirty years, Charles, you've used the same pomade for your hair.'

He leans forwards. He keeps hold of his frustration, but she can see it. It boils inside him, like water in a pan. 'Pomade? Jeanne, for thirty years I've been a warden. And in that time I thought I'd seen every kind of broken mind and trouble and self-harm. But him? Not him. Not his kind. And I'd sooner have a dozen patients who were constantly fretful and violent to themselves than have even one like the Dutchman who's perfectly calm and clear-thinking for much of the time, but then capable of being so ill ... You saw. You were there.'

She was. She looks into her husband's eyes.

'Don't you remember Rouisson? The bruise that he left? It could have been far more than a bruise. I make rules for protection. Jeanne, what's happened to you? Why are you being like this?'

With that, the Major sits back. He rubs his eyes for a moment. Then he takes hold of the bridge of his nose, as if pinching there, and like this he stays very still; he keeps his eyes closed, breathes in and out.

'How is the Dutchman now?' Said quietly.

'Sedated. He'll be kept indoors for weeks, at least. We have no choice in that. The seizure's passed but his brain is exhausted and he'll be haunted by it, distraught. He said he thought he was mended.' Charles lowers his hand.

She looks down at the table. 'Do you think he wanted to die?'

Charles is quieter too. The frustration's drained away from him, or he's too tired to show it. 'I don't think so. We spoke of it once, he and I. He said that even in the deepest water one must always swim for shore.'

'I thought he was swimming. His arms.'

'Were you hurt?'

'No.'

'He didn't grasp you?'

'No. I grasped him. I hurt him, perhaps.'

She finds he's looking at her. His head is slightly tilted, which is how he looks at a printed page – as if he's trying to read the lines in her or has found a new chapter. Can't fathom a word. 'If he worsens, it will ask far more of the nuns and Peyron and myself, and all I want is rest, Jeanne – for all of them. Do you understand?'

With that, he leaves the room. Jeanne looks at the chair he has risen from.

A month without the Dutchman in the fields. At first, knowing this, Jeanne tucks herself into corners. She makes her way to the chapel in the afternoons, settles herself down on the pew she's always known. The same old prayers.

Also, there are the chores she has strayed from and must return to – the sweeping, the reaching up to cobwebs and the cleaning of windows. All the laundry, scrubbed and hung out.

But they are not enough. She finds herself starting to run – down to Saint-Rémy and through its streets, or to the west where the cemetery lies. Schoolboys see her. Madame Lenoir too: she looks up from the rug she's beating.

Or she goes down to the canal, takes off her shoes. The water is greenish; she hoists her skirts high, lowers her legs in as far as the thigh and finds she can walk into it – that the canal's depth, in this part, is not deep at all.

She tries to spit, in the lane.

She fits her foot on the sides of trees, pushes herself into branches to gather the fruit growing there – figs, or plums.

And one afternoon she reaches under the nursery bed. Retrieves the trunk. She's right: the yellow dress is too small for her. But she holds it up against herself, looks in the mirror and turns from side to side.

To keep the Dutchman near her, she lists what she knows of him.

How he is copper and rust. That he sliced at his ear, took half of it away. That he knows the flat, watery country and felt, at times, like the tallest thing. That he misses the north. Sees colour in a cypress tree. How he found it hard to say *Les Alpilles* and liked to hear that Les Deux Trous can, sometimes, sing. That he will be an uncle. Doesn't sleep. Has no need of lavender. Spits. Reads Shakespeare, who Jeanne knows nothing of. Has hands so dry that they've cracked between his fingers and are red around the nails. That he painted a moth that no one else saw. Drinks water as if he's lived a desert life. Doesn't go to chapel or ever speak of God. Worked in a mine and looked up at the sky. Drinks absinthe, or used to. Knew the street by the city wall where women sold their bodies and walked into the Place Lamartine on a rainy night. That he took off his straw hat like a crown. That he clutched her hand as he swam in the high grass. Has brown-coloured teeth. Smells unclean. That he paints with such force and passion and fire that a proper fire could be raging around him in the fields as he worked – the wild fires that come, sometimes – and he'd never notice; he'd paint on and on. *Le fou roux*, to some people. That yellow and blue are his colours of life. That he hates English coldness. Has a mother, still living.

How she could sit by his side and watch him for hours, for days. How he told Jeanne that stars have movement – swirled and wild and bright.

At night she stares into the bedroom's dark, sees those canvases. The olives. Wicker chairs and avenues. *I treasured Sien, while I had her.* The nude with the heavy breasts, the forehead on her arms.

Eighteen years old. Until that age, her life had been spent in the haberdashery or eyeing Claudette's withered hand. Climbing out of attic windows. Once, she'd begun humming in the schoolroom so that Madame Desmarais had asked, Who's that? Making that sound? And Jeanne stopped. Then started again. Stopped and then started. She'd lie down on the steps of Saint Trophime to see its gargoyles better.

Then she was eighteen. And in the hospital at Arles a doctor with colourless eyes had looked at Jeanne and talked of the brain. 'Mademoiselle Lafayette?'

'Lafuye.'

'*Pardon*. A rupture. A vessel in the brain has ...' And he gestured with his hand. Exploded. Burst. 'The paralysis is permanent.'

'His speech?'

'Sometimes it improves.'

'Sometimes?'

'If he tries. If you help him. We've seen some slight recoveries.'

Her sadness showed itself as anger, first. She reached for her father's hand – the one that still had life in it, could move and take hold of things – and wanted to make promises, to assure her father that the doctor was wrong. Tell him that the doctor was too young to know, and to be a doctor at all – *don't listen to him* – and she and her father would prove this in the months to come.

Then the pastor came. 'I'm Frédéric Salles,' he told her. 'I work here, Mademoiselle. I've come to ...' To soothe. To pray. And Jeanne hadn't wanted to pray with a man called Salles, or anyone else. Hadn't wanted for any single thing to come forward and present itself except a cure, a turning back of time so that it could be yesterday or the day before and not now. 'We don't need you here.'

'I understand.'

He bowed, went. And then Jeanne left her father's bed-side, found a corner of an empty room in which she sobbed, struck the side of the door and cursed fortune or God or the doctor himself. She grappled with her own skin; later she'd find bruises. Then her sadness rushed in.

The pastor came back at dusk. He stood very close to Jeanne. 'Your father will need care now. For the rest of his life.'

'I know. I'll care for him.'

'You have a mother? Brothers or sisters?'

'No.'

'You're alone?'

'There's Claudette. But I don't think she can stay.'

He spoke very gently. 'How old are you?'

'Eighteen. I'll care for him.'

'What of the—'

'Cost? I know. I'll sell what I must.' She knew there was a meagre dowry for her. They'd blow the dust off it, use it for this.

So as winter crept in, Didier Lafuye was pushed through the streets of Arles in a wheeled chair, his face as strange as melted wax. In the rue de l'Agneau he slept downstairs. And Jeanne became the daughter of blankets and warmed milk and pails. She moved silently, asked nothing of him except to turn, in her washing of him – and she'd tell him of what she'd seen from a window in the hope that her words might take his mind, and her mind, away from the fact that this brave, proud, intelligent man was a child again. Being cleaned by his daughter and read to at night.

They sold the shop. They had no choice. On hearing that Didier Lafuye was ill, a short, hard-eyed woman knocked on their door in December. She talked of her love of fine silk. Picked at her teeth with a splinter of wood. Said her name was Marguerite Lafuye Saint-Pierre – 'I'm your aunt. Didn't you know?' – and shouldn't the shop go to her? The sister? The adult? The capable heir? 'You can hardly be choosy, can you?'

Jeanne knew very little of her Aunt Marguerite. All she knew was that she'd worked as a maid long ago, and fallen in love with a beaded glove. Claudette had heard rumours since. She passed them on with her damp lisp. 'Your father's sister? Sour piece. Drinks. The husband gambles, I hear. As wanted as rotten meat, that one . . .'

148

But money was money. Jeanne was unmarried and her papa was ill.

Jeanne went back to the shop just once more. The day before they sold it she used her key and stood in the place where her father had fallen and looked at the black-handled scissors, the velvet like breath. The counter. The lace.

They couldn't afford to keep Claudette. She nodded at this news, sucked her teeth. 'Well, then.' That was her goodbye.

She left the house on a windy day, clutching her coat with her uncrippled hand, and as Jeanne watched her from the window she wondered what the future would be for the woman who had no faith in love, believed a bath of vinegar would keep the fever away. Her hand like a claw. There was no way of knowing. But Jeanne knew her own future, at least. The seas and promontories and forested places, and even the thought of them must be swept up or folded away. The trunk that she'd carved *JL* onto was left in a corner where it gathered cobwebs, and where leaves found themselves in the autumn months.

Still no Dutchman. No blue overalls moving through the trees.

'He's weak,' Charles tells her when she asks. 'Not fitful or distressed, but very weak. He's not painting.'

'Not painting?'

'I won't allow it. Can't.'

They've often eaten in silence. But Jeanne knows that Charles, too, is aware of the silence between them these days – how their knives seem louder, how the pages of *Le Figaro* sound when being turned.

Charles. His scent. The skin beneath his eyes.

Jeanne used to dream of the man who'd marry her. She'd help her father dress or undress, look up to hear the cheers from Les Arènes and wonder where he was. When he might come for her.

To be cherished, looked at. 'Look at me.'

He lowers his knife and fork, looks up.

She wants words from Charles at this moment – of her, of their marriage. Something that is theirs and has nobody else in it, not their boys or Peyron or a patient. Just them.

She waits. *Speak.*

He rises, thanks her for the meal which wasn't much. Eggs, onions, a little stale bread.

After Claudette, there were no other women until Laure. Laure came, stood beside Jeanne and smiled – and, in doing so, became the only woman in twenty years to have felt even close to a friend. Laure was younger than Jeanne. The backs of her hands were less weathered; there was less stiffness in her when they rose up from benches or rugs on the ground. A waist too; Laure still had that feminine inward curve that Jeanne had lost with her pregnancies. Her own waist felt long ago.

And Laure looked younger. There was no doubt that she knew she had beauty. For all her love of patting the mules, of gathering herbs or wading through streams, she still knew what she had. She'd catch her own reflection as she walked through Saint-Rémy. On rising up from her prayers in chapel, Laure felt her hair to check it was still tied as she meant it to be. And sometimes she'd say, Jeanne, why don't you try . . . ? Offering things to her. A ribbon, a pair of gold earrings. Just to see, that's all.

In the beginning, when Laure was still unsure of her new, southern, married life and the fields around it, Jeanne brought her here – to Les Antiques, where the women are so worn down by centuries that Jeanne can't see their expressions or the intricacies of their hands and feet but she knows they're women, at least. Their skirts. Ropes at their waists. 'I'm friends with them,' Jeanne confessed. 'With these women.'

'With the carvings?' Laure paused, then smiled. 'I like that.'

Jeanne feels the stone now.

She presses her cheek against it, closes her eyes.

From time to time Jeanne had thought of their marriage – the Peyrons', not her own. Laure and Théophile. She pictured them in bed. It felt the wrong thing to do, but sometimes the thought swooped in, filled her head – as when she saw their difference in height, his limp or her litheness, or saw Peyron's hand on the base of her back as they walked. Their bed sheets, hung out. Her own marriage was chaste, by then. By the time Laure came to Saint-Paul the Trabucs were parents to three small boys; their beds were kept apart by three strides of wooden floor. And so, if she ever saw Laure's undergarments drying in the sun she pictured limbs and breathlessness. *Don't stop* . . . Peyron with his glasses off.

Of all the things Jeanne wondered as she walked by Charles's side on the boulevard des Lices, one of them was this: what does he know? Not of wars, or countries. Not of the old port of Marseilles or how to discipline a child. But of female bodies. What did Charles *know* – this military man, five years older than her – of the curves and tastes and entrances that every woman walked with, underneath her clothes? She wondered what he'd seen. If army men saw more, or less. How his hands would feel on her waist or thighs or belly or breasts.

*

That night, Jeanne makes her way downstairs. She wears her nightdress; her hair is unpinned. At the table, Charles is writing by a single lantern's light and she stands in the doorway, watches this. How he pauses, dips for ink. How he frowns – as he does when he does all things carefully. He isn't aware of his wife at first.

Then she walks to him. He looks up. And without speaking Jeanne takes her husband's hand and removes his pen from his forefinger and thumb and lays it down. Charles says, 'Jeanne?'

She presses his hand against her breast. She holds it there, breathes in. She pushes his fingers down so that he's grasping her, feeling the shape of her.

Then Charles pulls his hand away, stands up. He steps backwards, saying, 'What are you doing? Jeanne? What?' – and he looks from the table to the floor to the parlour walls as if these things have the answers, not her. 'What are you doing, Jeanne? What are you thinking?'

She has no words. Only, 'I—'

'Go upstairs. I'm writing. I'm writing a letter and I want to finish it. Go, Jeanne.'

What can be wrong in climbing a tree for figs? In talking to a man who likes talking to her too? In taking her husband's hand and pressing it onto a part he's touched before, seen before? Which he has weighed with his palm, wordlessly? This part that has fed his own children?

Look at me. See me. But she says nothing.

She steps back. Turns, goes upstairs.

Those two things in the trunk: the letter and the dress.

The letter is addressed to Jeanne.

My dearest Jeanne.

I hope this letter finds you. I also hope that it finds you well – and not sorrowful or angry or resentful of my leaving. You may well feel angry, but I hope not. Only a month, and you feel so far away. Saint-Rémy too – I thought I'd never see elsewhere but I write this to you with a view of a huge white cathedral and there are flocks of birds flying over it, and after writing this I think I'll walk up to it. They say there's a bleeding heart in there that really does bleed, or has done – just once.

I write to tell you that I miss my friend, to reassure you that I'm safe and well and not to trouble yourself with thoughts that might say otherwise. I can't imagine what they're saying of me in the marketplace, but I know you love me well enough to know the truth of it. You understand, I know that. Whatever rumours you hear will not be the truth, as they never are. Jeanne, I also write to send you an address. I won't be at this place for long – a week or so longer, no more. But any letter you might send will always find me, if posted to this place. Its residents are kind people, and will always know where I am, so they'll either send a letter on to me or save it for my return. Will you keep the address safe? And pass it on to no one? It is for you and you alone, my friend. If you ever came here they would welcome you too.

I wonder if Théophile is in such pain that you wish to reassure him. I hate to think of that – for I do love him. But he'll receive his own letter very soon. As for this letter, please keep it as our secret.

Be brave and strong, as I know you are. These are small days and you are not small-hearted.

Your loving friend,
Laure

Eleven

Jeanne came to know of her body's changing shape and the monthly bleed from Claudette, who had no care to talk in any intimate way. She spoke of moons and curses. The burden of their sex. One day she eyed the teenage Jeanne and hissed, 'It won't be long now. Look at you ...' – as if disapproving, and the bleed was Jeanne's own fault. Told her to chew willow bark. 'There are belts these days.'

'Belts?'

'So I hear. Or just bleed freely.' Shrugged.

'Which do you do?'

'I don't bleed at all now.'

As to what the female parts could do or make or feel, Claudette said even less. 'I'll tell you what it is. It's a man climbing on you and puffing and licking your neck like a thirsty dog, and then climbing off and walking away. That's what it is.'

'But I thought you never married, Claudette.'

A pause. 'Sweep that floor.'

The maid, surely, was wrong. Jeanne felt certain that Claudette had to be wrong – for if the act of making children was such a vile and painful act, would there be children at all? Wouldn't the human race die out? Jeanne had seen the stray cats. The dogs, too, hadn't seemed distressed as they'd

154

shunted themselves over the grass or under the market stalls. Furthermore, if love's expression (as she'd heard it called) was so unwanted by the female sex, why were there shawls of pure silk and the finest lace in her father's shop? Women thrilled at seeing them. Such things weren't made for outside.

Jeanne wanted to know so much more. Hoped to see truths in the rue du Bout d'Arles, through a keyhole or two. She'd wanted to ask the woman she met there, leaning against the white wall. And when at last she felt Charles's hands on her waist in the simple hotel room on their wedding night, she'd whispered, *Show me what you know.*

As it was, in the half-dark of their hotel Charles asked her, 'How's that? Like that, do you think? Or should I . . . ?' He laid his forearms either side of her, tucked his knees into the space between her own – so that his groin was the only part of him to be touching Jeanne at all. 'Or maybe like that?'

And in time they both learned more. Jeanne and Charles both came to understand this act, this joining of two bodies – what fitted, which parts grew hard or slick. She'd turn onto her side or front; he'd move slower or faster, or reach down with his hand. *There? Yes, there.* And they'd smile, sometimes – at the bed's own sound or at the first frail cries of a hungry son that stopped his hips, or her hips, or they'd smile in the hush that came when the act was done.

Her back, sometimes, would arch. He'd clutch the sheets when his turn came, breathe fast, say her name.

As September moves on, the plums come in. Their trees grow heavy, lower themselves. The nuns come out to pick them – Yvette and Marie-Josephine, and she sees that Patrice is with them. He sings, as always. He helps the nuns, looks at each plum as if holding gold.

Also the reapers come. They bring their carts and mules up the lanes, walk into the fields that border the olives and take out their scythes and work. Skin as thick as the mules' hide. In the heat of the day they sleep in the shade of their carts, pass flasks between them. At dusk they roll past her without acknowledgement, the wheat piled high.

The Dutchman comes, at last.

Jeanne sees him on an amber-coloured day. Has to pause at the sight of him, dragging his easel out through the grass with his hat and overalls – in case it isn't him at all.

She offers him water in the brown cup. '*Bonjour.*'

He is impossibly thin. He's so thin that he makes her think of the bones that she might place in a saucepan to boil away the last of the meat. Like a structure of a human, not a proper one. And he looks older – by years, not a month. A falling in of skin.

'You've been ill.'

He takes the cup with both hands. 'I know. You were there, weren't you?'

'I was. I heard you. Saw you.'

'I ate paint. Poulet said.'

'And grass.'

He drinks carefully.

She watches this. 'How are you feeling now?' Wants to embrace him, to absorb him as she's wanted to with her boys.

The Dutchman swallows. 'It stays with me. I feel its shadow. I said that I'd lost the fear of it, do you remember?'

'The fear is back?'

'Back, yes. And I don't think it will go. I think it will always be with me. I thought I'd mend here, Jeanne.'

The boy in him – a small, solitary boy from the flat country, not the grown man – and if he had been her own child she'd reach for him and hold him, or hold his head in her hands and tell him to be brave, and strong. That he's not alone. These motherly things.

He looks into the cup. 'I know how they are, these attacks. How they must look. I've frightened people with them.'

'I wasn't frightened. How do they feel? Charles told me you remember them.'

He shakes his head. 'I can't tell you. I can't describe it. I am left feeling frightened.' He looks up. 'Did I fight you, Jeanne?'

'No. You fought yourself. I tried to hold your fists. Do you know what I thought, when I saw you? You looked as if you were swimming. Laurent liked to swim. He'd taught himself. I didn't know it, but sometimes he went down to the canal when I thought he was playing out in the fields. I saw him, that's how I knew of it. You looked like that.' Jeanne tilts her head. 'He stopped you painting – Charles did.'

'He thought I might eat paint again. Thought it might worsen me to work, but how could it worsen me? What colour was it?'

'That you ate? Blue.'

'Blue . . .'

'But you're painting now?'

'Indoors, yes. The studio. I think the Major would have me indoors for the rest of my life if he could. But the reapers have come. Have you seen that? I asked him. I begged. And here I am.'

Jeanne says, 'I've been thinking of you. All this time. I've been seeing what you could have painted if you hadn't been indoors – how the light catches the sides of things like hoes or troughs, an empty cup. I've been thinking about your face in a mirror. Aren't all of your paintings the wrong way round? A mirror image of yourself?'

'What choice do I have?'

'Will you paint me?'

'What?' Turns to her.

'Aren't I the right kind? No duchesses, you said.'

He blinks rapidly. He also moves his jaw from side to side, as if trying to speak but lacking the words, and in doing this she sees the movement of bones and sinews – in his neck and collarbone. She could grasp each bone. Pluck them, like strings. This thinness. 'Paint you? What? How? How can I paint you? I'll be back inside by dusk. And they'd see. And—'

'I don't mean today. I mean soon.'

'Still. How can I do that?'

'The kitchen has a back door. It isn't locked by day.'

'And Charles? The Major?'

'Why should he have to know? And what could he do, if he did find out? A time will come – when he needs to go down to Saint-Rémy for an hour or two. Leave Saint-Paul.'

The remnants of the missing ear are scarlet in this light. A flower, closed up – or it's a flower that has bloomed and is wilting and folding back into itself as flowers do, when they're over. His eyes have redness in them too. 'I don't understand why you're asking me.'

Her friend. Shrunken down, as if he's been cooked: a reduction of himself. He sits very still. Then, slowly, he reaches out. He takes her wrist, as he has done before – still a light touch, as light as the ostrich feathers she's known, and yet what's different is he neither turns the wrist nor moves her. He only holds it. He holds it solely for touching's sake.

'You're a curious thing. Bold. If you think you can come to the studio without the nuns seeing you, and if you believe that Charles won't know, then I'll paint you.'

'You will?'

'Yes.' With that, he lets go.

Nothing moves faster than rumours. It's as if they have feathers and fly, Laure said. No net to catch them.

And of the rumours, none has a faster, lower flight than the shameful ones. If there's lost dignity, if it's scandalous or ungodly or unfortunate then it carries itself on dark, oiled wings. The news of Jean-Charles's birth — and Laurent's, and Benoît's — all moved far slower than the news of her two daughters. The rumours, not those babies, had the lasting life.

Knowing this, Jeanne walks into the marketplace at Saint-Rémy with a hardness to her. She lifts up an aubergine. '*Bonjour*, Madame. This please.'

Madame Arnoux closes one eye, half-smiles. 'It's been a while, Madame.'

'Our vegetable patch has done well this summer. I've not needed for much.'

'Busy, then. With the garden. With friendships.' Opens the eye. 'The redheaded man? His attack? Madame Gilles said he soiled himself. There's talk of the Devil being inside him.'

'There's no Devil in him.'

'Is any of it true? You were there, after all. It's been said that you're often with him ... '

'Our cottage is next to the olive groves. He's been painting in them.' She gives this as explanation.

Jeanne pays, moves. *This.* This chorus of birds, this gathering of tales of what has been, or might be. What good does it do? How does it help a single life? How they loved Laure's vanishing. How they murmured over each rumour as if they'd cupped jewels in their weathered hands: that Laure had taken to drinking too much, or had caught her own madness as others might catch a cough in wet weather and this made her senses go. That, and so much more.

But Laure survived them somehow. As Jeanne has, and the goatherd and Charles have done. Maybe their skin has thickened against the whispers, like bark. If someone has not survived the rumours that wing through the olive trees – or not managed them, at least – it's the man that Laure left. *Poor Peyron* ... His wife walked out of his life. And afterwards there came tales – that he'd never cared for Laure, that he used to strike her, use the hospital restraints. That his cruelty led her to lovers. That he may have seemed kindly and cheerful but, in fact, he'd treated her like a patient herself and governed every hour of her nights and days. Or that he preferred the young patient who talked of being an owl – because she'd been a frail, bright thing. *That's what I heard* ...

Those lies. They were hard enough to bear, but as the weeks passed there came darker ones – darker, and yet somehow a little easier to believe. For which man in Provence might not have seen Laure's girlishness, not admired or envied it? For the briefest moment, at least? Yet no children came. No little Peyrons – and so in the streets and under the planes there came the hardest tales: *He's broken that way. Which way? You know* ... That Laure was an unhappy wife. That she'd walk through the house on full-moon nights, turning the ring on her left hand and wishing she'd done differently. She'd taken a lover or many lovers, in different towns – Nîmes, Orange, Avignon. And so whose fault was it? That she went? Might she have stayed if Peyron had been more skilled in the act of love? And so when he knelt down on that Christmas Eve, punched the ground until he drew blood, they knew. They decided this: *He must have done something . . .* Or rather, he'd not done enough.

She buys a clutch of plums, yeast for bread. She wants to tell each person in the Place de la République that none of it is right, and none of it is true. That Laure whispered of their lovemaking once, and smiled as she did so – or a faint smile, at least. *He isn't broken, you see?* And Jeanne wants to tell them, too, what will soon happen – which is that Jeanne will be painted. Painted by him, *le fou roux*. And so they can sell their eggs. They can sell their lavender, sit in the shade with their sleeping dogs and embroidery and say what they wish about people they don't care for, and places they don't know, and they can talk about Jeanne if they want to.

I will be looked at, painted.

There's been no talk, between Charles and her, of her gesture. Of the evening she took his hand, pressed it to herself. The day after, they'd not spoken. The day after that also passed without it being mentioned. Perhaps it never happened.

As she rinses the floral plates he comes to her.

'Yves cut himself today. Took a stone from the garden, cut his arm. Not deeply, but still.'

'How is he now?'

'Resting.'

She looks at the nameless blooms. Surely he has more to say. Surely he's not standing beside her, watching her work, to tell her of Yves and a stone. He must have thought of it in these past few days: the feeling of her, under her nightdress; the message within that action of hers. How they used to be.

'Jeanne?'

'Yes?'

'I need to go to Arles.'

A pause in her work. She looks at the water. 'Arles? Again?'

'For the last of his paintings. The Dutchman spoke of them when he was ill. He wants them here, not in Arles.'

'You'll take him with you?'

'No. He's too frail for that. Just me.'

She returns to work. 'When?'

No talk of her body, or of touching it. 'Friday. This Friday. You'll manage?'

She walks out to the kitchen, says over her shoulder, 'Of course.'

He's still working on the reapers and their wheat; the colours on his palette are yellow, orange and brown. 'Friday.'

'Friday?'

'Charles is going away for the day. To Arles.'

'He is? For my paintings?'

'Yes.'

'The sunflowers?'

'I'm not sure what they're paintings of.'

'Sunflowers. I did several of them. They're good – my better work. He must be careful, bringing them. He'll take care with them?'

'Charles always takes care. I'll come to you Friday, then?'

His old, tired face. His body that looks as if it's been emptied and has nothing to support it. 'Jeanne, are you sure? What if Charles—'

162

'Yes. I want this.'

He gives a sad smile. 'One. Can you come at one o'clock? It's a quiet time. Lunch will have passed.'

'One. Yes.'

'And Jeanne? I want you to wear black for me. To paint you in black.'

'Black?'

'Yes, black. Do you have a black dress, a mourning dress? Wear that.'

A dream of the Pegoulado. The festival in Arles that she never took part in. At night, a procession of lights and tambourines and dancers, and all the Arlésiennes in their lace.

Jeanne is there tonight. Bells tied onto her skirts. She dances past Les Arènes and the shops and the towering church. The stars are moving, like balls.

She wakes, out of breath. 'Jeanne?'

He frowns down at her. Charles is fully dressed. He has dressed without waking her, wears his travelling coat. 'Did you have a bad dream?'

'No. What time is it?'

'Early. Still early.' He nods. 'I'm leaving now. For Arles.'

'Yes.'

A pause. 'Right.' Nods to himself. 'I'll see you tonight.'

She watches him from the window. The sky lightens in the east. She thinks of the *tap-tap* of a globe as her husband crosses the yard, walks down the lane.

Twelve

When her father's death lay quietly in wait for her, its shadow lying over her life like a shroud before his proper one, she made this dress. She knew where to buy the black crêpe, how to measure herself – her waist, the length of each arm. By lamplight, she sewed. Thread by thread. When it was finished she tried it on and looked at herself.

But Jeanne has changed since then. The black dress became too tight. So she searched for more crêpe in the market of Saint-Rémy, found none – only a darkish blue that she stitched into the back of the dress to widen it. She replaced its black ribbon with a single, durable cord.

Jeanne works the dress up over her thighs and has to breathe in, but it comes over her body and her arms find their sleeves, and then she reaches round behind herself, takes hold of the cord.

She finds her reflection in their one, tarnished mirror. A woman in mourning, yet fire-eyed. She decides to leave her hair pinned.

The Dutchman is waiting for her. He doesn't ask how she knew where to come. Nor does he mention or excuse the room's disarray – the canvases and flattened tubes of paint, the stiffened cloths. He's bare-headed. It surprises her; she has rarely seen him hatless, or without the band of sweat that darkened his hair. He sits with his back to the window. His easel, his palette, his box of paints. A chair sits, expectantly.

'You said black.'

'Yes. Sit there.'

'This chair?'

'Yes. Were you seen, do you think?'

'I saw the back of Mère Épiphanie, but only her back. No one else. Like this?'

'No, don't face me. Sit at an angle and look straight ahead. Find a thing to focus on.'

'So many paintings.'

'Not as many as there have been. Most have been sent to Theo. Keep still.'

'That's your starry night. The one you said. And is that—'

'Keep still ... Or I may as well be painting a dog that never stops moving.'

'A dog?'

'Well, then. Stay still.'

She finds a painting on the far wall. A field of wheat, not harvested. In its foreground there is the high wayside grass that borders the fields and orchards here; beyond the wheat, at the field's far side, is more of this same grass. But there is also a cypress and a row of olive trees, and beyond this greenery is a small house with a tiled roof. It feels familiar to her. Not their house, but like others. All houses seem the same in Saint-Rémy.

'I can't talk at all?'

'No. Or if you do, I won't answer.'

'What shall I do with my face?'

'Your face?' The sound of his brush on the palette. 'Think of what you love. I've not painted many people but I always tell them that. Think of what you love. It seems to occupy them and stops them from distracting me. Now, let me paint.'

It enters the room. It comes in as if she can see it, as if the light changes as the word *love* comes in. And it's her father who comes to mind – how he'd take a feather and find the back of her ear with it, or his love of roasted chestnuts, or how he'd fall asleep in his chair with his chin reaching down to his chest. *Jeanne-Jeanne.* His sore, cold feet.

And *love* makes her think of being young. Of lying in her single bed on summer nights when it was too light to sleep, and imagining a future for herself – of cities, stars, the Camargue, lovers who might fill her with brightness or with tiny human lives that would grow inside her. Impatience, for this. *Bring them to me . . .*

Pipe smoke. Geraniums. Resting her belly on the sides of bridges and looking down into the Rhône.

Then it's Les Antiques. Can ancient stones be loved? But if love is a strong, settled fondness – a vine that takes hold and grows and wraps itself about you, as she's imagined it to be – then perhaps her fondness of the swallows that nest in the crevices and of the goats dozing in the olives' shade and of the Romans and their slaves and wives that Jeanne has pictured have all grown into love.

And, of course, her boys. They had their own clear love for Les Antiques. They chased and clambered there; Jeanne's heart would clench for them as they climbed higher, looking for footholds amongst the old stones. There's no doubt in this: Jeanne loves every part of her three boys. She loves the birthmark on Laurent's thigh, the stubbornness in him that is also bravery; she loves the way Jean-Charles's tongue used to peep out of his mouth's corner when he was writing or playing cards. How Benoît came back from Les Antiques with their dust on his elbows and knees and asked Charles about what lives came before his own life – of continents, battles, emperors of Rome. How she had to shush them in the chapel sometimes. How Laurent belched. How they loved Christmases and birthdays and all had poor singing voices. How all of them looked when sleeping. Thumbs in their mouth, perhaps.

Charles loves these boys too. He's never said so, of course. His feelings have never been spoken of, not once – or not the strongest ones. And Jeanne made allowances for that, for years, told herself that her husband was haunted by war, and that lacking the word for love didn't mean he lacked the feeling itself. Claudette had had her views. She's said, once, that to use a word too often was to lessen it, as if the tongue was a hammer on a silver-bright word that, with use, thinned and thinned its meaning so that *love*, said too often, became *like*. *Hot* became *warm*. And so what's the point of saying it at all, Claudette asked. Or even feeling it? As foolish, to her, as fine lace.

Jeanne saw Charles's love for their sons. From the start she knew. Telling him about her first, new pregnancy had made his hands tremble. 'You're sure?' On passing his sons, he'd often cup the top of their heads as if blessing them and he'd tell them well done – for reciting the alphabet or listing every Shakespearean play, or for showing such physical strength as harvesting or chopping wood for the fire. Tasks that men should do.

But what of Charles himself? On their first meeting she'd been amazed by the beauty in his face. It wasn't an unlined, perfect face; not handsome in the truest sense. But it was formed. It seemed strong; it had both authority and a boy-ishness that felt right to her. Perhaps a little sadness. Perhaps a little need. On their wedding day he turned to look at her as she'd walked towards him and she'd smiled, felt undone by him: *this is my husband*. This man, who stood by the altar; *him* – which seemed hard to believe. As for love itself, she tried out the word just once: while he was sleeping she whispered *love* to his pale, bare back. Charles didn't hear it. He wasn't meant to. But Jeanne liked to think his deepest parts heard her, that her love made its way under his skin and filled him as he slept. For yes, she's loved Charles Trabuc. Oh, how she has.

And Didier Lafuye. Jeanne loved him too. She was by his side when he died; she'd sat by his hospital bed in Arles and thought, Don't go, please don't. She'd told him that she loved him – said it in his final hours and wished suddenly that she'd disregarded Claudette's claim that saying a word thinned it each time; she wished she'd said *love* over and over when her father had been well so that he might have always known. And what chance had Jeanne had to tell her girls? Their creased faces like buds that wouldn't unfold? The nurses had gathered them and the bloodied sheets and taken them out of the room.

'Jeanne? Jeanne?'

She blinks, stirs. Exhausted.

'Jeanne? Enough. I'm done.'

'Done?'

'Yes. You can go.'

She stays where she is, too tired to rise. Looks at him. 'Sien.'

He slows, in wiping his brush. 'Sien?'

'You spoke of Sien. Said that you loved her. Cherished

her. Would have married her. Vincent, do you still love her? Or can love go away?'

'I don't think it goes. I think once you've loved it stays in you. All we can do is survive it, if we can. Some people can't. Jeanne,' he says. 'Leave here. You must, before you are seen.'

Charles returns after dark. He eats quietly, doesn't look up. 'Salles sends his regards. And I brought the sunflowers back, and the train made good time. So it's been an acceptable day.'

This man who knows, instinctively, when a window is open but who can't hear his wife's quickened heart at this moment, or feel the anger that's rising up from her, or smell the turpentine.

Thirteen

Jeanne first heard the name *Trabuc* when she was twenty-five. She'd been by the hearth of the house in the rue de l'Agneau, rubbing salve into her father's heels. Seven years since his brain had ruptured. In that time there had been no meaningful change in the movement of him. His right side could not bear his weight; on good days his right arm might rise from the mattress, but never far, and Jeanne had to fold his fingers over his palm if he wished to hold a thing. But in seven years his mouth had found new shapes. He couldn't speak as he used to, but his tongue had altered itself to say old words in a new, understandable way. Or Jeanne, at least, could understand them. A language of wetness.

'Papa?'

'There is someone' – he swallowed – 'who I'd like you' – a pause. In that pause, Jeanne tended to him. She laid down the salve, covered his feet. She straightened the blanket, lifted his arm to tuck the wool closer to him and reached down. 'To meet.'

'Meet?'

'A man.'

With that, he came into existence: Charles-Elzéard Trabuc, a military man who'd served in the Crimean War – served with distinction, which was a hard, drooled word for a half-paralysed mouth. On return, he left the army. Was older than Jeanne by four years, or five. Not yet married, as she was not.

'How do you know this, Papa?'

He prepared his mouth for the single word: 'Salles.'

Nothing else was said for several days. But no more was needed: it was clear what was meant by a meeting. Jeanne understood that in the long hours of lying or sitting, unable to move, her father had looked at the far wall or the dark and worried for her – for the fate of his daughter once he was gone. Jeanne was getting older, the money from the sale of the shop had been spent and her dowry was growing less and less with the cost of fuel or yeast for bread. So he'd spoken to Salles at some point, and . . . Jeanne remembered Claudette's warning – *Say yes. It won't happen twice.*

He came in the bright spring weather. The almond trees were blossoming when Major Trabuc came to the house on rue de l'Agneau, his hat in his hand. His suit was pressed, tightly buttoned. She wore her hair in the loose, long braid she'd always had. '*Bonjour.*'

When he shook her father's hand he reached for the left, undamaged one. 'An honour, Monsieur Lafuye.'

They walked side by side, to the walls of Les Arènes. Charles told her the things he felt she should know: his age, his rank, that his parents were dead, how he knew Salles and the fact he'd been offered a job at a hospital in the nearby village of Saint-Rémy – did she know it? – and he told of what he was hoping for. 'I'm nearly thirty now. I would like children. A wife.'

Did it matter that Jeanne came with so little? No mother, a half-living father? A dowry as small as her travelling days? 'I've never left Arles. Do you mind that?'

'No, I don't mind.' What Charles Trabuc minded, she learned, was order and routine, good manners and a clear sense of right and wrong. For him, tortoiseshell combs and pearl buttons weren't the necessary things, there was inner beauty as much as inner strength – and this made Jeanne think of Aurélie, who had frowned at the shop's display, been untouched by everything except the man at the counter, watching her. *She'd have liked this man.* And Jeanne realised that she liked him too. How he paused on their walk, if there was a view.

She wasn't sure he'd come back. But he did. And they walked through all the streets of Arles, talked of the mistral and bullfighting and different kinds of lace. Of the countries he'd been to, and which he preferred. In turn, Jeanne showed him where the roses grew on the boulevard des Lices, might have showed him jasmine if it had been in bloom. She liked his perfect moustache. Liked how he seemed a little shy in asking 'Can I call you Jeanne? And please call me Charles, if you'd like to.' She did, after that. *Charles* – which sounded like a sigh. And the first time he ever touched her was when a beggar came too close: Charles took Jeanne's elbow very lightly, moved her to a safer place. She watched as he walked back and gave the man a coin.

'I'm sorry. About your mother.'

'*Merci.*'

After the fifth meeting he spoke to her father privately. Jeanne waited in the street. She watched the swifts racing along the rue de l'Agneau and knew what lay ahead, knew that this moment would always be inside her. She wouldn't forget. And when Charles emerged he walked her to the Rhône and a breeze came so that she had to hold back the loose strands of her hair, and as she did this Charles asked if she would marry him. And Jeanne nodded, said yes.

This black-eyed, thoughtful, principled man.

Her father tried to pat her hand that night. 'He will take care of you.'

A wedding in early September. A simple dress, save for the collar of lace. Lavender stems in her hair. When they'd walked back out into the sunlight he'd said, 'You look ...' And never finished that sentence. Only smiled.

Salles had been there. He'd brought Didier in his wheeled chair, sat with him at the side of the church. For Salles had assured Jeanne that he and the nurses would care for her father now, that Charles would meet the cost of it. 'Rest assured,' Salles whispered. 'But I must be honest, Jeanne. I fear he doesn't have long.'

Before leaving for their hotel she bent down to her father, pressed her cheek against his cheek. All her daughter's gratitude. Her love.

Only one wedding since then. Laure and Théophile's is the only other wedding that Jeanne has ever been to – in the chapel of Saint-Paul. The bride had to stoop to kiss the damp-eyed groom.

Jean-Charles has married too. Three years ago, last March. But his bride was from Normandy so they married in the far, far north of France – and it was at a time when Peyron was trailing his grief like rags, making no sense and unable to work, so Charles felt he couldn't leave the place. 'Who'd run it? Give orders? Take care of the nuns?' The woman who claimed that she ate an owl's heart was at her worst too, that spring – tugging at the bars, hissing for meat. 'I know you want to go, Jeanne. I know. But how can we? I'm sorry.' He'd exhaled, looked away. 'It's just too far.'

*

The slightest northerly breeze. She sees it in the grasses.

'What have I told you about standing behind me? Creeping up like an imp?'

She stands beside the Dutchman. She looks at each part of his face.

'Before you ask, no.'

'No?'

'You can't see it yet. It's finished, but it's drying now.'

'How long will it take?'

'A week, maybe? Have patience.'

'I don't have patience. You told me that. And you lack it too.'

'Me?'

'You paint so quickly. And you don't hide your feelings.'

He eyes her. 'I can't argue with you on that. Sometimes I think humans can be like an invention that holds steam or heat, and holds those things so tightly that it starts to shake with the effort of containing it – and what happens then? I've talked and talked in my seizures. I must have said some hateful, wretched words, done wretched things, for who'd make a petition against any reasonable man? I took my ear to a girl on the rue du Bout d'Arles, did you know that?'

She'd heard the rumours.

'I had a brother.'

'He died?'

'At birth. A year to the day before my own birth. He wasn't spoken of, not once. All I knew was that I was named after him, and that I am alive when he should have been. It makes me want more, perhaps.' He reaches for paint. 'If Theo and Jo have a boy they'll call him Vincent too. They've said so. But I've told them it will curse the child. Vincent feels like a curse.'

'I don't believe in curses.'

'No? It becomes easier to. With each seizure or mis-fortune.'

She frowns. 'But I know misfortune too. Are you saying I don't?'

He glances up. 'There's a change in you. You seem ... angry, I think. Are you angry? Jeanne, I'm not the one you should be speaking to.'

In the first days of October the mistral shows itself. She feels it in her skirts as she walks out of chapel. It seems to blow the nuns along the length of the boundary wall. Some of them smile as it happens. But others glance up, fasten their arms through those of other nuns or patients, or cross themselves.

In Arles, everyone feared it. This wind blowing down from the colder, stranger north. Jeanne recognised it not just from the wind's direction or the time of year, but the speed of it: it always seemed fast, and low. In the streets the mis-tral turned corners; it caught hems and tablecloths and the feathered feet of horses and all the other low-down, unseen things so that it felt like a river was rushing through the squares. Almost white.

But to be afraid of it? Jeanne never was. Perhaps there was a slight unease in her, when she saw an unlocked, north-facing door begin to shake on its hinges, or when dust ran down the street and coated the glass. But mostly she liked to throw open the attic window and haul in the taste of it. All those rooftops and clouds.

'I like to swallow the air. Treat it like water.' She tells Charles this. 'We married when the mistral was blowing. Do you remember?'

'It was September.'

'It was still blowing. It caught my veil, and you caught it. Remember?'

Charles pauses, thinks. But then he shakes his head, says no, he can't. 'It was a long time ago.'

On a Monday he comes back from work with an envelope. Jeanne washes the flour from her hands, sits down.

Dear Papa and Maman,

Forgive the long wait for this letter. As you know, there is so much life and bustle in Paris and work takes up so much of my time that when I'm not working I tend to enjoy the city too much to sit down and write. I'm sorry for that. But I hope you'll understand further when I tell you that I am in love. For a time, I've been courting a girl. I mentioned her in my last letter, in the spring. At first, she resisted me! But I was always the stubborn one, as we all know, and I've persisted enough for her to warm to me. My heart is entirely committed. I wish to ask for her hand in marriage before too long, although I am yet to meet her parents and this will have great bearing on my success, or lack of it. I am buying a new waistcoat at the weekend.

I must keep this short, for I promised Jean-Charles that I'd visit tonight. He's as many questions to ask me about love and my affairs as you must – but he also reminds me that Petit-Jean is growing fast and I must be a good uncle.

More soon, I promise it.

Affectionately,

Laurent

Laurent – who'd make swords from old branches, played war amongst the olive groves. Who grew bored at school so Jeanne saw herself in the long, heavy sigh, the wail of *But why?* Wanting to go to Avignon. Wanting to peep over the hospital walls, to see where the invalids lived.

That night she says, 'Laurent ... '

'I know,' says Charles from his bed.

'He's in love. Loving her.'

'Yes. Our boy ... They grow up so quickly, so ... ' He pauses. 'Jeanne, is the woodshed door locked? I think I can hear it.'

The bed creaks with his weight, so Jeanne knows he's turning onto his side to sleep.

All night, she hears it too: the hushed, distant *knock ... knock ... knock ...* of the unlocked woodshed door.

Laure used to clasp her hands when she heard a good story. *That's wonderful, Jeanne!*

She'd have done this with Laurent's news. Love, for Laure, was meant to be this way: exciting, shy, undiscovered. The last conversation they'd had between them had been a few days before she went. Laure found Jeanne in the vegetable patch. They'd talked of herbs, and the warm weather, and Laure had glanced up at the cloudless sky. Still glancing up, asked, 'Jeanne? May I talk to you?'

To leave. To walk away from her husband and home, the life she'd known. To head north. Stand on a bridge and look down at the Seine.

Jeanne had asked, 'Why? You aren't happy?'

'Sometimes. And he takes good care of me, I can't say otherwise. But surely there's more than this. The same views, the same walls. There must be more out there ... ' Her smile. 'Come with me.'

'What?'

'Come with me, Jeanne.'

'With you?'

'You could. You talked of the globe you used to have.'

'The boys.'

'Men, now. And they have all gone.'

'And Charles. What of Charles? He's in my life too.'

'You think he wouldn't survive it? He was in the army. And when I once asked if you felt loved by him you couldn't say yes – remember? Come with me, Jeanne.'

She cannot sleep. She rises.

Jeanne carries the lantern downstairs and into the yard. The woodshed's door is open. She had entered the shed at daybreak. Surely she had closed the door behind her? It knocks as if it has news. She holds up the light, steps in. And what she sees inside the shed is what has always been there – logs, the metal tub, cobwebs, feathers from a long-dead hen. The broom and a pail.

But one thing is new, and it's this: a large rectangle of cloth.

The cloth is grey. Grey, but also dotted with paint – red and dark blue.

It covers a hard, clear-edged shape. She reaches out, touches it.

As Charles sleeps Jeanne carries the rectangle of cloth across the yard and into the house. She holds it against herself like a child. The lantern swings from her hand.

In the nursery she lowers herself down onto the floor.

I will look old is what she fears – that she will uncover this painting and find a woman who's heavy, fleshy, plain. No semblance of a waist. Lines on her brow and a jaw so slack she could grasp its skin in her fist, hold it tight. Jeanne fears he'll have painted exactly what he saw.

She inhales. Pulls off the cloth.

A woman. Briefly, Jeanne thinks *I was right* – for this is a woman of age. A woman she recognises – soft jaw, prim mouth, greying hair. And the dress is too tight in places; it shines on her chest, on her widest parts.

But then something changes. This painted woman alters in her sight. There is a rush of tenderness. For in those polished, round, rabbit-bright eyes Jeanne can see it all: the market days, the marriage, the births, the countless times she's walked into the yard at dusk and watched the birds winging home or seen the tiny cracks in the Virgin's porcelain face. The girl who'd saved her milk teeth, named stray cats, who'd dreamed of saving a bull from Les Arènes and riding it through the streets of Arles, her hair down her back.

Charles's face, she thinks, would have been reflected in these eyes; his own eyes, looking down tenderly as he tried to find the place to enter her, or after he'd found it. It is loss she feels, as she sits there. Loss, and love, and waste.

The portrait fits in the trunk beneath the bed. She wraps it in the yellow dress, lowers the lid. Pushes the trunk back into the dark.

There had been no way of leaving Charles. For a few moments, Jeanne had considered it. But then she'd looked up to see Charles crossing the yard with a whistling tune, that scent of pomade, and he scratched the tip of his nose in the same way that Benoît sometimes did. He told her, too, of a frog that Gilles had found in the hospital grounds – Charles called the frog *a fine fellow, Jeanne* – and these things had been enough for her to know that no, she couldn't leave him. She didn't want to. She was his wife. So she'd smiled, looked up from the coffee pot and said, 'A frog?'

I do love him. Days passed, and nights. Laure left and Théophile cried – and her neat, strong military man walked into a new kind of war in which his soldiers were the quiet, padding nuns and his battle was for the mending of the thirty lost souls in Saint-Paul. For the care of the building itself, in which the walls could crumble to the touch. Those were the things to be fought for and saved. And so Charles became older, further from her.

Yes, I was right to stay with him. Or she had been. But Jeanne knows that same question asked a second time is not, in fact, the same. That answers can change, as people do.

Fourteen

Charles had not been the first. Not quite.

There'd been a boy. Years before she'd met Major Trabuc, Jeanne had hoped to see a different man in rue de l'Agneau.

How old? She'd been fourteen, perhaps. No idea, yet, of the possibility of bleeding in the brain. It was July, she remembers. The shop's doors had been kept open, held back by two copper hooks that fixed the backs of the door to the wall so that the breeze, if there was one, came through them. Summer's heavy heat. In Arles it seemed to mean the dust was quick to rise from the dry streets, so her father had to be careful. All his lace and velvet was kept under glass – a glass that Jeanne cleaned with a rag. Hand mirrors were kept face down.

In such weather the ladies came for fans. Handles of bone or elephant tusk, with so many feathers that somewhere – far off – a bird must have given its whole wing away. The draught that had lifted it into the blue sky now dried the damp beading on a lady's upper lip. 'So hot,' they said, 'in that arena . . .'

For the heat didn't stop the bulls, or the men who came out to fight them. This was the bullfighting season. Outside Les Arènes, people dried their clothes against its baked walls;

inside, the dust rose where it wasn't dampened down with blood – and from the shop they could hear the crowds. She knew, from the sound, of the fates inside.

'I don't understand it,' she told her father. 'How they can enjoy the death of a thing.'

'Nor do I, *mon chou*.'

Then a bullfighter came into the shop on rue Diderot. A shadow in the doorway. He took off his hat, stepped in. *Young.* Jeanne had thought the bullfighting men older than this, but he was twenty, no more. She lowered her scissors; he moved his hat round, between his hands. 'In Catalonia,' he said, in an accented voice, 'we carry a talisman for luck. A miniature or a crucifix.'

'Catalonia?' Her father smiled. 'You've come a long way.'

Dandella lace from Lebanon; silk from China. *He comes from Catalonia.*

'Do you sell such things? Crucifixes?'

Her father shook his head. 'Not those. But we have things with the good symbol on it. Objects that would fit in a pocket. See here . . . ?'

His first bullfight in France. He'd only fought in Spain before, he said – on the outskirts of towns and with smaller bulls. 'No crowds. But here . . . ' His hands shook as he talked. He looked at the handkerchief with a crucifix stitched on its side in gold brocade. 'I'll take that. Thank you – to you both.'

She looked up, turned away. Looked again. He was dark-haired but light-eyed – his eyes were a far paler brown than Provençal eyes; nut-brown, or how the Rhône could look after rain when the earth of the higher land had washed down into it. The colour of pathways where men played boules. His bottom lip that was fuller – far fuller – than his upper one, and when he thanked the haberdasher for his kindness he smiled easily.

'Good luck.'

'*Merci*, Monsieur Lafuye. Mademoiselle.'

She dreamt of him that night. Her thumb touching his bottom lip.

It changed Les Arènes for her. What had been a place of cruelty was where he might be, where he had been. So she'd walk a little slower when she passed it. And with every bullfighter who passed their shop – their jackets, their scent of leather and heat and animal musk – she'd glance up in the hope she'd see his eyes or height.

One meeting was enough. She'd lie on her bed at dusk, think of the muscles under his sleeves. How he'd taken off his hat as he'd entered and worked his fingers round and round the brim as he had talked of talismans.

How do you kiss? She hadn't known. Mouth open? Or maybe mouth closed.

She hoped he'd come back. She had dreams of being kissed in alleyways by a man with Spain on his skin, Spain on his breath. *Mouth open, please.* But he didn't come back.

His smell is strong, as if the sweat is trapped in the cloth itself. His beard looks clotted, unwashed.

'The woodshed?'

He keeps his eyes on the canvas. '*Bonjour*, Jeanne. Where else? I couldn't knock on the door.'

She knows this is true. 'I was afraid.'

With this, he looks up. 'Afraid? Of me?'

'Not of you. Of the painting. I didn't expect to be, but I was afraid to take off the cloth. In case of what I'd see.'

'In case you didn't like it?'

'I've always liked how you paint. It was knowing that it would be me, my face – not olives or an iris bed.'

'You asked me.'

'I know.'

'And? What did you think of it?'

So often she's wanted to cup this face of his. No matter that it's lined or spotted with paint. 'How do I tell you? I don't know how to tell you. I saw a fifty-five-year-old. But then I saw my younger self and my boys, and how you've painted my mouth ... It is like my father's mouth.'

'You like it?'

'Yes, Vincent. I've never had a gift like this.'

With that, he looks at his hands. And Jeanne looks out across the olive groves. The trees are starting to lower themselves with fruit. All the other trees in Provence bore their fruit in the summer and are free of fruit now – but not the olive. It's autumn, for these trees. The olive harvest will come within days – the trees will be plucked and the grass between them trampled down, and this landscape will be stripped bare. Grey. 'Part of me wants to show them all. The nuns and Charles and Peyron. To say, *look at me*. Hang it on the wall.'

'You can't hang it.'

'I know.

'Where will you keep it? If you can't hang it?'

'It's in the nursery. Under the bed. There's a travelling trunk – it belonged to my mother – and I'll keep it in there. I'm sorry.'

'Sorry?'

'I feel it deserves better than to be wrapped up in a trunk.'

'It's for you. You can do with it what you want to.'

She tilts her head. 'Are you well?' He doesn't seem well.

'Me?' He breathes out, with force, through his nose. 'I fear it coming back. An attack. There is this wind, and ... Jeanne, I can never be well. The Major told me that; I have to see these attacks as part of myself, as much as everything else is about me. My illness may come and go, like the moon's phases, but there can't be a cure. I must accept this, he told me. That I'll carry this illness with me when I leave.'

'Like love? Surviving it?'

'It wasn't just Sien that I loved. There was Kee too. Others. Sometimes I feel I'm my own hearth that no one sees — or they see the wisp of smoke from it, rising from a chimney, but no one cares to come closer and sit by it. Sien came closer but it wasn't enough.'

'How do you survive?'

'Me? By painting. Drinking and smoking helped. And I chose to move on, away from her.'

'Moving on? That's the best way?'

He shrugs. 'It was my way.'

She goes upstairs, pulls out the trunk. She lifts up the yellow silk, unwraps it. She leans the portrait of herself against the nursery wall.

Thirty years. And her bones are too old to carry her weight on her hands or head, and her hair's half-grey, and Claudette and her father and the stray cats are all dead. But here, in this portrait, is *her*. Her hands are her hands. Her heart is still there.

Paris isn't so far. Nor is the marshy land of the Camargue. Nor Catalonia, which her father found on the globe that night and struck with his nail, saying, 'That boy? Who we served today? That's where he's from, just there.'

Fifteen

October moves into November and the cypresses fill with air.

The olive pickers come. She hears them – the women from Saint-Rémy, their low voices like water and the padding of their feet on the lane that leads south, towards her home. The men too. They bring ladders and baskets and the wide nets in which to catch the olives that drop of their own will. These nets are laid out, pulled tight.

Madame Arnoux and Madame Lenoir and Madame Gilles. This is the only time of year that they choose to come so close to the hospital. Every other month, they distrust it – call it *up there* or worse. But with the olive harvest, there is money to be made; there's fruit to be preserved or pressed into oil and bottled, sold in the market – and these trees are no one's trees, as such. What a person picks is called their own. So for this, the women come.

Bread is wrapped in cloth and kept to one side; stoppered jugs of water are leant against walls. The children from the village run in between the olive trees, calling to one another in thick Provençal. Her boys used to do this too. Soldiers with imaginary guns and demands, grasping one another's shirts and tumbling down. Breathless with effort, half-laughing. *Don't run on the nets! Don't knock the ladders!*

The sudden halt and wide-eyed stare when, sometimes, they did.

And they come for more than olives this year. Looking across for a glimpse of the man known as *le fou roux*. One-eared and unwashed, a mouthful of blue. They're like hens in how they straighten their necks and move their heads from left to right, as if being tugged by a string, in order to see more. 'Look? Is that him?' And trying to see Jeanne too.

Gusts of wind find the hems of skirts, and make the women hold onto their headscarves or boughs. The Dutchman himself seizes his easel when the wind comes, braces himself. He waits for the wind to pass, and as he does he looks, narrow-eyed, at everything around him: the snapping of hems, the blowing over of baskets, how the grass flattens and splays. And when he looks south Jeanne follows his gaze to the five cypress trees that have been filled by the mistral and are shaking. They bow and toss themselves.

The harvest lasts a week. All week, they are there and Jeanne is amongst them – taking her own ladder out of the wood-shed, propping it next to her own tree. She climbs into its branches, picks. She listens to the clicking of tongues.

He spat! Did you see?

There he is. The mad one. Dutch. See? Don't stare.

Why is he out? He shouldn't be out. I heard he . . .

Bites? I heard he bites.

Dirty. That he's dirty, even with the baths.

Why isn't the warden with him? Shouldn't somebody be?

She holds her shawl to her chest as she makes her way to him. Offers him the brown cup.

He drinks. 'Water? It's been a while since you did that. And why today? It isn't warm.'

'I want them to see. I want them to see me talking to you.'

'Ah.' He looks across. 'I feel I've got a thousand eyes on me. I'm not sure that woman's picked a single olive.'

'Her? Madame Lenoir. You know they're talking of you.' She would seize them, if she could. She'd go from tree to tree, look up into their ladders and tell them that he's painted moths and starry nights, loved with his whole body and risen out of mines. And Jeanne turns back to the painter, opens her mouth to speak of Laurent's heart, when she hears a cracking sound, a rushing and a falling down, a calling out for help.

Vincent. Her first thought. But he's beside her, and well.

It's Madame Gilles. She's fallen; reaching for the highest branch she leaned too far, so that the ladder tilted and fell. The ladder cracked, not bone; as Jeanne hurries, she sees this – the broken, splintered wood. But Madame Gilles is damaged too. Blood on her cheek and right arm. Blood on the palm of her right hand.

'Let me see,' says Jeanne. She's not the only mother, but she feels these trees are her trees. This land is the land she walks on each day, so Jeanne crouches down. 'Can you move your hand?'

Madame Gilles winces.

'Open it and close it?' She tries to. It moves like a heart. 'Madame, the wounds aren't deep but I think they need a little care. To be cleaned. Can you stand? Our home is just there.'

It doesn't matter that her husband is the Major. Nor does it matter that Jeanne has been seen running through fields, or talking to the one-eared man. For now, Madame Gilles is in pain. She nods, tries to stand. Jeanne closes her arm around her waist, helps her to walk through the long grass.

She looks up, just once; the Dutchman is hurrying away from her, towards the hospital. His unweighted stool has been blown over by the wind.

The gardener's bird-like wife is helped into the parlour chair. She talks of the wind, the ladder, her wounds – and then pauses. Scans the room. The Trabuc house with its kettle, its stove. Floral plates. A ticking clock.

'Here.' Jeanne offers water.

She takes it, unsure.

'You must be shocked. It happens, with falls.' Jeanne kneels, unfolds the wounded hand. So long since she was last this close to another female, aware of a female heartbeat or breath.

Charles's footsteps; a change in the kitchen's light.

He rushes in. 'I heard. Madame Gilles.'

'A fall, Monsieur . . . '

He kneels beside Jeanne. He takes the sore hand away from his wife so that she rises, steps back, watches the Major as he works and handles the wound. As wardens do. 'Jeanne? A cloth. A damp cloth, if you please.'

'Yes.'

'And don't we have bandages?'

'Yes. Upstairs.'

So Charles goes upstairs for bandages and Jeanne looks down at the tiny wife who flexes her hand but looks, in fact, at the wallpaper and the cobweb, high up. They hear the sound of his footsteps – on the stairs, and then overhead. She hears the sound of a trunk being pulled out from under a bed.

Charles's weight comes back into the room, makes the floor-boards creak. He carries a crate that holds what they used to use far more, when the boys were still with them – scissors, cotton bandages, a brown glass bottle of iodine.

Jeanne watches.

He sets the crate down. He says, 'Here. Iodine. A little of this, Madame Gilles … It may sting, but it will help you. And then you can make your way home.'

Silence as wide as a river. She stands on one bank, looks across.

Just him, and her. Madame Gilles has gone.

'Explain it to me. Explain what I've found.'

'Found?'

'Don't. I found it. A painting in the trunk. You sat for him.'

'You looked in the trunk? Why did you look in the trunk?'

'Does it matter? I saw yellow silk, and opened it. You sat for him.'

'Yes.'

'When?'

'September. The day you went to Arles.'

'When I went there for his sunflowers?'

'Yes.'

Charles lifts his hands, palms up. 'What? Why? Don't speak to him – didn't I say that? To leave him alone?'

'Yes.'

'You think it was for my sake, Jeanne? God knows I've endured too much. They all see you talking to him in the fields – the nuns, the wives, Peyron. They all see! And I saw too – from one of the windows. My wife sitting down in the grass at his feet, laughing. You think I'm a fool? That I

190

didn't know you were breaking the rules?' He paces back and forth.

'Breaking the rules? I told you: I'm not a patient.'

'No! But there are patients all around us. And these people are here for a reason, Jeanne: they're unwell! They're too ill for a life without care – and no one can be sure that they won't strike out or use their teeth or hurt themselves. Cut off an ear! And yet you sat for him ... ' Charles scoffs, looks away. 'He asked you to?'

'No.' She puts her hands on her hips. 'I asked.'

'You asked?'

'I wanted him to paint me. I asked him to do it.'

'You? Asked him? Do you know who else he's painted?'

'Himself. The postman.'

'And more! Shall I call them bohemian? You know who he's painted, Jeanne. Do you think there aren't enough rumours about us? The Major at the hospital with his murderous hands and his Arlésienne wife who rarely talks? By all means, be painted. Let's give them more.'

With that, Jeanne hears her own voice. It rises, seems louder. 'What right do you have to give orders? Not ask for my views or thoughts on these things, or ask what I want. It's me! I'm tired! Tired of being instructed as if I've no mind of my own. Tired of being unseen by you.'

'Tired? I pay for this life! I earn for you and keep you! You're tired, you say? What about me? Tired of the hours I work for us – for the food on the table and fuel and the clothes. Tired of having to work in a place where people are broken and tearful and who rage so that sometimes they have to be restrained. My God, Jeanne! You are my wife. I *married* you.'

'Was that so hard to do? Charles, it's a painting – that's all.'

His frustration comes out in a hard, rasping sound. Scorn.

'Not to me. It's not just a painting: it's a lie from you, and a whorish thing.'

Charles goes upstairs. She follows – but before Jeanne can make her way to the nursery he's coming back down, carrying the portrait so that it bangs against the wall and he pushes past her, throws open the door. Walks into the yard.

Wind. It's strong, blows against them. Jeanne raises her arm, calls out. 'Charles!'

With that, he lifts his foot. He holds the portrait, kicks it – three times, and on the third time he breaks through the canvas with a loud, ripping sound. It falls to the ground.

For a moment Charles looks down. His chest heaves in and out.

Then he walks past her, back into the house.

Les Deux Trous can sing in the wind. Jean-Charles thought its wailing was a monster. *Is it a monster?*

No, little one. Back to bed.

She hears Les Deux Trous now. Two stones worn down by water and the years, hollowed out.

She stands in the yard, listening. Lime leaves and flakes of paint are blown down to the south.

Sixteen

The fever that seizes Jeanne in those last days of November is so strong that she can't open her eyes. She sweats. It hurts to be touched. She hears her husband's voice saying 'Careful with her . . . ' Feels herself being laid down.

After this, she loses the world. Jeanne's only awareness is of the body that she's in – unable to bear the weight of the blankets or her body's dampness or the pain there is in swallowing. She aches. Too stiff to turn. There might be frosts or fires beyond her, a thousand people in their house. Her boys could be standing by her. But all she knows is that stones can sing in wild weather, and she's too hot, too hot.

She burns. In her dreams, Jeanne is on fire. Like the other Jeanne who was strapped to a stake as others looked on. Jeanne d'Arc. A flaming end to a flaming life.

Jeanne says, 'Marie-Josephine . . . '

'Are you asking for her? I can bring her.'

Her lashes are thick, gummed. She can't open them fully, but through them she sees a face she knows – from the side of the Rhône, and from their marriage bed. It's a face she's kneeled before, missed. A good face. 'I don't know your name. I'm sorry.'

'What? I can't hear you, Jeanne.'

'I don't know your name . . . '

Jeanne knows him then. She made her own versions of this face in those three boys who sang for their plums, who shouted their voices against the white stones of Les Antiques so their names came back. An echoed *Benoît*.

'It's Charles . . . Jeanne? Can you hear me?'

Sometimes a hand on her forehead. With it, she flinches, moans.

Later she feels a cool, wet cloth on the sides of her neck and on her chest and this, she knows, is a woman's care. A female touch.

Her father's ostrich feathers had been as long as the arm that offered them. She'd take them from him, wonder at the size of the birds that had made them. 'How big are these birds?'

He said, 'Very big. Bigger than you or me.'

'Where from?'

'Africa.'

This is a dream she has. But there are lucid, waking moments within her fever too. Sometimes, beyond the window, there's a pause in the mistral as if it needs to find its breath. The silence wakens Jeanne. Amid her sickness she finds enough sight to look at the stained, papered wall and study the pattern on it. She has moments when she thinks she can stand, and tries. But there's no strength in her. She has no wish except to stay as she is. To sleep. She closes her eyes.

Cups are brought to her lips. Mostly they hold water. Sometimes the taste is thicker, like broth. There's also the feeling, from time to time, of hands beneath her arms and the cold, cold porcelain of the chamber pot against her skin, and like this she hears her body's sound. Rain. She asks, 'Is it raining?'

'No, no rain. I've got you, Jeanne.' A nun. 'There, now.'

Didier Lafuye died in early autumn. Rose season was nearly gone. The last blooms of the summer hung on their branches in the rue Molière, outside the hospital, so that his death seemed sweet-scented. Those hours of slowing down.

She learned he was dying from Salles. He'd written to Jeanne. She'd read the note, turned to Charles and said, 'I want to be with him. He's dying.'

'I know.'

They took the train together, through Les Alpilles. But in Arles Jeanne let go of Charles's hand and hurried through the corridors of the hospital, found her father and pushed her fingers through his own and didn't leave his bedside for his last four days. Jeanne didn't eat, didn't sleep. She only looked at his dying face. *Don't go.*

'You must eat. Please eat. Salles has offered to—' – Charles, stepping forwards.

'No.'

Didier. If she were to name each small, loving gesture he'd shown her she'd talk for weeks or months. She might never stop talking. His grief – the widower's kind – had been packed away as much as it could be so that he might be a good father – knowing and gentle and bright. And he'd been these things to her. He had, he had.

I love you, Papa.

So he died. And roses dropped their petals when they took his coffin out. And when Jeanne had paused in the street to retch they said it was sorrow. Said it was her body

195

trying to rid itself of pain – and she, too, thought that. It was only much later, in Saint-Rémy, that Jeanne learned a child grew inside her – that as she'd stood by his grave she'd had a second heartbeat, that she hadn't been mourning her father on her own.

She told Charles. Having learned of the child, she turned on her side in their shared, warm bed to face him and whispered it. He'd listened. Then, slowly, he'd cried. His face moved through so many colours and shapes that Jeanne could only watch; she'd had no words, could think of no word to say except *love*, which neither of them had said. So she reached for his hands and held them. The Major – the man they called fearsome, a murderer perhaps. But here he was, lying with her, saying, *A child? Jeanne, is this true?* Here he was, crying. Here he was, reaching down for her abdomen as if it were gilded and tender, and he'd whispered, *How did this happen?* Jeanne smiled. She laughed in his ear, said, *You know how . . .*

For those months Charles touched his wife as if she were as fragile as dust. Then Jean-Charles entered the world – by tearing her, so that she flooded the bedroom with all manner of blood; clotted or blackish or thin. When the nuns had taken the soiled sheets and buckets away his eyes had been on this little boy. His son, his heir. He'd marvelled at him. 'We shall call him Jean-Charles.' And Jeanne had been unsure of who she'd wanted to embrace more, or have pressed against her – the wailing boy or her husband's hands and her husband's face.

The truth she never spoke is that her love for her infant son didn't come at birth. It took a handful of days. Jeanne knew she felt something – deep, unspeakable, as if an animal's nature were prowling nearby. But how could she name it? Was this, indeed, love? Before this, she'd imagined a strong maternal love would rise up in her breast instinctively when her child was placed upon it – her heart's love finding his own newborn heart. But Jeanne just watched as he suckled. Later she searched for the name of this feeling as she might search a bottom drawer – what *is* this? *Keep looking.* For it felt too hard for love. Love was what she felt for Charles – not this. A walled Jeanne, in that handful of days. She was a fortified town. And she'd wanted sleep. She missed a full night of sleep.

But yes, it was love. Love was its name; it was simply a form of love she didn't recognise – a new, mothering kind. And Jeanne knew this with absolute certainty when her teats cracked and her milk became bloody and she couldn't feed her little screaming boy so that she suddenly wanted to feed him and warm him and comfort him more than she wanted any other thing.

Charles's boy. Mine.

Then Salles, with those green leaves. And as Jeanne watched Charles cradling their baby she knew there were these two, wild loves – love for the boy she had birthed, and love for the man who'd made him. She nearly said so, that night.

More children, after that. And she recognised the love that came with each one. As they stirred inside her, or as she kneeled on a blood-soaked mattress and brayed for God, she thought, *I love you. Come out of me.*

Once, Charles said that he felt one of the world's most beautiful sounds was the chapel bell ringing out across the fields. 'Don't you think so, Jeanne?'

No, she doesn't think so. There are a hundred thousand sounds that she likes, but they all lack beauty compared to Benoît's cry. In that second between Benoît's slick emergence and his first, frail calling Jeanne had clutched the side of the bed and prayed to the woman she'd never seen but imagined so often. *Please.*

Aurélie Lafuye. Who would have lifted her head off a damp bed and looked down through her knees, said *Does she live? Tell me.*

'What was that, Jeanne? I can't understand you.'

Charles. Her moon and sun. Whose mouth she would kiss both open and closed, lovingly.

But after those babies he'd moved their beds apart. Read the newspaper. Retired to bed before her, not at the same time. Or he'd sat at his desk, written letters long into the night.

Close windows. Never walk too far. Wash fruit.

'He broke it,' she murmurs.

'Broke what?'

Her portrait. Jeanne tries to speak but it feels too hard.

'Hush.' A woman's voice. 'Here, Jeanne. Here is water. Drink.'

December. Jeanne opens her eyes.

The fever has passed. She looks at the ceiling, knows it. Her skin isn't burning now. The fever has risen and left her behind.

Slowly, Jeanne climbs out of bed. She goes to the window, looks at the fields.

The mistral has blown through the world. Trees are bare. She sees her grey reflection in the glass.

Seventeen

The fever leaves her parched, as light as bone.

Sœur Yvette comes to her. She carries the metal tub into the kitchen, fills it with water she has warmed on the stove. Very gently, she helps Jeanne's body from its clothes.

'Lean forwards a little . . . There, now.'

Jeanne rests her forearms on her knees. She puts her forehead on those arms, feels the water as the nun washes her – on her spine and shoulders, running down. The crust of the fever is washed away, as is the smell of herself. What's left is clean skin, cold air.

Charles sits very still. 'You've been ill. So ill. It's been nearly a month.'

She watches his face, how it moves when he talks.

'You were almost too hot to touch. We put poultices on you but then you shivered. You soaked through the linen with sweat. Here.'

He hands her a plate. There's bread on it.

'You should eat something. Try.'

She doesn't want to eat. Nor does she want him to speak of her fever. She wants him to talk of the portrait, the yard.

'Salles came. We were so worried. I thought to take you to the hospital in Arles, or Avignon.'

'Hospital?'

'Yes. But Salles said there was no more that could be done in a hospital than here. Water and rest. The nuns prayed.'

She looks at the bread. 'Was it just me?'

'Who's been ill? No. Others have had sicknesses and I heard there were fevers in the village too. But none lasted as long as yours.'

'The Dutchman?'

Charles shifts. 'Not with a fever, but yes, he's been ill. A seizure again. Near the cypress trees. The goatherd saw him and came for us, and when I found him in the grass I thought he was eating paint again but it was blood. His tongue.'

She waits.

The clock ticks. If he has an apology he must say it now. Now is when he must tell her that he regrets the breaking of what was hers, and the words he said – and if he doesn't say these things she will find the strength to rise and walk into the cold, dark blowing afternoon.

She waits, waits.

'Jeanne ...' But nothing else follows. So she stands. And as she stands the floral plate drops to the floor and cracks and she steps over it and makes her way out of the room.

Ignoring a thing doesn't kill it; the flies still rattled against the schoolroom's glass and the stray cats still crept through Didier's legs, and there have been times when Jeanne has felt rage turn inside her, or make a fist of her heart. She's never asked about the damaged ear. Yet it doesn't stop the ear being half-gone, doesn't stop her sometimes imagining it: the mirror, the bowl, the razor, how he'd cut through the flesh of his lobe as she has cut through herbs, with that bright nick as the stalk breaks free. What had he felt as he did it? He told her that he'd raged. She can believe that: a deep, rising anger that had, at last, burst through. A pouring out.

Rage has been inside her too. She's felt it; as she stood in the shop and felt aware of the passing day, or when she was spoken to by fine ladies as if she was worth far less than them. *Bring me that lace.* She hated that. Hated what was unfair – how her father was robbed of himself, struck down as he stood with a glass jar. With that, Jeanne moved from being the teenage girl with the attic view and a knowledge of all the country's rivers to mashing her father's food so that his mouth could manage it. And she never felt rage at that, as such – not at him, or her new role. She might have crawled inside her father and tucked up within his heart, for how much she loved him. She would have done anything. But sometimes, Jeanne was aware of it: how, deep down, she'd think of how he used to be, before the stroke, and seethe.

When he died she could have roared as the patients do in Saint-Paul-de-Mausole. There is a pain beyond measurement. She felt rage at his loss.

'I've got you,' Charles said in that moment in the hospital room. He'd tried to embrace her brittle, resisting frame. 'Jeanne, can you hear me?'

And no, she has never felt rage at her boys – not once, not for the briefest time. But sometimes she's sat in a quiet room and imagined the life she might have had if her body hadn't made them; if she hadn't strained on a mattress and broken herself for the sake of their making. As babies, they cried out for her. She stopped being Jeanne; she became *Maman*, and loved the name – *I do, I do* – but with it came a lack of sleep and loss of time and a draining of herself that no one ever saw. She'd sit by their bedside with love. She'd listen to their sleeping breath and have no regrets – not once did she wish that Jean-Charles's frown didn't exist, or resent the slapping of Laurent's shoes when he ran, or fail to love Benoît's care in lifting a snail from the lane and carry it to safety as he'd seen his father do. But she might think of the other life. She'd imagine the woman whom none of them knew, the Jeanne she locked up and left in order for these three boys to thrive. A mother makes that choice. But she still thinks of Jeanne the explorer, from time to time.

And this: Aurélie. She had no choice but to accept that loss. She died – and Jeanne had never known her, so how could she miss what she never had to lose? Even so, the anger has stirred inside her, as a child does. How she never got to see the body that she grew in. How Jeanne has never held the hand or seen the face of the woman for whom all the freedoms and adventures and nights of deep sleep were worth the sacrifices, in order to make this single life.

When Charles tells her to stay indoors for she's frail, still, and the mistral hasn't fully gone, she says, 'Don't tell me what to do.' And Charles looks as if something has been taken from him.

It is hard to stay upright in the wind. She's half-pinned her hair so that it's like the cypresses – full, and wild.

He looks up. 'It's you. You were ill. I heard.'

'Yes.'

'You look thinner, Jeanne. I painted potato farmers once. They were walking bones, or ghosts. You look like one of them.'

'You're thinner too. Charles told me – a second attack in the fields. He said you hurt your tongue.'

He turns away from her stare.

'Why did you ask me to wear black? In the portrait?'

'Why?' He cleans his brush. 'Because it felt right. I felt it was the right colour for you.'

'The right colour? That was my mourning dress. I made it for my father's funeral. A funeral dress.'

He looks back up. He looks older than he's ever looked to her. Tired, with bruises under his eyes. 'You're angry, Jeanne. With me?'

'Not with you. The black dress.'

'I don't think it's that. It's something else. Don't *les Arlésiennes* wear black?'

She reaches for a branch. She takes it, steadies herself.

'You're still unwell. Sit.' He offers his folding chair.

'No. *Merci.*' The wind finds every edge of every hem and leaf. She looks at Les Alpilles. She wonders if the echo of fever is still inside her – a strangeness of thought, a heaviness. 'I need to tell you,' she says. 'I went to your studio. I went in there without telling you. You were in Arles. With Charles.'

'You went in there? That's my room – mine.'

'I know. I used the back door, in the kitchen. I wanted to see.'

'See?'

'What you did. What you painted.' Jeanne looks back at him. 'I don't think I've ever seen so much. A room as full as that. I cried out when I entered it. It was like a cave, and they were all things that you'd seen or been part of – bridges and streets and rooms and fields. I saw your starry sky. I saw a nude woman with her forehead on her arms and you'd done several paintings of yourself, and I wanted that.'

'Wanted it?'

'To be part of it. To be seen by you, marked down. When you said what it felt like to be painted … That others had cried and thanked you for it.' She pauses. 'The portrait is gone.'

'Gone?'

'He found it, destroyed it. Said you only painted whores.'

Hard eyes. 'Don't call them that. Don't judge them.'

'He used the word, not me.'

'He broke the portrait?'

'Kicked it.'

The Dutchman spits, wipes his mouth. 'That doesn't sound like the Major.'

'He did it. I was there. And he hasn't mentioned it. Hasn't said sorry.'

'Go home, Jeanne.'

'I don't want to.'

'Leave me alone. Go and tell your husband why you broke his rules.'

She won't, she won't. She has no wish to look at the face of the man who asked her to marry him by the Rhône with such a slow, respectful voice that he might have been asking for help in a task, as if love was hardly required. His hands had shaken very slightly. Jeanne liked to think it was affection that shook him, but she was the fool and sees that now. He shook from being unsure. Or his head had been certain, but his heart had wanted more.

For he knew. He must have known from the way Jeanne had blushed or smelt any flower he picked for her, or how she'd wanted to look at each part of his naked body on their wedding night that she loved him. He must have known

Jeanne felt love. And he, in turn, made a promise in church. In God's sight and hearing he'd made his vow in spite of his less loving heart. He'd renewed the vow with each child made, or each attempt at making one – an act that some men might buy in dirty beds but that most knew was kept for husband and wife and was called *sacred*. Physical love. So he lied with each pushing against her. Each little shudder in the Provençal night.

He stands beside her now.

Jeanne is washing the plates. When a plate is done, she passes it to him; he takes it. 'Dry that.'

He finds a cloth. 'How are you feeling?'

She feels it's all too late. The mistral should have found their cottage long ago. Blown away the shadows and walls. 'On our wedding day,' she says, 'you looked at me and said, You look ... And nothing else. What did I look? You've never said. Do you remember?'

He flinches, steps back. Says, 'Jeanne, I ... I wanted to talk to you. About Christmas.'

'Christmas?'

He nods. 'Yes.'

The boys won't come for it. Nor did they come last year – with their lives and adventures, their duties elsewhere. 'A letter came from Jean-Charles. I read it to you, by your bedside, when you were ill. Thought you might hear all the same.'

His thoughts for Christmas are this: that for the meal itself, on the night before, it would be a right and proper gesture to ask Peyron. 'It worked well enough last year, didn't it? It's a hard time of year for him. And Poulet too.'

'Poulet?'

'What do you think?'

Jeanne looks at her broth, remembers the days of hiding sugared almonds in the corners of the house for the boys to find.

'A simple meal, that's all. Perhaps a little beef? That will be enough.'

In the days before Christmas the market expands and grows brighter. There are more lanterns – on stalls but also on the ground, and pushed into the cracks in walls. Candles nestle in groups on steps.

Jeanne walks past them all. Past the women of Saint-Rémy who talk even more than they usually do, as if noise and chatter can keep the chill away. She moves past the meat, plucked birds, picked fruit and garlic bulbs.

What might they have made of Claudette? If they think Jeanne is not to be trusted they should have seen Jeanne's old maid – slurring through her splayed teeth, suspicious of marriage and sunshine, hiding her hand like a weapon. And so it's Claudette that Jeanne thinks of as she walks through the market. How the tufts under her arms turned grey.

Jeanne's rage clenches like a fist. And she stares as she goes – at each stall or rug laid down on the ground, and at each woman who looks up at her. For what gave them the right? To judge or tell stories? There are no perfect people. Even the nuns had a life before their vows; even the goats and trees and stone walls grow old – and these wives are women as much as Jeanne is. They, too, have missing teeth. They have blemished skin or the thickening of flesh at the tops of their backs that comes with age. Their dresses are also too tight in places, which tells her they were thinner once. And what of their bodies? Under those clothes? The women say *Trabuc* as if it has a bitter taste, but aren't they like her? If not exactly the same, then with similarities? They have their own puckered thighs, their own violet web of lines over their bellies from the swell and fall of pregnancies. They all have their own cracked heels, their fur, and as Jeanne buys meat from Madame Porcher she thinks, Does her body leak too? Do her knees crack when she kneels or stands up? And how did it feel for Madame Porcher when Monsieur Porcher climbed onto his wife for the very first time and pushed himself in? Perhaps she lay on her front. Or perhaps she looked up at the ceiling, considered its peeling paint.

'Beef,' Jeanne says. 'Enough for four.'

This woman – the butcher's wife – was the first to raise her eyebrows at Benoît's bright-coloured hair; she'd said *it's not like your own, is it? And your husband's hair is so black ...* Twenty years ago. Yet Jeanne can remember it – how this woman had licked her teeth, half-smiled. *How dare she?* This, suddenly. Jeanne tightens her fists and wonders how this woman had dared to slander Charles, had slandered her and her last boy. How can she, Madame Porcher, think it's fair to talk of Jeanne – or anyone else – with such casual fire? To cut her meat so poorly, sniff or roll her eyes? The ladies who came to the shop on rue Diderot were the same, exactly the same: they'd eye the girl in the corner, exchanging glances between themselves as if to say, *Aurélie's girl? Are you sure?* Did they think Jeanne never knew?

Madame Gilles. The birdlike frame of her is half lost beneath a woollen shawl but Jeanne knows she is watching her.

Most of all, she seethes for his sake. The Dutchman's. For if there was a single person who wasn't deserving of rumours and lies, it's him. A man in need. In need of his own sanctuary, as Deschamps had found his form of it by sleeping under the cypresses. In need of rest from his life before Saint-Rémy.

'You're better, Madame?' Jeanne asks.

Madame Gilles presses her lips together before she speaks. 'It wasn't a broken bone. But the bruising was deep. Lasted a long time.'

She waits. 'I helped you, did I not?'

The wife shifts. She feels the sharp edge to the words. 'You did.' She pauses. '*Merci.*'

'And did you hear I was ill? After your fall. I caught a fever. Everyone heard, I'm sure of that.'

She tenses. 'Yes, I heard.'

'Am I better? Mostly. I've lost so much weight that my garments don't fit. I tie my skirts with string. But I'm blessed to be here, I know that. I know that fevers can kill.'

An unease between them.

'Mind you don't catch it yourself, Madame.'

The words feel simple to say. Cold and metallic in her mouth. And maybe that is how anger tastes and Jeanne is only learning this now – at last, after all these years.

On her return to the cottage she puts much of what she has – the meat, a little cheese – in the hole beneath the floor.

Laure. Her. Her face swoops in, settles down. It feels hard to see this truth. But just as she's resentful of the deaths of her parents or the sparseness of Charles's love, so Jeanne resents this: *you.* Laure. Laure, her friend, who'd had the boldness or bright selfishness to choose to pack her single bag and slip out at dawn, and not come back. Jeanne wants to shout, What of the rest of us? What of those you left behind?

But she's angry, too, at Laure's foolishness. At the fact she failed to see how loved she was. That no one else wore a pearl – *ma perle* – around their neck.

But you went. And look.

Look what your foolishness did. In Laure's wake a husband whose heart and mind have undone themselves equally. An asylum that is not what it was. A fountain that has greened, and a list of patients that's grown less and less, and a warden who has to work twice as hard to make up for the grief and shock in Peyron. Charles has aged since Laure's leaving. And it's Jeanne who must cook for Laure's husband on Christmas Eve because Laure herself isn't here.

You did that. You did.

All this rising up in her.

Eighteen

Christmas Eve. The house smells of pine and the roasting meat, and Jeanne comes downstairs in the dress of her youth – as yellow as the sun. It's too tight to wear as it ought to be worn, with the buttons on its back done up to the nape of the neck. A blue shawl covers the unfastened buttons and her exposed flesh.

Her skirts sway as she walks. Charles looks up. 'Jeanne? What's this?'

'A dress.'

'It's yellow.'

'Yes.'

'Jeanne ... Not that dress. Not tonight.'

'Why not? It's the colour of life. The Dutchman said.'

With that, there's a knock on the door.

Poulet is flushed as if he's been elsewhere before coming here – a tavern or a younger man's house. 'Jeanne! *Merci*. A happy Christmas to you ... ' He steps into the parlour with his arms outstretched.

He seems not to see the dress. But Peyron follows him, wipes his feet carefully on the threshold and looks up. He sees the full skirts and yellow silk waist, and he blinks several times as if this colour's too much for him. A pause. Then he smiles. He clicks his heels and comes forwards to Jeanne. Kisses her three times, in the Provençal way.

Four at the table. Jeanne comes into the room carrying the meal; the three men look up as she enters and they say what they must – how lovely it looks, how lovely it smells.

'Jeanne, our thanks.' A raised glass.

Poulet cuts into the meat. 'And it's peaceful tonight. In the hospital, I mean. It's as if they're all exhausted from the mistral. Or perhaps the whole year's tired them. Patrice is still singing, of course. And I believe Sœur Maude was playing cards with Rouisson an hour ago! Out in the north wing. But otherwise we have a tranquil Saint-Paul. Even the nuns said so.'

'All of them?'

'Yes, all. Although the Dutchman's peace is our doing, of course.'

Jeanne looks up.

'Sedated,' says Poulet. Eats.

'Sedated?'

With his mouth full, he tells her. 'He was ill again. Remember how he was, in the olives? When you found him? It happened again today. So yes, we sedated him. The Major and I.'

'When?'

'This afternoon. He's sleeping now.'

To Charles, 'And you didn't tell me? Where was he?'

Charles swallows. 'The quarry,' he says. His warning voice.

Peyron pushes his spectacles up his nose. 'It's curious, what he chooses to paint. He paints the orchards and the wheat, and he worked in the garden for a time. But he's not painted the cloisters. We have fine cloisters here.'

'He isn't too fond of God,' Charles says.

'Ah, no. I see.'

'And what of how he paints!' Poulet reaches for wine. 'Is there a name for it? That style, of layering paint onto paint so that it's so thick it looks like brickwork and takes three weeks to dry? Looks like a child's effort.' He sips. 'It's not a well mind that paints like that ...'

'I remember,' says Jeanne, 'when he came. Salles brought him here, and called him unique. I remember that very clearly.'

'His painting's unique, yes, for sure. And,' says Poulet, with his mouth full, 'I'd say the rest of him too. I can't think of any other patient whose affliction has seemed so ... strange. Unpredictable. And severe, with that wound. Didn't he used to drink absinthe, Charles?'

'He did. Too much.'

'*La fée verte,*' Jeanne says. 'I know of it. It gives you strange dreams.'

'Your wife know absinthe, Monsieur? *Mon Dieu!*'

'She's knowledgeable, my wife.'

'But it's not just the absinthe,' says Peyron. 'There's the epilepsy in him, the mania, the nerves ...'

Poulet laughs at that word. 'Nerves? Is that what we call it? If a man is prepared to visit the women who—'

'Poulet. Enough.'

'The rue du Bout d'Arles?' says Jeanne. 'Streets like that? Don't worry. I know what they are.'

'Jeanne.' Charles's voice is steely, low.

'Why can't I talk about it? I know where that street is. I know what's sold on it. I walked down it once and I spoke to a woman who sat there. You mean diseases, Poulet? I think you mean diseases.' Jeanne reaches for wine. Senses her husband's stare as she fills her own glass to the brim. 'He painted those women, I know. He painted me too. Did you know?'

212

Silence, now. Forks pause in their journeys from plates to mouths.

'Clothed, of course. I wore a black dress. Very proper. I asked him to paint me because I like how he paints, you see. I've never seen anyone paint that way. And I don't think a child could do better, Poulet. Not at all.' She turns to her husband. 'Tell them, Charles. Of the portrait of me.'

There is almost a plea from him now. 'Jeanne . . .'

'What did you do with it, Charles?'

It's Poulet who steps into the hush. 'Mind you, we've had others that we could call unique too. Remember the man who laughed all the time? Couldn't stop? Who was he? He left long ago. I didn't mind him at all. He was rather fine company, I thought. And the woman who thought she was a bird.'

'An owl. Eaten the heart of an owl.'

'That's it. We won't have an eater of owl hearts again.'

Peyron nods, but seems lost. He looks at Jeanne's yellow dress, then he looks at the window where the ivy is tapping against the glass and she knows he isn't thinking of the Dutchman.

Then he turns to Jeanne, smiles a little too brightly. 'The beef is so tender. I must thank you again – for having me here. A treat.'

The wind brings a light rain. 'Hear that?'

'Yes.'

It grows late. They make their awkward goodbyes. 'It's been . . .' Unsure of the words to say to Jeanne as they kiss her cheeks.

'Yes.' Like Claudette, she sniffs and gives a tight *joyeux Noël*.

*

Charles closes the door behind them. For a moment he looks at the closed door, and then he turns to face her. Rubs his eyes. 'What happened tonight?'

'What happened?'

'How you spoke. That wasn't you. And this yellow dress, this half-pinned hair . . . Please, Jeanne. Where is my wife?'

'Why can't I talk of the patients? I live here. I have eyes and I see. I've spoken to Vincent far more than Peyron or Poulet or the nuns or you have.'

He raises a finger. 'But the painting? How could you have talked of the painting in front of them? Of all people? How do you think that makes me look?'

'Makes you look?'

'Only nuns and doctors can enter their rooms, you know that – and yet you tell them both that you walked in and sat for him? I was embarrassed tonight! To hear my wife talk like that. And they were embarrassed too.'

She shrugs. 'So I can't go into their rooms and can't enter their grounds. Can't open our windows. Can't wear yellow. I'm one of the tethered ones. Ask Jeanne Lafuye to marry you because she'll say yes and always be grateful, and easy to rule.'

'You feel that?'

'Of course I feel that. I've spent this marriage in five small rooms.'

With this, Charles reaches out. He takes the back of a chair, steadies himself. He breathes in very slowly, then out. 'Jeanne. Do you think this is what I want? As we are? All I do is work, since Laure went. I have boys I hardly see and a wife I hardly know.'

'You don't try to see them. Or to know your wife.'

'That's not true.'

'No? Yes, you work. But *Le Figaro*? And you chose the

single beds, not me. And you sleep on your left side so you're always facing the wall and I can't remember the last time we walked upstairs together, by the same lamp. We used to laugh. Eat honey in the grass. Sit by Les Antiques.'

His whole face looks sad.

They sit at the table, as they have a thousand times. The fire is almost gone and there is no candlelight left. What they have is a single lantern. It sits on the parlour table; Charles looks at the flame. Half of his face is lit by it and one side is dark.

'We don't talk. Do you see that? We wake and you go to work and I bake bread or I sweep and you come back and we eat and we go to bed . . . Or if we speak, it's of things that don't matter. The weather. Eggs. If I've polished your shoes.'

'We talk of the boys.'

'Sometimes. But they've stopped needing us. They hardly write and that's how it should be.'

Outside, the rain is harder.

'I wish he'd never come.'

'You think it's his fault?'

'Isn't it? You changed when he came here. Within days of him coming you seemed different to me.'

She nods. 'A bird flew into our nursery once. It came in through the window, flapped against me and cut me, and I thought it might hurt Benoît. But then it flew back out again. He felt like that to me.'

'Do you care for him?'

'Love him?'

'Is that what this is?' Charles stands, lifts the lamp. He walks to the stairs, pauses and turns back to her, but looks at the floor. 'Sometimes I feel unmarried. I come home to a woman who doesn't speak, just stares out of windows or watches me eat.'

'I feel it too. Unmarried. Or not a true wife to you.'

She stays downstairs by the hearth. It is embers now. The only other glow is from her dress.

For a long time, she sits.

Then she stands, makes her way to the wooden desk where Charles keeps his ink and paper and pen. She takes what she needs, carries it back to the fireside.

With her knees as her table and by the fire's light, Jeanne writes to Laure. Then she folds the letter, hides it in the hole beneath the kitchen floor.

Nineteen

In the days that follow, they pass on the stairs. They eat meals without words or glances. No speaking; the only sound in their cottage is the creaking of floorboards and the closing of doors.

The rain passes through. They have three clear, cold days in which there is no wind; the cypresses stand still. Jeanne walks out to them, looks up at their stillness. Charles works longer hours, coming back in darkness. He writes letters, saying nothing. It's Jeanne who goes to bed before he does. She lies in the dark, listening for his weight on the stairs.

Before the year's end, there's a knock on the door.

She looks up at the sound. *My boys.* But she knows it won't be her boys.

'*Bonjour*, Jeanne.' The man raises his hat.

Salles. Jeanne blinks. '*Bonjour.* Charles is working today. At the hospital.'

'And you? Am I disturbing you?'

'No.' She thinks of the *suck-suck* of his pipe.

'Will you walk with me to Les Antiques? It's been years since I saw them.'

A bitter day. The weather has stripped the landscape to rock, bark and earth. Jeanne wears a plain brown dress.

'Charles asked you to come here. Didn't he?'

'Yes. I can't lie.'

'He wrote to you?'

'He did.'

'Does he think you should take me back to Arles? Lock me up?'

A pause. 'Even if he did, I wouldn't take you. I don't believe a small room with little company would serve you very well, Jeanne. You've known too many.'

'Too many?'

'Small rooms.'

She looks across at him. No wife and yet he knows that a woman's life can be a life of standing still and looking out. 'What has he told you?'

'Charles? That you had a fever.'

'He said you came to see me.'

'Yes. Fevers come and fevers go. But yours lasted for nearly a month and that's a long time.'

'Water and rest.'

'Yes. Mostly that's all that can be done in such cases.'

'You were kind to come. But it's passed now, Salles. I'm better.'

The ruins of Les Antiques appear. In the hard winter light the structures look bluish. Salles pauses, look up at them. 'There they are ... So old!' he breathes. 'Look at them. The aqueduct at Nîmes is a near miracle to me. They only had their hands! Yet look what they built, and it's lasted all these years ...' He nods in thought. Still looking at the ruins he says, 'Don't forget what he's seen.'

'Who?'

'Your husband.'

'Seen? In Saint-Paul?'

'Elsewhere.'

'Do you mean in the war? The Crimea?'

'Yes.'

'He never talks of it. I asked him once, and he told me not to ask him again.'

'He saw sickness there. Fevers, like yours. More men died of fevers than of fighting – and he was a major, in charge of those men. He left the army afterwards. He didn't want to stay. Came to work here' – Salles moves his arm, as if showing her – 'in an asylum in quietest Provence. Goat-bells and cypresses . . . Only Charles can tell you why he did, but I believe he saw so much that he was ruined by it – that he saw too much of the damaged human body, how it breaks down. The physical decay of it. Cholera. Dysentery.'

'Chose human minds instead.'

'Perhaps. Tell me, are you sleeping?' They walk on a little more.

'Mostly. Sometimes I have dreams.'

'Of what?'

'Many things.'

'And when you're sleepless?'

She wonders if she can lie. She also wonders if her words to Salles will find their way back to Charles and she decides no, for both. She can't lie; her words will stay with him. 'Did you know Laure?'

'Théophile's wife?'

'Yes. She asked me to go with her. In the days before she left.'

'To go with her?'

'Yes. The two of us.'

'To leave Charles?'

'I said no, when she asked. And when I can't sleep, I keep thinking of that – the answer I gave, and—'

219

He stops, touches her wrist. 'Are you saying you think you should have gone? Said yes to Laure?'

Is she? Is she wishing she'd caught that morning train and seen nothing of Saint-Rémy, in four years? Nothing of Charles? 'No. No, I'm not saying that. He's my husband and I am his wife. And I know how much Peyron loved Laure, how much he suffers. But since Laure went . . .'

'Charles has had less time for you? I know he's so busy.'

'There's never been much time. But when there's time he reads. I feel he's closed up, gone from me.'

Salles seems to straighten. 'You don't think he cares for you? Why would he write to his old friend Frédéric if he didn't care? If he wasn't afraid?'

'Afraid? He's never afraid.'

'Oh Jeanne, he's been afraid. Of losing you to the fever, but in your pregnancies too. He wrote to me before each of your labours. He wrote to me after . . . Shall we sit?'

There's a bench, and they lower themselves down. From there she can see the carvings on the Roman arch and the vague, weathered faces. 'I've never seen it – fear. In him.'

'Not seeing something doesn't mean it isn't there.'

She nods. She knows that. 'He's written to you about the Dutchman too?'

'Vincent? Yes, he's written several times.'

'Disliking him?'

'No, not disliking him. Fear again, I think; he knew that you were spending time with him. Knew of the petition. He wanted to know my thoughts on it.'

'On him?'

'On him, and on him talking to you. And I told him that I like the man. He's strange and solitary and his attacks are very severe and like nothing I've seen before. But for all

220

their severity, he's never hurt another. He's only ever harmed himself – and so I felt he wouldn't harm you.'

'He painted me. Did Charles tell you that? And did he tell you what he did, when he found the painting?'

He nods. 'Yes.'

She looks back to the stones. As she does, there is a sudden, growing breeze that comes from the south and blows the dust of the Roman road.

'Do you remember meeting me?'

'For the first time? Yes. Your father's stroke.'

'You were so kind. You handled him so gently. One doctor was rough with him and talked as if he couldn't hear him, and I hated that. But you felt Papa's pulse as if he were your own father. When I said that I'd take care of him myself you asked if I was sure. Asked my age.' Jeanne turns to him. 'What about you? The things you've seen? You've also been near sickness.'

'Not the war's sickness.'

'But how long was the war? Five years, or six? You've been in that hospital for far longer. Prayed with the dying.'

The pastor shrugs. 'I have faith. I can comfort them. We have the medicines to calm them, which they lacked in the Crimea. In that way I've seen less pain, or a different kind of it.'

'I think that's what I wanted, at first. To comfort the Dutchman. He was the first patient in so long, and I heard he wasn't sleeping. I wanted him to sleep.'

'You felt motherly.'

'Yes, motherly. Also, Place Lamartine: you said he'd walked out in the rain, unclothed. I envied him for that.'

'Envied?'

'Not for the act. But for the fact he dared to, felt he could. He hasn't lived a little life of washtubs and duty.'

221

'Listen,' he says. 'When your father fell ill you cared for him. You did that on your own. And since then you've raised three strong, bold, adventurous men who are forging lives of their own. You have Charles. These are not little, unremarkable things. I heard stories of you. Before we met.'

Jeanne looks across. 'Stories?'

'Yes, one or two. Or rather, I heard stories of a girl and I'm sure she was you. Sleeping in Les Alyscamps? Handstands?'

'Ah.'

'Pushed feathers into your hair in the shop? Then I met you in the hospital, at your father's side. You seemed so strong.'

'Strong? Or stubborn?'

Salles tilts his head. 'Most people I meet think that the patients of an asylum are weaker forms of human, that a tormented mind is of less value to the world or to God than a sound, strong one. You think otherwise?'

She sniffs. 'Yes, perhaps. But it's more than that. To have disregarded rules ... To have had his kind of freedom. He seems so brave to me.'

Salles reaches into his coat. From its pocket he finds a handkerchief, unfolds it. 'Take this. Jeanne, there are many forms of bravery. I've have seen grown men cry at the tiniest of things, and others make no sound when their whole world is lost. Be gentle with yourself.'

'The Dutchman talks of that.'

'Of survival?'

'Yes. I feel I've been asleep for years and years. I feel he's lived as I should have done.'

'Jeanne.' The pastor leans closer to her. 'Talk to Charles. Because he doesn't know how to talk to you and he wishes to. Tell him these things.'

*

They walk back. Jeanne looks up at the pine trees, and sees the sky through them. To her right, she sees the hospital – its roof and boundary wall. 'The cabbage leaves,' she says. 'He asked you to bring them – didn't he? I've never been sure how you knew.'

'Yes. Charles told me you moaned as you turned in your sleep, wept when you thought he couldn't hear you. Talked of failing your child.'

'He thought I was failing?'

'No, he did not. But he feared you thought you were, asked if I had remedies. Jeanne, he's written to me more often than you know.'

She looks back across the fields. How has she lived without knowing this? For years she's believed the pastor simply sensed her tenderness, came of his own accord. When she saw Charles with a pen she believed he was working. Accounts, or placing orders. Making notes of something in the hospital that had broken or rusted, or been worn away. She never thought he was writing of her. Asking for help from the pastor in Arles.

Charles is waiting for them. He stands at the kitchen window but, on seeing them, steps back – not wanting them to know he's been waiting.

'Ah. Salles. *Bonjour.*'

He must have tended to the fire in her absence for it's brighter than it was. They stand in front of it. Rub their hands.

'Salles, will you eat with us? We have a little salted pork.'

'Are you sure?'

'Quite sure. Charles?'

He nods. 'Of course. Yes. And we have the second bedroom, if—'

Perhaps one day the pastor will nod, stay the night in the bedroom that looks into the lime tree and snore gently to

223

the sound of its branches on the window pane. But tonight he only shakes his head. 'I'd love to eat with you, thank you. But as for staying . . . I'd like to see Peyron and the nuns have already made a room for me – in the east wing, I think.'

Later, Jeanne washes her nameless blooms. She cleans the table and sweeps the floor.

Upstairs, she finds that Charles isn't sleeping yet. He's shifting, tucking the blankets around himself. In doing this, he looks old.

'You wrote to him,' she says.

'Yes.'

'And you've written to him before. Before each birth, and when I couldn't feed Jean-Charles.'

'I thought he might know how to help you.'

'You heard me crying. He said.'

'Yes. You thought I was sleeping.'

No childbirth, she thinks, in a war. He'll have seen every wound and death in those fighting days, but not that. Not the pushing out of life or the sores and indignities that follow it – the seeping or looseness. The tears that always come. He'd have had no knowledge at all. 'Why didn't you tell me? That you'd written to Salles?'

'It was a private matter for you. I thought . . .'

'Or me? Why didn't you talk to me, Charles?'

He sighs. 'You didn't tell me. I knew you were in pain, but when I asked how you were you wouldn't speak of it. You didn't want to tell me.'

'I didn't think you'd care to know.'

'Care to know? That my wife was bleeding? Crying at night?'

Jeanne sits down on her bed. She stares at the far wall. She'd thought, my breasts are on fire. I'm still bleeding between my legs from the birth and it hurts, hurts, and I can't feed my child – but how could she tell him these things? The man who sat with his pen? Who wouldn't undress in front of her or let her reach down to his most intimate part? Who'd wanted routine, steadfastness and order. Not a broken wife.

It's an old, old version of the painter that she finds – as if a week has been a year to him. She hadn't expected to see him. His seizure at the quarry had been his worst so far, they said – yet there's a man in the fields with an easel and it's him. He wears a coat like a bear. He's muffled against the cold and yet she can tell he's thinner. A sinking of the eyes.

Old hands too. To hold the brush seems hard for him.

The Dutchman lowers his hand, looks up. 'I wanted to paint the rocks and bare trees, and it was windy. Christmas Eve.'

'A windy day.'

'A gust caught the easel. After that, I don't know what happened. I made it back to the hospital but I don't know how. I don't know.'

He has his stale fox's smell. A slur to his words.

'And now? How are you?'

'No use thinking I'll mend. I'll never mend.'

'I saw Salles yesterday. He came. We walked to Les Antiques.'

'I know. He saw me too.'

'He likes you, you know that?'

'There have been kind people, as well as unkind people. Salles has always been good to me.'

She smiles at him, feeling sorry. 'What news from your brother? The child must be due soon.'

'It is. Jo cannot sleep or sit comfortably. She says her back is tender.'

'Still thinks it's a boy?'

'She's certain. I want to paint something for him, when he comes. To paint something for his nursery or to paint something for their own bedroom. Flowers, I think. Buds. Something clean, new.'

At first, she wants to be on her own that night. After their meal, she wants to wrap herself up in all her thickest clothes and sit out in the olive groves, beneath the cold sky. To look at the stars without company. And so she finds her shawls and walks out.

But, in the yard, this changes. She stands and looks back. The lanterns shine through their windows; their light finds the sides of the ivy and the metal bench and all the shadows of the yard seem more pronounced to her. The wood store and wash-house. Tools propped against the wall. The path of flattened earth that leads across their yard, into the lane. Hollows made from scratching hens.

She sees all of this, and looks up. There are more stars than she's seen for months or years. More white than dark, as if the stars are made of darkness, black marks on a canvas or sky of light and she could look at them all night. Lie out amongst the trees.

But she doesn't lie down. Instead, she walks back to the house, wanting him.

'Charles?'

'Yes?'

They choose the bottom step of the stairs. She isn't sure why, or how it comes to be that they walk past the chairs and find themselves sitting side by side on the stairs, as if young. But they are here, now.

'How long have you been worried for me?'

'How long? Since marrying you, Jeanne. But since last May most of all.'

Jeanne can see his hands. He has placed them over his knees, protecting them. Like this, she can see the broad expanse of them – strong, capable hands, with a fleshy web under the thumb. She looks, then, at her own. She has her hands together, her fingers linked.

'You never saw our shop.'

'No.'

'I wish you had. I wish you could have opened its drawers and smelt it all . . . Touched what we had. We had so many things – satin, gold, tree sap that had hardened and looked like caramel. Cloth that was dyed with the ink of fish or the crushed shells of beetles. Can you picture that? And our counter was mahogany. Each day we polished the glass . . . I wish you could have seen it.'

'I wish I could have done too.'

'And Papa. I wish you'd known him before he fell ill. How he'd teach me where each shell or button or polished gem had come from in the world. Abyssinia. Isn't that a beautiful word? Don't you think it must be a beautiful place?'

'You wanted to go there?'

'For a while I did. I grew so bored of Arles, and I wanted much more. The Dutchman?'

'Yes.'

'He reminded me of that time. Reminded me of how it was to be like that, to hope for those things. I'm fifty-five,

Charles. How did I become fifty-five? And I've been a mother and wife, and Salles told me these were not minor things and I'm grateful for being both, but I'll only be fifty-six and then fifty-seven and fifty-eight, and there'll be no change. When he painted me … It felt new. I felt I was being looked at, Charles. I felt as I might have felt if I'd ever got there – to Abyssinia, or anywhere else on the globe. As if I was mattering. You asked me if I love him.'

'Do you?'

'Yes. But it's as I love our boys, or maybe as I loved Laure.'

In the hours that follow, she talks to him. About *l'espionne*. About looking through keyholes and telling herself, *she is your mother*, on seeing Claudette. About how she'd hear the crowds from Les Arènes at dusk and think of the life that waited for her. The cheering and brightness. A vow: *you'll see*.

How she'd count the hairs on her forearm at school, too bored. Used to peek under market stalls in the hope of finding a dropped coin or fruit too ripe to sell, and would take any treasures to Les Alyscamps. 'I liked it. Never minded that they were tombs, or that it was sombre there. Lovers walked there sometimes. They thought no one could see them, but I'd see them while I ate my pears or apricots. I imagined my own too.'

'Your own? Lovers?'

'And the act of it. And love itself. In my father's last hours he said my mother's name. Even with his damaged mouth I knew what he was saying.'

'Aurélie?'

'Aurélie.' She leans her weight against him, a nudge. 'It was you who came to me. I had daydreams of who I'd marry, but a major? I never thought that. You seemed so proper. I liked you from the beginning.'

'You did?'

'I did. I was so happy when you wanted to see me again.'

'You thought I might not want to?'

'Me? I climbed trees and wore my hair down. Forced doors, if they were locked.'

'Forced doors?' His eyes widen. 'I didn't know that.'

She smiles. 'Only once or twice.'

His weight presses against her in return. He opens his mouth but says nothing, at first. He only looks at her face. Then, 'I hate that you've been unhappy. Jeanne, I've never wanted that.'

When he stands, he says, 'Come with me. It's late.'

'Let me show you something first.'

She takes his hand. She leads him into the yard. The air is so cold their breath is white; they stamp their feet for warmth.

'Look up.'

More light than she has ever seen. Above the limes and roof and olive trees and hospital, and Saint-Rémy, are all the stars she's ever seen. 'He painted a starry night. Did you see it?'

'Yes.'

But even so. Even though he had painted a night of such movement and gold that she'd lost her breath on seeing it, she would choose this moment over it. This sky.

Upstairs, they unclothe. They do so privately – keeping to shadows and facing their walls. She takes down her hair.

'Jeanne. Would you . . . ?'

Yes. She joins him in the same, single bed. There is less room than there used to be; their bodies are larger, softer than they were and she feels less able to bear her weight on one side for too long. But like this they face the same wall; with her back to him, Jeanne looks at the same cracked wall, the same discolouring from years of damp and candle smoke.

Outside, the blowing wind.

'This?' He means his arm, which he's placed over her waist. 'It's not too heavy for you?'

It's not too heavy for her.

At dawn, Jeanne wakes to find him standing by the window, looking out. He doesn't know she has woken, or that she's watching him.

His nightshirt. His bare feet.

He is my husband. He is. Watching the first dawn of the year.

Twenty

'Charles, come back to bed.' She whispers this.

He climbs in very slowly. Settles down beside her, lies on his side.

For a long time, Charles says nothing. He doesn't look at her face; rather he seems to look at her arm, the shape of her collarbone.

'What were you thinking, when you looked out of the window. I saw you.'

He says, 'Peyron. In the marketplace. How he fell, and the sound. And there have been times when I've gone to his house to see how he is, or found him in the corridors, and he's been so ... Four years now. He tries to carry on. But in truth he's still a shell of himself. It's as if she took out his bones and organs and carried them with her, and there's nothing left.' He looks at her. 'I've wanted to help him. All this time.'

'I know.'

'I was thinking of him as I looked out of the window. And I was thinking of you.'

She takes her hand, lays it down on his nightshirt. Beneath it, she feels his chest.

For a while, he looks at her neck. Then he lifts a curl of

her hair between his thumb and forefinger, feels it. He does this for a long time. 'Twenty-three.'

'Twenty-three?'

'I was twenty-three years old in 1853. When the war began. I joined to help. Some people join for the act of fighting itself or because they want to be patriotic men but I just wanted to help where there was trouble. I remember that very clearly.'

'Twenty-three is young.'

'The war came quickly. I wasn't a major then. I was just a soldier like thousands of other soldiers. I knew medicine. I wasn't a medic but I knew enough and I helped where I could and that made the difference. We landed on a beach near Sebastopol. The injuries.' His fingers grow still. 'Cold. Only September, but I remember the cold. The British were already out there and some of the battles were theirs and some were ours, and some we shared. It went that way. At Balaclava there were horses. That's what I remember – this strong smell of horses and gunpowder, and—'

'And what?'

He's hesitant. 'Humans. The smell of human bodies, living and dead – that's what battlefields smell of. With terror, the body can fail you in ways you can't imagine, worse than I've ever seen at Saint-Paul. I turned twenty-five that winter. I've tried to forget this, Jeanne.'

He takes her hand, looks at it.

'You want this? To hear this?'

'Yes.'

'It took a year for Sebastopol to fall. That's what we wanted – to take the city because it was the heart of it; take a heart and you have the rest. But each time we got close there was something. The cold grew worse. A Russian winter, Jeanne. You think it's bitter here, with the mistral? There was frostbite in our troops. Black toes. Blood too frozen to flow so the skin died and if we came near a fire to warm ourselves ... The smell of dead human flesh. When the cholera came it took off half our men. There was a small hospital and I knew enough to help them. Boys, mostly. But there are no remedies for cholera, Jeanne, and the beds we used had holes in them, with pails lined up underneath, and there were girls whose only job was to empty those pails. Weren't enough girls. Dysentery too. You think you'd remember each face but you don't. There were too many. There stopped being any difference between them – all dirty, all scared, all exhausted and streaming with water so that they looked shrunken in their last moments because there wasn't any water left in them. They all pray. Perhaps not always to God, but they pray for something. For mothers or wives. Childhood things.

We couldn't bury them. Not in the winter with the ground so hard, and it was too cold for decay so there was a street where we left them until the thaw came. Just piled them up. But rats came, and then dogs. Our major was one of the dead so I ordered five men to dig despite the frozen ground. We had to try. We'd have started fire if we'd had enough wood.' Charles looks at their fingers. 'You turn blue, with cholera. Before you die, you turn blue so you look dead before you are. They call it that sometimes: the blue death – did you know that? We had to be careful – to make sure a patient was dead before we took them out and piled them up.'

Charles shifts his weight. In doing this, he comes closer to Jeanne. 'They made me a major, by the end. Said I'd earned it, but how had I earned it? By not dying? By burying my friends? I couldn't stay. I felt I'd done nothing, deserved nothing.' He pauses. 'I was lost, for a time. I had an acquaintance in Salles and so I went to see him. Heard of a job in Saint-Paul-de-Mausole. I felt so old. And I wanted what matters most of all – which is peace, and a family. A wife.'

For a while they stay very still. She wants to ask why it has been this way, for both of them. How did they think that keeping a silence would make the hurt less? It hasn't made it less.

'There are things you can't forget. Why would I share those things with you? So you might not forget them also? That would not have been fair.'

All these closed windows. The rinsing of fruit. Bringing in the washing before the dew comes down. This need for safety.

'How Peyron has been, since Laure went. How Rouisson can be. I know I'm the Major but that's how I'd be without ...'

'Without what?'

Charles gives a soft, single tap on the back of her hand.

Later in the day, he cuts the bread. Jeanne leans against the wall and watches him. She has a blanket wrapped around herself. He wears only his nightshirt and the brown woollen socks that she's darned through the years.

'How did my father find you? Hear of you?'

'He didn't find me. You think that? That he heard of a man back from the war and seeking a wife?'

'Yes. That's what happened.'

'No, it's not. I found your father, Jeanne. Monsieur Lafuye knew nothing of me.'

'What?'

'Didn't you know? Salles told me of you. One night we sat at a café in the Place du Forum and I told him what I was wanting and he mentioned you. The fabled haberdasher's daughter. Said you were different – unconventional. Capable. Wild-haired.'

'Unconventional?'

'That's what he said.'

'And you didn't mind that in a girl? Plain and unconventional?'

'Salles never called you plain. Why would he say you were plain? Because you're not a wearer of pearls or sealskin gloves? That doesn't mean plainness. It only means you've no care for them, or need to add to your own beauty; that's what it means. I saw you in the street, Jeanne. Salles described you so I went walking and I knew you when I saw you.'

'You followed me?'

'Not far. Not for long. Only enough to be sure who you were.' He looks up from the bread. 'Then a few more times. To Saint Trophime, and you went inside. Once, you crossed over the Rhône and sat on the stones of the old Roman bridge. Am I saying too much?'

'What then?'

'Salles visited your house. Perhaps you were in the kitchen or market, or upstairs, I don't know. But he told your father about me then. My interest in his daughter. Spoke well of me, I hope.'

'This can't be true.'

'Why can't it be? I even know where I saw you for the first time, Jeanne – what you were wearing. Carrying.'

There can be no way of knowing. Not for Jeanne. She was the watchful one in Arles. There was never a moment when she believed she might be followed, and not by a man – and not into the cloisters or dark, cool interior of Saint Trophime where the candles burned like eyes. If she felt seen in there she felt it was by statues. By the pained Christ or the grieving saints.

As for the old Roman bridge, yes, she used to go there. Her father slept in the afternoons; for those two hours she'd scrub the floor or scald the pork to take off its hair or wash his clothes and hang them out. Or she explored – and once, yes, she crossed the Rhône with her hair untied, sat down on the plinth of the old Roman bridge and ate a little cheese and bread, sharing her crumbs with the gathering birds. She'd swung her legs. Tried not to lose a shoe.

She remembers that day exactly. 'You saw that? Saw me?'

They eat, aware of each other. There is the sound of their mouths, the tap of their spoons on their bowls and, afterwards, Charles rises. Takes the bowls away.

'What was I carrying? You said you remember.'

'The first time? I do. A basket on your arm. There were lemons in it. You wore a grey dress with a darker hem. And you carried that basket as you always carry a basket – on the crook of your elbow, your forearm pointing forwards.'

'That dress was always too long for me.'

'It wasn't too long.'

All the old, known things are in this room – the brown cups of water, the plates, the linen, the clock that has accompanied their days and nights. Yet there is a difference now, in the way she sees them. As if they've been cleaned, held up to the light.

'And then our first meeting. I remember that. We walked, and you told me you had pity for the bulls in Les Arènes. I saw how tiny your hands were. I wanted to hold one.'

'On our first meeting? You thought that?'

'Yes. I know I don't say these things. But I loved you early, Jeanne.'

The word is like a breaking thing. A jar of buttons, dropped. Or it's a bird flying in or unexpected

236

light – moonlight that wakes her – or it's the emergence of a child with its own, hard voice so that she has to pause, blink at it as if it can't be real. And she looks at Charles. This winter afternoon in which they haven't left the house, in which they haven't even dressed. He stands in his nightshirt, offers her bread.

On their wedding night Charles had cupped himself. She knew she'd never forget that – how he'd blushed and cupped the private part of himself. *He doesn't want me to see* – when she, Jeanne, wanted to see every fraction of him, each crease and hollow, each different texture or colour of skin and to breathe him in and taste him. Nor did he seem to want to see her. He touched her so cautiously, as if he felt obliged.

'I thought it was duty, maybe. Why you married me.'

'Duty?'

'You wanted children.'

'Duty? Jeanne, you have no idea.'

She should have reached for his hands on their wedding night. Said, Show me, and parted them. She should have said what she felt – which had been love, and luck, and awe, and fear, and impatience in wanting to see every inch of his body and share her own with him. How she liked the name *Trabuc* because it was both their names now. 'The two beds? You asked to push our beds apart. After Benoît. Why?'

'Benoît was the last. We knew. You were so tired, so sore.'

'Yes, but the beds?'

'What choice did I have? Did we have? Jeanne, we'd have only made more.'

That night, she isn't shy. Nor is he, in how he lets her look at what he'd cupped before – his maleness, the part of him that entered her to make their boys.

Jeanne looks at it for a long time. Then she no longer sees it. Instead, she feels it – how it pushes against the part of her that he, too, has never seen. Like this, he finds her opening. He sighs as he moves in.

She also sighs. 'Charles? Charles, I want to see.'

She lifts herself up, looks down. He pauses in the act. He, too, looks down and slowly, very slowly, Charles starts to move again and he watches this, as she does – in, and out, and in. 'Jeanne . . . '

She loves how he says her name. She loves his face and always has.

'Jeanne,' he says. 'Jeanne.'

Twenty-One

His body is both changed and unchanged. The two, fleshed discs on his chest are the same shape and texture that she remembers, but the muscles that they rest on have slackened and dimpled with age. A puckered belly beneath them. Hair has turned white, or grey.

He sleeps. She watches her husband, sleeping.

A day passes, then two. They push the beds together to make one bed, from which they have the same view of sky and distant cypress trees. The January mornings are quiet, a shade of blue.

The birds come. Later there are flashes of green in the soil by the garden wall which she knows to be snowdrops. Every year, without fail. New, but not new.

Spring brings the sound of water. What has frozen in Les Alpilles thaws and makes its way down to them. Rivulets in the lane. Charles comes back from Saint-Paul to tell her that the hospital gardens have music in them.

'Music? What music?'

'The fountain. Gilles has cleaned it, would you believe? Spring has invigorated him, perhaps. The moss is gone and the leaves have been cleared out. It's like how it was.'

239

A fish, arched back. Spouting water high, so that it catches the light.

With the weak new sunshine Jeanne opens every door in the house. She moves from room to room, throwing the shutters and windows wide and letting the cool, bright air move through. She sweeps all of it – coal dust, leaves, cobwebs, hair, the residues of winter – out into the yard. And in the vegetable patch, which Jeanne has neglected through fever or her preoccupied mind, she finds the tufts of vegetables and bends down, tugs them out. Too early for sorrel. But there is chicory. Also, there are three earthy cabbages, which is too many for Charles and her – so she carries them and the chicory under the pines to the hospital kitchen, and to Sœur Marie-Josephine. An armful of greenery, handed over as a child might be. The nun is bright-eyed, thanks her. 'How have you been, Madame?'

Walking back, Jeanne pauses. She sees the bell tower, high up. She sees the goatherd making his way through the fields with his goats, the line of cypress trees, and the sky.

They have to talk of rules. Jeanne understands why he made them, the purpose they served. But it's the season of thaws. 'Charles, they can't last. I don't want them to.'

They walk, in the early dusk, to Les Antiques. There's no reason for it except to be walking, and side by side. To see the stone faces with him. Her arm is through his arm. 'Didn't you break them anyway? Open windows and swim in the canal?'

'Talk to the Dutchman?' She smiles. 'Yes. But . . .'

'I know.'

There have been boys in Saint-Rémy who have tied strings around rose beetles, walked with a cloud of fluttering wings, and such beetles never lasted long: they either escaped or damaged their wings and died – and this is how she thinks, suddenly, of tethering. Let it be what it is. Jeanne looks up. 'Did you know I used to tell you I loved you as you slept? I wanted to tell you. I had to tell you how I felt about you, as if it needed releasing – but you'd never spoken of love yourself, or been near to speaking of it. So I didn't feel I could. I whispered it instead. Into your back, when you were sleeping.'

He says nothing to this, but hardens the arm through which hers is linked as if bringing her closer, as if answering her without words. 'There is talk,' he tells her. 'I think the Dutchman will go.'

'He's said this?'

'Not to me. But he's talked of it to Poulet, and seems to be making plans. It doesn't surprise me. He wanted a cure.'

'Will he go soon?'

'I think so. Quite soon. And others have talked of leaving – Michel, and Evelyn too. More empty rooms.'

'There won't be new patients?'

'None have asked to come here and Salles has no patients to send.'

They stand by the mausoleum, look up. Birds are nesting in its highest parts; there are feathers, the occasional soft clap of wings. 'How long can this go on for, Charles?'

'This?'

'The hours that you work. Too few patients, and even fewer staff. We aren't young.'

He also looks up. 'I don't know what we do. Hope that Benoît comes back. Hope that Laure does, so that Peyron's well again. Hope there's money.'

'I miss Benoît.'

'I know. I miss them too. How I spoke to Benoît that night . . . '

'You were worried.'

'Why couldn't I have been calmer? Done as you did, which is understand that they have to go?'

She turns to him. 'Charles. He's Benoît. He understood.' Kisses him, by the tower and arch.

When she goes to look for him he isn't in the olive groves. Nor the quarry, or the fields of wheat that have long been harvested. In these places she looks for his overalls but there is no blue except overhead. She walks down lanes. She stands beneath the cypresses, looks up.

Perhaps he doesn't paint at all. Not today.

But in the end she finds him where he has never been – on the northern side, near the boundary wall. Him and his easel. His brush held like a lamp.

'Vincent?'

'Ah.' Brightly said. 'I was thinking of you.'

'Of me? Why were you thinking of me?'

'I have news. From Paris.'

She comes to his side where he can see her. Like this, she sees blue. There's more blue than there's ever been – not Prussian blue but something lighter, blue mixed with white, and this shade's in his beard and on his collarbones and hands.

'Jo was right. A boy.'

A rush in her. 'A boy? Is he well?'

'Healthy and strong.' He smiles as he looks up at her. She sees the brown teeth and the lines by his eyes and yes, she loves him. 'He's Vincent, as they said he'd be.'

'A good name. You know that? It is a good name.'

'Maybe things will be different for him. I must believe that.'

'You've got paint in your beard.'

She reaches, picks at it. He lifts his jaw to help her. 'Theo is so happy, Jeanne. His happiness comes up from the page. I'm not sure I've read of more happiness – and look at this weather, as if in celebration. Such sunlight.'

'And you?'

'Me?'

She means if he is happy.

'He likes what I've sent him too. My latest pictures. The stars? And a self-portrait in which he says I think I look quite healthy. He says some might sell.'

She takes her hand down from his beard. 'I'm so sorry,' she says.

'For what?'

'For what Charles did to my portrait. That no one else saw your portrait of me when you'd worked so hard, and I liked it so much.'

He frowns. 'Jeanne? What do you mean? Theo did. Theo saw it, and Jo. Others, I'm sure.'

'What? How can they have done?' It was stamped on in the yard as the mistral was blowing. Thrown into the wood-shed to be burned in winter months.

The Dutchman seems confused. 'Because I painted two of them. One was a gift to you, of course. But I always want Theo to *see* what I paint, to see what I've been working on here in Saint-Paul. He's been paying for all of this, after all.'

'So there's still a portrait of me? A second one?'

'Yes. Didn't I say?'

*

243

That afternoon he paints an almond in bloom. Above the easel and their heads it twists up, stretches its branches like arms, as if waking from a sleep. And in her lifetime Jeanne has never really noticed it. Perhaps she has eaten its seeds without knowing; perhaps the grazes on Laurent's knees were from a day of climbing it, or the handful of almonds that Laure would roast with honey and salt came from the branches of this one tree. Jeanne can't know. But she sits beside him as he paints it – and she knows she is seeing this tree now.

'It's for their new arrival. My gift to them. Blue is the colour of life.'

'And yellow. You taught me that. They're saying you want to leave Saint-Paul.'

The painter pauses. He spits into his hand, looks at it momentarily. Dries the hand on his overalls. 'It's been ten months since I came. And this place has been strange and kind and like nowhere else, and I've painted well. But it's time to leave it. You understand?'

Elsewhere. Surviving. 'Yes.' Moving on.

It is not only the almond trees. As she makes her way back she sees buds everywhere – open or half-open, unfolding themselves after the winter – and seeing them, she thinks of how patients come and go. This was her belief: that no patient ever truly left Saint-Paul. That their bodies might rise and go elsewhere but they'd leave a mark behind – if not a physical mark such as a stain or scratch on a wall then an echo in the corridors. A slight scent in their wake. Now she's not sure if this is true. The owl girl? She left a memory, that's all. The woman who, years ago, cut the flesh of her thigh with broken glass has left the fear of glass with the nuns, and nothing else. Deschamps left, briefly, an indentation in the grass beneath the cypress trees, but that has gone. And memories themselves are as frail as lace. Fading over time if handled too much or exposed to the light – and a mark on the wall could be caused by anyone. Rising damp, or rain.

People go. And some will be remembered, leave their mark. But some will not.

Him? There won't be a nun in Saint-Paul who will ever forget he was here. Who won't have their own tale to tell of his fox hair or turpentine, how he grew bored of beans. Swam in grass. Fought the leather straps they forced him into. And if nothing else, there will always, always be that: cafés and irises, a wicker chair, a moth. There will be signs of him from the pictures on the wall.

That night, for a while, she watches Charles sleep. He lies on his front, head to one side. His mouth is open, and these sounds are like those that Benoît used to make when he, too, slept this way. Palms down, on either side of him.

She wishes she'd known him before. If she'd been in that distant, cold besieged town she'd have sat beside him; if there had been any way of telling futures she'd have sent out a note to Sebastopol, to Major Trabuc, that said, You will survive this war. Marry. Be loved. Live in *la ville verte*, where your sons will gorge on fruit and grow strong.

Gently, she touches his back. Then she rises from the bed, goes downstairs. From the hole beneath the kitchen floor she takes her letter to Laure, reads it once.

She tears it into pieces, adds these pieces to the embers of the fire.

In the marketplace there are radishes and early peas, the thick, white asparagus Jeanne used to eat with Claudette, butter dripping down their chins. Goose eggs as large as her fist. And she makes her way across the square, moves under the shade of the planes and pauses in front of each stall.

Tables have cloths laid upon them. There are crates and baskets with fresh bread lying in them, or the trotters of pigs with dogs sitting near by. There is fruit and honey and fist-fuls of herbs, and all the women are here – Madame Gilles and Madame Arnoux and Madame Leblanc and the elderly woman who used to teach the three Trabuc boys, and the fisherman's wife who brings fish from the Durance or the Rhône, and travels here by night.

It is as the market always is. Yet something has changed. And the change, Jeanne supposes, is in her. For she used to see them as tribes. There'd been the wives of Saint-Rémy and the wife of Charles Trabuc: two armies, facing each other, with different hopes for life. That's how it felt, for years. And yet where, truly, is the difference?

The Dutchman had talked of survival. Salles had talked of this too. And so, as Jeanne moves from stall to stall, she decides to believe this entirely: that they, like her, feel the bones of their childhood dreams stir in them sometimes. Or they miss their husbands' touch at the base of their back or under their breasts, or they miss their dead parents, or hear their children reading from the Bible or *L'homme de bronze* or a poem and feel their own shame that they aren't able to. Or they never had children at all, or lost them. Or their brief moment of beauty is gone. And just as they have these pains in them – unspoken, or buried in a part of them they're scared to venture to – so they have their comforts.

The fat, earthy leeks of Madame Gilles.

Jeanne smiles. '*Bonjour.* Two, please. No, three.'

'Three?'

'Please. They look very good.' She watches her lift them.

'How are you? And your husband? I hear that he's mended the fountain. Charles says it's as good as new.'

So many comforts too. How they find their rest must be, she thinks, as varied as the pains that they seek rest from. Patrice sings. As for Michel, he finds a solace in feeding the sparrows and doves. And there's absinthe, self-harm, the crying at night, the holy orders that must feel like safety and painting – ochre, vermilion, Prussian blue. Reading novels. Leaving one's married life. Or choosing to be mute, to say nothing at all and to sleep up in Les Alpilles with the goats as company. Feeding the stray cats of Arles. Breathing in jasmine until she felt light-headed, drugged.

'*Merci à vous.*'

The rumours? It's harder to see them as comfort. But perhaps, yes, they help. Perhaps they're reassurances, that these women – daughters, sisters, mothers, wives – tell their tales because it helps to reassure them that there are other people who hurt more than this, who have had worse losses, whose lives are even emptier or darker or stranger than their own. *Take heart. At least you're not him* . . . The Dutchman who cut off his ear and gave it to a woman who sold her own body like land.

A form of survival in each face.

'*Au revoir*, Madame Gilles.'

'*Au revoir.*'

Honey from Charpentier. Two eggs, with white feathered tops. She pauses to pull, very gently, the ear of Monsieur Porcher's sleeping dog. And in the shade of the south-western corner of the market square, near the old road to Arles, Jeanne sees a rarer sight. The goatherd is here, sitting on the ground with his knees tucked up. Bottles by his feet. They hold, she knows, goat's milk; that this is the season when goats will be nursing, that udders will be brimming with milk and so here he is. In the shade of the planes. He's plugged each bottle with cloth.

He looks up as she comes across.

'One, please.' She says no more than that, pays him. Puts the milk in her basket, smiles and makes her way back.

She wants to tell him all of it. She waits in the yard, looking for him. *Come to me.*

But when Charles comes he takes her hands and says, 'Jeanne, don't speak. I have two things to tell you. Two things have happened today.'

He sits her down beneath the lime. 'What is it, Charles?'

He feels his moustache. Looks into the leaves, down to the ground. 'I did something.'

'What did you do?'

'Jeanne . . . I—'

'Tell me.'

He looks at her. 'I sat for him.'

'For Vincent?'

'I know. I know how it sounds. I ruined your portrait, I know. You've told me there's a copy and I'm glad but that one was yours, a gift to you – and I tore it apart and ruined it and I always spoke dismissively of his work, I know that too. But how you spoke of being painted . . . How you said it felt, and what it meant to you. And I broke your portrait, Jeanne! I destroyed it! I've not forgotten a second of that. It's stayed in my mind and hasn't left. I am so sorry.'

'He asked you to?'

'No. I asked him. As if he could paint me just as he painted you. I wanted to sit in the same chair. Look at the same wall. Feel as you felt, I think.' He holds his breath, waiting. 'Jeanne, are you angry with me?'

It isn't anger she feels. What she feels, sitting there, is relief. Or she feels as she does when Charles holds out an arm to her and she takes it, so she can move against him and there's no space between them at all. She smiles. 'Of course not.' How could she? 'Have you seen it yet?'

'Not yet. It's still drying. But he says it will be ready soon.'

A kiss with mouths open. Under the lime.

Then Jeanne pulls back. 'What's the second thing?'

Charles reaches into his pocket, takes out an envelope. 'A letter. From Mexico.'

That night, Charles looks down at her. A single candle's light is a star. 'Like that?'

'Like that.'

He smells of himself. In his kiss, the tang of red wine. And she thinks his mouth is a pool she can enter. Her hips lift up to meet his own. Charles, with veins like rivers. His dark forests of hair.

Twenty-Two

The last time Jeanne saw her youngest boy he'd been climbing onto the train at Saint-Rémy with a book under his arm and a bag slung around him. He'd paused as he'd hauled himself up – one foot on the train and one simply held in the air. He'd looked back at his parents, called out, 'I'll be safe!'

'Promise?'

'*Oui, Maman!*' Blown her a kiss which she'd tried to catch and press to herself, before blowing a kiss back. And she'd stayed to watch the train move away. She'd stayed until the train was entirely out of sight, while Charles had begun to walk back through the streets and poured himself a glass of brandy and said nothing of it for nineteen months. Hardened his jaw.

'I wasn't angry. I just didn't want him to—'

'To go so far? And for so long? He understood that.' She takes his hand.

These buds, breaking open. She, in turn, has spent so long misunderstanding *Le Figaro*. Believing Charles had read it at meals because a newspaper was far better company, or because it felt like a different world for him. 'It was our boys,' he now tells her. No quicker way for news of foreign wars or droughts or distant natural disasters to find its way to this father, in his house beside the lime.

*

She finds him – but there's no easel with him. He sits on a stone bench near the avenue of pines, looks south to Les Alpilles, Mont Gaussier and Les Deux Trous.

'Not painting today?'

'Yes, but not here. In the studio. Just sitting, for now.'

'Just sitting?'

'Looking.'

'May I sit too?'

He smiles very slightly. 'Like you used to? You always sat down in the grass.'

She sits at his side.

Once, he asked her the name of these hills. Had needed a little help in how to pronounce them, as children do.

She thinks, friend.

'You're going soon. Aren't you?'

'Yes. To the north.'

'Paris?'

'Near it. Auvers-sur-Oise. There's a good doctor. Gachet, he's called. Theo wrote to him, told him all about his mad brother, and Gachet thinks he can help. I'll stay in his home with his family. He has a fine garden, I hear.'

'Better than ours? Than Gilles's hard work?'

'Let's hope. Although some of my best work has been of the weeds he's failed to dig out, so I'm grateful Gilles is rather lazy and old.'

She smiles. 'He sounds kind. Gachet.'

'Yes. And I'll be near Theo and Jo. Little Vincent.'

In the beginning, she'd wanted him to sleep. That had been what she wanted for him, why she had given lavender. Now she wants him to be contented, to be safe and well. 'Have you been happy enough? Has it been so hard for you here?'

'Hard?' He looks back to Saint-Paul. The chapel's tower and blue sky beyond. 'All hospitals are hard. And the cracks

251

in the walls, the dust in the curtains when I open or close them ... When Rouisson was troubled at night. These things are harder than you know, Jeanne. But I've worked well — or rather, I've produced a great deal. Many pieces have failed and aren't what I've hoped they would be. But some I am pleased with.'

'Like the moth?'

'You remember the moth?'

'And what of your portraits? Portraits of wardens, perhaps?'

'Ah.' He smiles. 'You know. Charles told you?'

'He did. It surprised me.'

'It surprised me too. I always thought he'd be a good sub-ject, with his strong face and a patience in him. But I never thought he'd come to me.'

'Did he say why?'

'No. But I'm no fool. I'm mad but not foolish and he talked of you. I told him to do as you had done.'

'To sit very still and not talk at all?'

'Yes. To think of what he loves.'

There are the first, few cicadas in the grasses. They hear them. 'What will you miss, do you think?'

'Miss?' He sniffs. 'The baths. I've liked the baths. These insects. The view from my window, especially at dawn. Do you know Michel? He asks for my bread when I don't eat it, and always asks so politely. And the nuns are all very kind. I called it a zoo at first, didn't I? A menagerie, perhaps.' He shakes his head. 'That was wrong of me.'

'Anything else?'

'Having water brought to me in a brown cup. I'll be thirsty in Auvers.'

She smiles. 'A letter came yesterday. Benoît's coming home.'

'Your youngest?'

'Yes. Hair a little like yours. And I have a fear that you'll leave before he comes here, that you won't meet him. I'd have liked that – you meeting him.'

'I won't.'

'Moving on. I know. Your way.'

'But I have a few days left. And I will spend them painting what I'll be leaving and won't find in the north. Cypresses and olive trees. Your musical rock up there. And Gachet might have a fine garden, but he may not have irises or roses or pomegranate trees or all the other things that seem to climb over walls and terraces and take over this place. I'll paint Provençal things, in case I don't come this way again.'

In case. But he won't come back. She knows this, inside herself. He must know it too.

'And so I must go . . . My studio. I have much to do.' He gives no goodbye. He only stands, says 'Charles's portrait is dry now' – and makes his way under the pines.

The Dutchman paints his last paintings. The blue shutters are pushed back. Charles walks with Rouisson in the hospital grounds, or takes the pulse of Dominique, or talks to Mère Épiphanie.

As for Jeanne, she readies the second bedroom that looks into the lime. Carries its linen and rug and blanket into the yard, hangs them on the line. This way, they take on the scent of April here – which is sunshine, the slightest hint of herbs. A little earth. Pomade. When she places the linen back on the bed she imagines Benoît sleeping there.

'How will you be?'

'When he goes?'

'Yes, when he goes.'

Jeanne thinks about this. 'I'll be sad, for a while. But it's right that he does. It sounds like he'll be happy there.'

'Gachet's a good man. I'd like to escort him.'

'All the way to Auvers?'

'No, it's too far. But halfway, perhaps. Would you mind? I'd be home by dusk.'

She moves against his body and thinks of a book closing up. She rests her cheek on the place that is neither his neck nor his shoulder. A hollowed place. 'I don't mind.'

Like this, they rest.

Charles says to her, 'What I said. On our wedding day. You asked me – do you remember? You said I'd started to say something, that I'd said, You look ... And never finished it, never said how you looked. Jeanne, I can't remember now. I can't tell you the exact word I'd meant to say when thirty years have gone by. But I know I loved the stems of lavender. And when I first saw you with the basket on your arm—'

'Of lemons.'

'Of lemons – I thought you looked like the Roman women that are carved into the sides of Les Arènes. That you didn't belong in a market, buying fruit and stepping round the dogs. I'd wanted to put my hand in your hair. Feel you. That's what I thought.'

Their goodbye, in the end, is small. It's under the avenue of pines. He stands with a single bag and his easel. He wears his travelling clothes: a shirt that is stained under the arms, fraying trousers. A jacket over one arm.

'What will you do?'

'Do? Benoît will be here soon. And we'll go to Paris before too long. Explore it. See our other two.'

'I'll think of you doing that.'

A breeze through the pines, so they look up. 'What I hope,' she says, 'is that you are well, in Auvers. That you stay well, Vincent. And that you might sometimes think of the south, and of a white house near Saint-Rémy and that when you think of it you feel a fondness for it. We'll think of you.'

There is nothing more to say than this. His eyes are his own shade of blue, his beard is his own gold and red – and the Dutchman offers his hand to her. She takes it. Jeanne steps in and gives the three, slow kisses as is the Provençal way and, in doing so, smells turpentine and the scent of him.

'*Au revoir*, Jeanne.'

'*Au revoir*.'

Charles waits in the lane. The Dutchman looks back at the hospital and the olive trees, the shutters with their flaking blue. Then he makes his way to him.

Jeanne watches them – these two men she knows the footsteps of, the inked shape of their names. They don't glance back; they seem to be talking as they walk beneath the plane trees towards Saint-Rémy.

Jeanne watches till they're out of sight. How they move through light and shadow and light.

In his studio, the shutters are thrown back. A warm breeze blows through the room. This breeze finds what he's left behind – hair, dust, a pencil's curled shavings. And here, propped against the walls, are the last works of his, the paintings he's done in the last two weeks of living here – side by side, drying.

She looks at them, one by one. There are flowers in jugs,

in this room: two of white roses, spilling like snow; two more of irises, with curling leaves and broken stems. They seem too large for the jug — meant for more than the jug they are in. A lane with a cart, and two men. A final view of Les Alpilles.

And there's a canvas of olives at dusk. It must be dusk for there's a high moon, and it gives a soft light onto the trees and fields beneath it. People too: a couple walking side by side. She bends at the waist, hands on her knees, for these two people are people she knows: a red-headed man in blue overalls and a woman who is gesturing as she walks — one hand raised, as if talking of love or her distant boys or the Place Lamartine. She wears a yellow dress. Her hair is pinned high.

Landscape with Couple Walking and Crescent Moon. She has never seen his handwriting before.

For a long time, Jeanne stares.

She could stare far longer, but a thought comes: that there's a portrait she hasn't seen and which must be here, in this room. She rises, turns. And there he is. There is Charles, exactly: he sits in his striped uniform, neither smiling nor stern, but how he looks when thoughtful, and his eyes are the polished black that she's seen her own reflection in. There are flashes of Laurent in this. A pose, too, that Jean-Charles might adopt. The look Charles has had, at times, when he's been watching her.

She crouches, smiles at her husband. Then she lifts this portrait carefully, carries it through the corridors and out into the sunlight to their home.

Twenty-Three

Jeanne doesn't think of him all the time. She does not even think of him often, but there are moments when she sees the Dutchman and has returned to them – and it is only by moving her head or stepping forth that she finds it's a shadow or half-lit tree, or her youngest son in the fields.

Since stepping down from the train in late May, she could believe Benoît never went away. He has the same tendencies – the same love of cherries, or cracking of knuckles when food's brought to him, and his voice is the same. She'd forgotten his voice. But that, like his freckles and hair and laugh are all the same as they ever were. 'Did you ever go?' Rubbing a little dirt from his cheek.

'Yes, I did.'

She knows. A broader, stronger man. Tales, in the evening, of rivers with strange names. Rituals. The bites of insects. 'One day, I went to a mountain town at sunset, and . . .'

'I wish you'd met him,' she says.

'The painter?'

'The painter.'

So there are times when she thinks of that man. She prays for him in chapel. And there will always be the second, painted Charles on their parlour wall. But mostly, when Jeanne shakes out linen or helps the goatherd milk his goats, she thinks of nothing but the task and the day she is in, at that moment, and has no sense of missing him.

'Did you hear?' Marie-Josephine. 'His work? The paintings that the Dutchman did? They're being displayed, I hear. An exhibition in Paris, no less. The ones that he painted here.'

The nun is standing in Jeanne's vegetable patch. She's come to help her; together they pick the peas and black-currants and peaches that they'll carry back to Saint-Paul.

'It seems he's getting known. Famous, even! There have been articles. Imagine! To have had an artist here!'

'I love that he's come back,' Charles says. 'Look at him.'

'Yes.'

The blessing. Benoît works in the grounds. He was never the man for rooms – so he spends the summer months with Gilles, stripping away the ivy that has plucked at walls and sealed doors. He digs a new vegetable patch. He cuts back the sprawling grasses and weeds to make paths in the hospital grounds and he walks with the patients, showing them the new, clean places to sit and where birds are nesting, where he found frogs. 'It's not Mexico,' he tells them. 'But I've been thinking. Les Antiques? Well, what if there's more to be found? More Roman ruins in the ground, hereabouts? I might have a dig, the next time I'm back . . . ' He eats every-thing Jeanne offers him. Drains every flask.

'Do you think he'll stay?' But Charles knows the answer. Their youngest has other paths to take, other countries to walk in. 'He's talked of Paris.'

'Of course he has.' She smiles. 'Charles, come back to bed.'

*

She thinks of him when a gust of wind comes so suddenly that it catches a chair and blows it over. With blue things. With a fox's scent. Each time she fills the brown cup and drinks from it as he did.

Jeanne thinks of him, too, when a letter comes – at the summer's end. A letter from Auvers-sur-Oise, written by a woman called Johanna van Gogh, who starts her note with, *I write to inform you . . .* And with those five words, Jeanne knows.

A gunshot. To his stomach. In the fields near Auvers. A slow death from infected blood. *Theo rushed to be with him, but . . .* – Jeanne kneels down in the yard. She kneels, passes the letter to Charles, who reads it and kneels down too. And that night she cries. She cries into the side of him – the place near his armpit, near his chest. And Charles whispers to her. He talks of the thoughts that came to him when the Dutchman had told him to think of what he loved. Fireflies. Honey. The sunrise he saw above a besieged town. How he'd felt when she told him of the newly made Jean-Charles growing inside her. The chapel's bell. Beetroot. The few, rare times when all three boys have been in their house, sleeping and safe. Letters from them. The house on rue de l'Agneau. Entering his wife. How he knows that, as a child, she'd imagine the places that water might go when she upturned a pail – rivers and seas.

'I told you that?'

'You did. You talked about tunnelling moles and it made me love you even more.' *Ma femme*, he calls her. *Ma reine.*

'Vincent was so—'

'I know.' Pulls her a little closer. Strokes the downy lobes of her ears until she finds her sleep.

*

Of all the memories Jeanne has of the man who came in May 1889 and stayed for a year, this is the clearest one: how he looked up and smiled. He was painting; she was talking of Les Alpilles, so he lowered his brush, pushed back the brim of his hat with his fist to see her better, hear her more clearly – and suddenly smiled. Teeth and bright eyes. A boy. A son. A beard of rust and light.

She remembers him now.

'Come here. Sit with me. Let me tell you about a man—'

'Which man?'

'A man I knew.'

Jeanne stands in a room that's new to her. From its window, a new view. Her grandson sits beside her – a boy with long lashes, a taste for pears. He swings his legs impatiently. 'A kind man?'

'Yes, a kind man.'

She cuts a pear, looks up. This is Paris, laid out. It is early October: the sky is pale and clear. The rooftops are damp from the morning's light rain and have smoke rising from their chimneys, and she knows he'd have painted this. 'He had coppery hair.'

'Coppery?'

'Like sunsets and sunrises. Here.'

She's learned the whole of his name. Sometimes, as this morning, she speaks of him and thinks of the hunters of old, the bearded men who chanted for boar as if the boar might rise up. And sometimes Jeanne likes thinking this – that the Dutchman might turn in his permanent sleep at the sound of his name, smile at it. But other times, she thinks, *Rest. Don't wake.* After his sleepless life, at last, a form of peace.

Yet her grandson doesn't wish to speak of van Gogh. He'd rather tell Jeanne of the sweet pastries that he's allowed if he's good, or the mice he's seen, or the big metal tower that he can spy from his bedroom. 'And do you know Uncle Laurent? He carried me on his back yesterday!'

'Did he?'

The boy sucks his pear, hums.

The heart, she thinks, is the painter. Love, and moments like this, are the art. The Dutchman taught her that.

Jeanne looks at the autumn sky. And then she, too, leaves her thoughts of van Gogh behind – for there's the sound of a door opening behind her, the sound of footsteps coming near and she doesn't turn around. She waits, waits, knowing who's coming nearer. She waits until she feels Charles's touch – his hand on the side of her arm – and with that she turns. She reaches, takes his hand in her own. Says no words, and smiles.

She is a woman whose looks have faded, a poor soul, resigned to her fate, nothing out of the ordinary and so insignificant that I simply long to paint that dusty blade of grass. I talked to her sometimes when I was doing some olive trees behind their little house, and she told me then that she didn't believe I was ill – in fact, you would now say the same if you saw me working, my mind clear and my fingers so sure ...

Vincent van Gogh, in a letter to his brother Theo
7 or 8 September 1889
Saint-Rémy-de-Provence

... a painted portrait is a thing of feeling made with love or respect for the being represented.

To his sister Wilhelmina
19 September 1889

Author's Note

The idea for this book grew as I read a few of the many letters that passed between Vincent van Gogh and his brother Theo. This contemplative, tender writer seemed so different from the man I'd assumed van Gogh to be. His year at Saint-Rémy, specifically, intrigued me – the asylum, the landscape around it and how he produced his finest work when he was, perhaps, at his most ill.

I've tried to be historically accurate – in terms of Vincent's attacks, moods and the paintings he created during his time at Saint-Paul-de-Mausole. But inevitably, changes have been made for the novel's sake. Furthermore, whilst both Charles and Jeanne Trabuc existed (as did Peyron, Poulet and Salles), I'd like to stress that their private histories, personalities, relationships, children and the events that take place within this book are entirely my own making. Wherever they are now, I hope they don't mind.

The portraits of the Trabucs can still be seen: *Portrait of Trabuc, An Attendant at Saint-Paul Hospital* is held at the Kunstmuseum in Solothurn, Switzerland; *Portrait of Madame Trabuc* is in St Petersburg's Hermitage. The painting described at the end of the book – *Landscape with Couple Walking and Crescent Moon* – is in the São Paulo Art Museum in Brazil. I like to believe it depicts what Vincent cared for most during his time in Saint-Rémy.

Acknowledgements

This book was written with the generous financial assistance of the Society of Authors, through their K. Blundell Trust, and the Royal Literary Fund's J. B. Priestley Award. I'm deeply grateful to everyone involved with both decisions. Their help made such a difference to me, and this book. Thank you.

Thank you, too, to Lennie Goodings and all at Virago for their faith and exceptional care; to Viv Schuster, as always; to Sarah Bower, Lisa Conibear and Suzanne Worthington; the staff in the Tourist Information Office at Saint-Rémy; and to Gilbert and Chantal Tardy and Ronald and Marie-Claude Bouchonnet for their patience and many kindnesses during my stay in Provence.

Lastly, to all of those who asked, listened, reassured or held my hand during the writing of this book – thank you. You know who you are.

Susan Fletcher was born in 1979 in Birmingham. She is the author of the bestselling *Eve Green*, winner of the Whitbread First Novel Award; *Oystercatchers* and *Witch Light*.